A simple story, simply told by a simple man

for Mahid

Hope you enjoy

MARTYN X

Martyn Benford

M Benford

Printed by Biddles Books, King's Lynn, Norfolk PE32 1SF

Acknowledgements

I would like to show my appreciation to Teresa for her huge input into this work, not only for her editing and proofreading skills but her insistence in getting it right. I will thank too, Rod and Nigel for their excellent camera work and Tim for his graphics.

I thank my friends Michael Gasson for his encouragement, Gordon for his belief in my work, Jay and Marie of the Maltsters Arms, Debbie and Ashley at the Mill House, Little Petherwick for letting me into their homes and the historical information they have provided. I will thank Jean, Charlotte and Dudley for allowing me into the home of Macdonald Tamryn.

I must thank the members of my own family for their encouragement, my late wife, Penny for her patience and especially my late mother who believed in me and supported me throughout.

My appreciation also goes to Sharps Brewery and New Age Publishing for their help and guidance.

Martyn Benford

Prologue:

'A simple story, simply told by a simple man.'

I once read a fascinating book, a story of hardship, romance and conflict. A bride shot at the altar. The narrator of the story was John Ridd of Oare, in the county of Somerset. John told of a hard life and what, one truly honest man has to do to get what he wanted in life. It is a story of a farming family who lived in the seventeenth century. John, a giant of a man, becomes head of the house after his father is murdered by a band of Brigands who kidnapped, robbed and murdered without reason.

And I, Macdonald Tamryn of Padstow Town in the county of Cornwall, think I am having a rough time of it in the twentieth century!

Macdonald Tamryn.

Chapter One

Under a Blood Red sky

An explosion of pink feathers flutter in morbid silence. We watch as they settle gently on the rippling surface. A warm, gentle breeze draws a handful further. The sticky feathers come to rest on the seating area of the empty quayside bandstand. The ancient and rickety bandstand is gradually detaching itself. It leans uncomfortably towards the gently lapping for now, Atlantic. The bandstand is tired, knackered!

Luckily for Lenny and I, the last of the late season coach parties have mostly disappeared as lightning continues to flicker around the enshrouding grey of the harbour walls.

Wet granite reflects a purple sky. A time honoured pastime of culling the seagull population might become dangerous with the sudden heavenly discotheque.

"It was mine, Lenny. Unless it swallowed them both at the same time."

"Might have, bit of a bleddy waste if it did buddy."

"I'm all for two for the price of one, one for the price of two idn't so bleddy good and baking powder don't come cheap!"

"Will us 'ave a beer on the way home, Maccy?"

"Skint mucker."

"Usual then?"

"Yeah, I'll go over. Your turn to be 'obby 'orse. I 'ave got me a bad back from last time. You should get smaller feet."

"Ow would I do that? My bleddy trainers wouldn't bleddy fit."

"Wear two pairs of socks Lenny, that would help. Did you bring your bottle opener?"

"Course I did. Never go anywhere without it."

"Nice one mate. Bend over."

"Don't hurt me Maccy."

"I'll take my trainers off. Things I bloody do for you." I am lucky not to break my neck, Lenny wobbles all over the place as I climb on his back and flip myself over the wall at the back of The Mermaid public house, missing the cemented in broken glass. I grab two bottles of Light Ale and call back to Lenny. "Brown Ale or Lager mucker?"

"Cider for me, Maccy. I wanna keep a clear head."

"Blackcurrant?"

"Naw, straight."

Lenny's right, he needs to keep a clear head. It will be a first for him! "Coming back, look out." I reverse my previous action and hand my mate two bottles of strong stuff.

"Didn't you get any glasses, Maccy?"

"Don't take the piss Lenny!"

Lenny Copestick and I, like it or not, are born and bred Padstownians. We are privileged apparently. That's what the old-timers keep telling us. "You'm Padsta born and bred and be bleddy proud of it lads, lessen you want your bleddy arses kicking." Sort of pain and gain. Us boys prefer painless, as you would. Most of them would fall over anyway. Two walking sticks can do that to a man.

My Ma subscribes to a different theory. Ma doesn't swear much. She might think of her children as affectionate arses. Physical punishment has never really been a part of our household. Ma would ask if we thought we'd done right or wrong. The kid, my younger brother and I should benefit from our own answers and the contents of our consciences, or the lack of.

The kid, Dusty is a year younger than I and my only sibling. Instead of participating in the gull culling, he's most likely in a bus shelter with a young maid; two, even three. The kid's not fussy what girls look like. He just needs to be surrounded. Who wouldn't want their own harem? Dusty has a magnetic personality where the ladies

4

are concerned. I don't do so badly, I just need to work a tad harder.

The gull rainbow effects have been caused by homemade sweets. The sweet consists of a small strip of foil, with a half teaspoon of baking powder inserted. Both ends of the foil should be twisted like a toffee paper. The silvery device is launched skyward with a good elastic band dropped by some careless postman. Padstow only has the one 'postie'. Proving guilt would be simple. He wears a blue shirt, jacket and shorts. He swears blue murder when stepping in anything brown. Everything about him is blue excepting of course his shoes.

Padstow gulls will eat anything. They fight to the death for every morsel. Gull fishing is an ancient local tradition passed down through generations of fathers. Not mine though. I have no idea who he is. If he ever shows his face to mine, I won't recognize it. It wouldn't be long before he could say the same. I'm not certain I want to meet the man, for want of a better description. To be truthful, I don't. I believe my brother and I are in complete agreement. He has been and he has gone, never to return. I have never lost sleep over him and never will. He isn't an elephant in my room, if he was, I'd shoot him and mount his head over the fireplace, if I had one.

To the task in hand, our Padstow gulls are the greediest. They will think nothing of stealing from a hand, even a half open mouth. They will return the newly compacted ration almost instantly. Sort of take with one hand and give back with, well just give back really.

It seems Padstow has as many gulls as it does people. Every rooftop has its squadron of snipers. There are lookouts on the tall bobbing masts in the harbour. The reconnaissance and individual fliers cry messages to squadrons who swoop down when the cafés, restaurants and takeaways open for daily business.

Lenny and I have been targeting members of the suicide squad until we spot the blue and white uniformed 'copper' passing the Harbour Commissioner's office on foot.

"Reckon his Panda car has broke down again Maccy."

"Can't be anything else seeing as he's walking Len. Tis bleddy unusual."

"I wonder if he needs a push mucker."

"We could push it in the quay and push him in with it. That would be best. Kill two birds with one stone that way."

"I suppose a couple more won't hurt."

"Maybe he has fallen out with the snack bar owner who has a backroom with a TV. More likely one of the shopkeepers has tipped Twotrees off to what we've been doing."

"Most likely."

"Leave him to it Len, we don't want to be seen talking with him. Our name would be mud hereabouts. Let's get on."

As for the half dozen or more floating corpses? Maybe it's time the mackerel got their own back. Mother Nature's justice! Mad mackerel disease? Maybe, but the fish could have been a little crazy in the first place. Who knows?

Padstows' old granite harbour is like a second home to Lenny and me. Truthfully, the quayside is a second home to any proper Padsta kid. The town is a lively little place in high summer. In high, or low if you prefer, winter, it's a virtual graveyard. Come spring it should blossom like a huge flowering weed. I'm not one for holding my breath.

Lenny and I avoid Twotrees grasp by slipping in the front door of The Sailmaker's Arms and out through the rear exit, through the yard and over the wall. A handy, well-used escape route. The cemented in broken glass has long since been smoothed out by wind, age and large boots. We stroll innocently up Padstow Hill with our T-shirts clinging damply to our backs as the sudden late Autumn storm waltzes off in the direction of Lundy Island.

My hometown of Padstow overlooks the sea. That's not to say the sea doesn't occasionally overlook the old town. With a Spring tide, a powerful Atlantic storm thrashing water might launder the narrow streets. One might even be able to row around the town's Market Square. Maybe tie up in front of the traffic warden, without fear of a yellow and black plastic envelope. If that official attempts to write the ticket, an accidental smack on a shin with a well-directed oar would bring him to his senses. It would never bring us to ours.

Little Padstow gives the impression of a town built on a cliff side, with narrow winding backstreets. It has almost everything we need. There's a cinema where the feature film might be changed once a year, twice if we're lucky.

Youth club? What can I say? Table tennis isn't my thing. Kiss-chase? I'm not keen on being chased by thirteen-year-olds, especially the girls. Of course, their elder sisters can chase all they like, and I would shout, 'Here I am. Where do you want me?'

Call me cynical, and you might be right. I believe the modern version of Kiss-chase falls under: 'Catch me and you can give me one. I'm over here behind the chippy. Mum says I have to be home in fifteen minutes for my piano lesson.'

I like to frequent the Methy' chapel. Not that I'm an over religious lad though I have shouted for the top man's help on occasion. So far as I know, I have never received it.

The old, grey Methodist chapel hides a twelve by six-foot secret. Upstairs above the altar, is a huge dusty loft. Hidden under old sailcloth, is a full-sized snooker table. If I can't be found, I'm up there playing snooker and having a few cans of cheap lager with the minister's wayward son, Michael.

Michael looks much older than seventeen. He never has a problem getting served in the towns' only off license. I look seventeen and I get served just as easily. Maybe I have that sort of face. It could be the result of my compliments, cheeky innuendos, and purposeful physical contacts with the middle aged, blonde who manages the smallest off license in town, the only off license in Padstow. It's also the largest. I think she likes me!

You might also find me at The Mermaid on occasion. The Old Mermaid is my other second home. Not that it should be. The very name suggests it is a pub. For legal reasons, my being only seventeen and a halfish, I still have a five month wait until I can legally fall down and lose my memory as often as I like.

The Mermaid has what we call the quaintly named Mermaid's Bar. The pub must have been lost in some previous century. Not sure which. It could be the last, maybe the one before. It's pretty much lost in this one. As it stands, it will stay that way, indefinitely.

Lenny and I had stood in the here in The Mermaid as we drank our first illegal pint. Until then we'd sneaked a few cans of cheap 0.1% strength cat's piss, or a litre of out of date dry cider beneath the bandstand with somebody's daughter. Or, on occasion, up in the chapel's snooker room with Methy Mick.

After two pints of Wrecker's Revenge, Lenny and I had thrown up all over the Mermaid, not literally as there has never been one in here as far as I know. Anyway, I'm sure we didn't coat the whole area. We did make an honest effort. You need to start somewhere.

The Mermaid's landlady chose me over Lenny that day, not that I was in any way grateful. She both carried and dragged me outside into the yard. Not kicking nor screaming. Nobody in their right mind screams at or kicks the landlady unless they have a strong preference for hospital food or a pre-booked plot in 'God's Half Acre.' She ushered me through the cellar with a well-directed foot, and into the back yard amongst the empty stacks of beer barrels. Once there, she proceeded to invade my body 'for your own benefit' as she will regularly tell it.

8

The woman forced what felt like a stony forearm down my throat to help me continue what I had started. It wasn't her arm of course. The searching and probing had only been done with the pinkie. The trick was done by she that day.

She' is Blencathra. She is enormous. Blen' is built like a pregnant Totem Pole. She has a voice like an iffy cement mixer, tits better suited to a dairy farm resident and the facial hair of a porcine. Blen' has designer stubble.

Her loyal partner is Bligh, Cap'n to some, but Bligh to most of us. He's the opposite of Blencathra. Bligh is a six foot two and a half inch fluffy-topped cocktail stick minus the sausage. Perhaps that's unfair, dear Blencathra must see something in him. The Cap'n says he is descended from the notorious Bligh of the Bounty. He could be telling the truth. Admiral Bligh hailed from St Tudy just a few miles away, as the crow flies. There goes another one! Crow to him or herself; 'right I will only fly in straight lines from now on'. It could be painful, certainly with the beak of a fellow bird almost stuck up one's Jacksy.

I recently discovered it was Bligh, at One-Armed Frank Pendragon's suggestion, who had tapped cigar ash into mine and Lenny's second pints of Wrecker's Revenge. We didn't notice at the time. We had something hugely more important on our minds.

I still remember it well. Lenny and I were engaged in ogling some young northern piece who subscribes to that most important of silent questions: 'What do you think of my arse in these?' To be fair, it wasn't bad, it wasn't fat. It was hardly in anything at all. Her dimpled buttocks were attempting simultaneous escape from both sides of her Hot Pants. The pants were far too tight which was obviously intentional. I suppose there's nothing wrong with taking in a bit of washing. The sotto voce answer to her silent question would be: 'it's okay!'

So, Bligh had induced our technicolour yawns while we two were predicting the maid's age. He'd done it to others before. There will be future targets. Oh, by the way, for the record, she was sixteen. Lenny and I were a tad thankful for that legal detail, on separate occasions of course. We Padstow boys do have some standards.

It is late autumn. In just a couple of months I would leave for London and college. Despite my teenage rampages, well practiced traffic warden and copper baiting, I have given some thought to my long term fortune earning future. I like to think of myself as a positive sort. I doubt anyone of unimportance would agree.

As you know by now, I'm a through and through Cornish lad. Not of a wondering and wandering nature. Many my age couldn't wait to get away to the newer university towns of Plymouth, Bristol or Exeter. There they could smoke it, club it, share breakfast with it and leave it, loved and forgotten. I am booked into London to learn it primarily, with no intentions of staying on. Nothing could change my mind. When I finish my 'further education', the 'Smoke' can do exactly what its nickname suggests, plus the flame bits.

I'd been to the big city once before. It wasn't a memorable experience; a school trip to London Zoo, with a 'farcical ending,' and long term recriminations. Apparently, feeding a rare Panda anything meat based and Ketchup coated is out of the question. Who the hell decided the Panda was rare anyway? Lenny, Michael and I were out on our respective ears, sharpish.

For Christ's sake, we were only ten or eleven. How were we to know? It might have been this outing that first steered me towards the catering profession. Anyway, it was the final school outing for us three. It was at least educational. We learned the Zoo burgers were crap!

My destination is to be the West London and Fulham Catering College. I'm told it's somewhere in Chiswick.

It's a mouthful so-to-speak, it is a culinary teaching establishment in or around the capital. With luck, when I have my credentials, I'll be back in the Duchy and rolling in it. Everyone needs food, tourists need more than most. It's needed to soak up all the alcohol they intend to consume while their kids are running amok. When college days end, I'll be on the first train to Truro. I'll fill my wallet and maybe my boots if you get my meaning. My little brother seems to be doing things quite the other way around. And, why shouldn't he? He's still a youngster.

The kid, as I like to call him, reminds me of the young bull who says to the more experienced bull, 'there's a field full of cows over there. Why don't we run over and get one?' The older bull standing nonchalantly by his side might reply. 'No, best we walk over and get them all!'

College must wait just a few more weeks. Until then, every day, hour, and minute is as precious as a Pearl filled Oyster. The coming days need to be filled. They will be, to the best of my ability.

"They ought to get quality cider, Maccy. I'm gonna complain, this stuff is crap. Tastes like bleddy virgins' water!"

"Yeah right, Lenny. I hate to ask but how would you knaw that? We live in bleddy Padsta."

"I wasn't thinking, Maccy, sorry."

"No matter."

"Maccy, why did they used to have bells on fire engines do you think?"

"Easy mate they didn't have knockers back then."

"Yeah but they never let you come in, so I don't see the point."

"They will if you wipe your feet."

"So then, what if your feet aren't dirty."

"Wipe your boots Lenny! Your sister Alice has some."

"What?"

"Knockers!" I knew it would set Lenny off. There is no risk as I know Lenny was the worst runner in the whole school, I wouldn't have dared otherwise.

Chapter Two

God's Eyes and Cod's Eyes

At age seventeen, I have my first opportunity to meet a member of the bloated seagull population, face to face. We are on a level playing field. I'm not certain the gull is overweight. I have no idea what an average seagull weighs. Who does? Who cares? Anyway, my train of thought is suddenly redirected by the voice of an invisible ventriloquist.

"What are you doing up there, Maccy?"

It's Lenny the ventriloquist. "Watching, watching and thinking, Lenny."

My close companion has what resembles a nasty look in its eye. Have I orphaned it at some point? I might have. I might have fed its parents a homemade hand grenade. I wished I had one with me now. I could hand rear it.

"You'll be wishing you're somewhere else when the bell ringers turn up, matey."

"Campanologists, Lenny. That's what they folks call themselves, I believe. Don't worry. I've been up here before when they have started at their bleddy racket. They buggers won't bother me. What do you want matey? What brings you around here now? Shouldn't you be eating something, somewhere?" I know Lenny better than anyone. Better than he knows himself.

If Lenny's not doing something, he's eating, with a maid, or between the two, sometimes doing all three at the same time. Lenny the human seagull. The thought makes me glance again at my close companion. I feel like Eddie Large. Sid is unmoving.

"I 'eard you are up here and thought to see why, mucker?"

"Tidn't anything for you to worry about matey. I'll be down when I have finished thinking. I'll be down drekly."

"What is it you're thinking about, Maccy?"

"To be honest I haven't really begun yet. I was just getting started when you arrived." It's odd talking to Lenny like this. I can't see him, but I know he's there. It's almost like a telephone call, without the phone. "When I'm done, I'll be down there where you are."

"T'was the harbour master told me to come and see what you're doing. The bleddy emmets did report you. Said they thought you might be a jumper. He said as we two are muckers, you and I, I should see what you are about."

"Bleddy nosey tourists. Do I look like a bleddy woolly?"

"Well, the buggers don't have anything better to do. What do 'e mean, 'woolly'? I don't understand, Maccy."

"Why can't they just go swimming at the beach and annoy the bleddy lifeguards. It's nothin' to do with anyone else. If I want to jump, I will. It's nothing to do with anyone else." I knew my little joke will go right over Lenny's head. Lenny is a tad slow with some things, many things. Lenny can do food and he can do females.

"I'll be off then, Maccy. If you'm okay. I got me a date, sort of. With a bird."

"That's good thinking, Lenny. They do say it's better if it's a maid."

"That's right, I heard the same thing."

"Do you know Lenny, I have myself a date with a bird too, it seems like." I flick another nervous glance at my fat, unmoving companion.

"Don't leave it too late coming down then, Maccy. I have to go in case I miss her."

"You go Lenny. I have started to think some now. Go and see to the poor maid. Which one is it?"

"To tell the truth, I can't bleddy remember, Maccy. Don't matter. I'll find out when I get there, if she's there. If she isn't, I likely won't."

14

"I'll meet you at the café later. You can tell me all about it. Where are you meeting the poor maid?"

"Behind the chippy."

"You can buy her fish and chips after."

"After what, Maccy?"

"I dunno matey, I won't be there, will I!"

"Don't make any plans for tomorrow morning, Lenny. We do have us a job to do out at the old station at Camel's Halt. Grandad is taking a tractor over there. He wants to steal some of the stuff that's been left lying about there. I told him you would help. Before daylight, six o'clock at our place."

"Six o'clock? Bloody hell, I idn't too clever at six o'clock, Maccy. Is it livestock?"

Lenny, master of the understatement. "I wouldn't have asked if it wasn't important. No, it's rolling stock." My mate is a tad slow any time of the day.

"I'll be there. Do I get my breakfast?"

"Do you never?"

"I'll see you at the café. Please don't jump from there, Maccy. You'll make a hell of a mess of yourself. You'll look like vegetable soup. The bleddy gulls will eat anything hereabouts."

"I'll mind what you say, Lenny. I'll be okay. You go and see to the maid now."

"Listen Maccy. If she isn't there, shall I come back and help 'e with your thinking?"

"Who, if who isn't there?"

"I told 'e before, I can't remember."

"Come back iffen you want but I might be gone."

"Gone, gone where?"

"Somewhere else I suppose." It had been my intention to only be up here for an hour or so. I wanted some time alone. Lenny is eating into my quality time now.

"Gotcha Maccy. I'll see thee later, at the, the….?"

"At the café, Lenny."

"That's it."

"Don't eat everything before I get there."

Lenny is my greatest friend, my soulmate. We two had once been the Padstow school teacher's worst nightmare. Very soon, I'll be looking for someone to take his place. Someone shapelier, prettier and eighteen. Lenny will have to do for now, despite his shortcomings.

Padstow, my little Duchy outpost, sits below a wooded hillside. The Atlantic Ocean waits at the bottom. Padstow is small and packed with dozens of tiny fisherman's cottages. They are so closely packed they resemble an overfilled sardine can. A stranger might think the cottages had been built on top of each other. To me, this hillside town is larger, bigger than the great salty expanse that licks roughly at its streets. In winter with a high tide, the water will flush into the ancient fish cellars that now serve as well-filled stockrooms to the parades of gift and antique shops.

Padstow isn't my home town to be truthful. I was born a Cornish mile away. A Cornish mile can be anything between just under one and five. We like to keep the emmets on their toes. Ma is from Padstow, a true local. Her father, Grandfather Tamryn is another. He was born in a quayside gift shop, though it wasn't at the time. It was a ship's chandlers, where fishermen could buy their supplies. Now, it's Cornish toffee, candyfloss and water pistols, cheap trinkets that won't last twenty-four hours. If they do, you have yourself a bargain.

I make little mention of my father. I don't have one. I do have one but have no idea who or where he might be. If or when we might meet, he can expect a good smacking from me and the kid, Dusty.

Dusty and I are in full agreement. We two feel the same about the invisible man. If he turns up and leaves, it'll be good riddance. If he doesn't, there'll be no need for fond farewells. Are we bitter? Yes, I believe we are.

Joy, our Ma, is our figurehead. Not in any nautical sense, as those things can be a tad saucy. Ma's no prude but Ma and saucy don't go together. Ma could not be called slap face ugly either. There have been various would-be suitors but mostly one-sided. Maybe when the two of us, there are only two, have left home, she will feel differently. She could take a hold of a man and march him down that which right now rests coldly beneath me.

Aye, if you hadn't already guessed, I am fully astride the church roof, sitting on the chilly castellated parapet.

I slide myself onto the whitewash splattered floor. 'Whitewash' being my polite pseudonym for seagull shit and I make a horrible discovery. My escape route is missing. My ladder has removed itself from its position or more likely it has been stolen. I'm temporarily snookered. I'm sure no one else around here has ever had to deal with a situation such as this.

As I begin to ponder my fate, I am suddenly side tracked. A heavenly apparition is even now appearing before me. What better place can one be for such, than in god's eyes? 'Forgive me lord for trespassing on your holy perch. And by the way, thank you for what I am about to receive'.

A dozen rooftops away a penthouse door slides open. She arises and unfolds her wings. She yawns upwards at the crisp, misty morning. I stare in wonder. It is hardly a penthouse in reality. A tiny redeveloped loft, bijou and full of rotting feline corpses I guess.

I am mesmerised by a halo of golden, shimmering hair. Thoughts of decency evaporate more quickly than the morning mist. She stretches, reaches out, in every direction and surveys the splattered slates. My eyes grow an inch and I want to believe she is reaching out to me. Suddenly her lips part. I wait in silent awe for my angelic message from this glowing, naked, nineteen-year old goddess. It soon arrives.

"Maccy Tamryn, you dirty bugger. Have you been spying on me?"

"Naw my 'ansome. I have been here for almost two hours. I didn't hardly know you were there sweetheart. It has come as a complete surprise to me, a complete surprise."

"You bleddy liar, Maccy Tamryn."

"Yes, I suppose I am. I have only been here for an hour and a half. I am considering staying another half hour. It does depend really, my lover."

"It does depend on what?"

"How can I put this, are you staying long? Do you come here every day?"

"Ais, I do, same time, same place, rain or shine."

"I had best remember then, hadn't I?"

"You best had my handsome lad."

Alice Copestick raises her chin. Her perfect breasts tremble as she laughs wickedly at her own final reply. She turns, sashays through the open glazed door, sliding it shut as she disappears. Inside, I see she halts, leaning back against the clear glass. It is all I can do to switch my thoughts back from gutter to street level and how I would physically achieve it with my ladder now missing.

By some quirk of fate, snooker becomes the operative word. Another message drifts up to me from the church lawns. "Maccy, Maccy, are you still up there?"

Michael in the nick of time. "I am Michael, I am. Thank the lord. How did you know?"

"Lenny told me."

"Not the lord at all. You will need to go inside the church, Michael and open the trapdoor to this tower. Only then will I be a free man."

"What are you doing up there matey?"

"I was thinking about things Michael. My thoughts have been regularly interfered with. It is time I got down but my escape route has vanished. I'm relying on you now." It's a pity I didn't think about some bugger pinching my ladder.

"I don't know, Maccy. It isn't as easy as you make it sound."

"Have they two daft buggers fallen out again, Michael, your dad and the vicar?"

"They have, Maccy. I despair of them sometimes. My father won't be happy with me going inside the church, as you know."

"I don't understand, Michael. They two buggers are supposed to preach peace and harmony to us sinners. All they do is bicker and squabble." I'm not what you could call a perpetual sinner. My recent discussions with the delightful Alice could change things somewhat in that regard, if she wasn't engaged to a one-eyed fisherman from across the estuary at Rock. Mervyn is an inhabitant of the posh place. He doesn't rise to such levels of the majority. Mervyn lives in one of the handful of council houses.

Poor Mervyn had lost an eye when he'd been out night fishing alone. The story goes Mervyn Trethewey lost his torch, tangled his hooks and lines, and in the dark had caught himself. It's the sort of thing that can happen to anyone. Mervyn might be best described as a tad dippy. Alice must see something in him. I'm not certain what. At school Mervyn became known as Conger during some shower room antics, after a rugby match. Mervyn goes under the nickname of Popeye too, but as far as I know, he's unaware.

"Come on Michael. I can't stay here waiting for my bleddy eyeballs to disappear before my very eyes." I glance again at my silent and still unmoving companion. The bird hasn't moved an inch since my arrival. I stretch across and gently touch a wing. The bird tips over. The gull is evidently stuffed and I confess I have no clue as to how it came to be here, unlike myself.

"I will, if you don't say anything to my father, Maccy. You gotta promise me."

"I do Michael, I do, I promise." Michael and I, like Lenny and I, go a long way back.

"I idn't promising, brother."

This is Dusty. The runt of a litter of two. "Dusty, you can come inside the church and let me down from here. Come on with 'e boy."

"Can't do it Maccy!"

"What do you mean boy, can't?"

"If Michael doesn't do it, I can't blackmail him at some opportune moment in the future, iffen I feel the need."

"Then don't feel the need boy. Do as I ask, or I might just jump right down on 'e."

"It is against my better judgement I do as you ask, Maccy but you understand money must change hands. Five quid?"

"Five quid?"

"Five quid and Michael's off the hook. Just drop it down over the side, brother."

I did as I was told and watched the note flutter into my brother's greedy hand. There would be a time to get it back. Dusty pockets the note. There is momentary silence and then I hear the distinct sounds of a ladder scraping at the wall. Dusty has kept his side of the bargain. I peer over the edge.

"Dusty, you bastard. That's my bleddy ladder." The kid meant no real harm. He has taken his opportunity well. It has all been planned.

We Tamryn's know how to make a few quid when we need to. Dusty usually makes his out of me.

My sojourn on the roof has told me one very important thing. There is a storm approaching. It might be a matter of hours away, even a day, but it is coming. We would have to move fast tomorrow morning. The quay is alive with seabirds of every kind, Guillemots, Shags and Cormorants and the common, local gulls. Seabirds will take to the confines and safety of the harbour at such times. Seals are diving and playing outside the harbour walls.

I can see it all as I stand the weird, potbellied gull back up on its hardened claws and depart from the roof. Dusty is gone when I step off the bottom rung of the now replaced ladder. I slide the extension down and tuck the double eighteen back behind the shrubs that line the church wall, exactly as I had found it on my arrival.

Michael tells me two panting teenage fillies had suddenly arrived and dragged my brother away before the completion of my descent. Just as well for my kid brother. The two of us stroll on towards the harbourside. We pause at the sight of the young kiddie standing alone and shivering with cold. The boy is fishing from the slipway below the bandstand. I lean over. The kid has a tacky, cheap looking rod. He reminds me of myself at the same age.

"How's it going, lad, any luck?" I smile down at the youngster.

"Crap, bleddy rubbish. Not even a bleddy bite, Maccy. I've been here longer than you were on the church roof, yakking your bleddy head off to Alice Copestick. I reckon you buggers frightened the bleddy fish off. It's useless."

"Sorry lad."

"You bleddy should be. Was she naked, Maccy?"

"That's just for me and her to know, youngster. Nothing to interest you in that direction."

"Come on, don't give me that crap. Was she naked or not, could you see her titties, could you see her Oyster?"

"I told 'e. How old are you lad?"

"Ten, nearly eleven. I'm older than you think."

"You can't be. What bait are you using lad?"

"Mackerel strips. I cut up a mackerel. I got plenty more."

"Why are you fishing if you already have fish?" Michael asks the very same question that is puzzling me.

"I dunno, I idn't too clever."

"That's true enough, youngster." I reply with honesty.

"I wouldn't let my brother steal my bleddy ladder."

"Look kid, mackerel idn't a lot of good in these waters. Listen to me, you need Cod's eyes hereabouts. Cod's eyes, best bait of all."

"Cod's eyes, where can I get some of they, Maccy?"

"From Cod, I suppose. Look lad, you will have to go over and ask the skippers on the fishing boats, over there."

I point at the neat line of brightly painted boats that are bobbing up and down alongside the harbour wall.

"Look after my rod and gear for me."

"Can't lad. Got important stuff to do."

"Arseholes!"

"Come on Michael, time to be going, methinks." I feel some pity for the youngster as he leaves his gear unguarded and strides smiling towards his destination. The skippers will be in foul moods this morning. They will know a storm is approaching. They can't leave the harbour. Beer bellies would be grumbling for a day or two without their earning enough to fill them. Moods will already be dark, tempers will be short.

Michael and I clearly hear the tacker's sobs as we stride up Padstow Hill.

"I believe the kid might have caught something, Michael."

"A clip around the ear, I suspect, Maccy."

"I told him he'd catch something, didn't I, I said so."

"Aye, you did. Dusty's bleddy smart, Maccy."

"He has a good teacher, too bleddy good."

"What were you doing on the church roof, matey?"

"Michael, I was seeing the light."

"The father has been good to you, Maccy. What a wonderful experience."

"Not sure about the father, Michael. Lenny says he and Alice's old man ran off a couple of years ago with a woman from the fish market. Says his dad now lives with 'Lobster Woman' out at Mother Ivey's Bay.

"Gross!"

"As you say, Michael, as you say!"

Chapter Three

Into the Frying Pan

Grandad has roused us two while it is still dark outside. We creep about the house. Ma would not be best pleased at being disturbed at such an hour. Lenny arrives almost on time for once.

We wash, dress, eat a 'Full English heart attack' and sip hot tea. Within the hour we are on the road heading towards the old station a mile or two away. Dusty sleeps. On our arrival at the overgrown station buildings I reawaken him. He is grumpy. It makes no difference. There is man's work to be done.

I study the ivy infested station house. I am certain there is no way we can tug the thing back to the Tamryn Farm; even with a good tractor.

"No chance Grandad; we can't move this, it's too bleddy big."

"We're not taking that boy. No, no we've come for they buggers there." Grandad points a gnarled finger at the two peeling first class railway carriages standing dejectedly to one side of the crumbling platform.

The powerful tractor should make short work of moving the beasts, even if it is only half their size.

We boys clear clumps of scrubby grass away from the steel wheels while Grandad secures two heavy chains from the tractors' hook up to the first carriage.

We watch anxiously as the tractor lurches forward to take up the slack in the thick chains. It's amazing to see the carriage suddenly begin its first movement in years.

One hour later, the first wooden beast is at the farm. It settles nicely on a level patch of redundant land.

The removal of the second carriage is much easier, a simple task to follow the same route as the first. Any low hanging tree branches having been torn off at the first removal.

At the completion of our work Ma shouts us for food and we sit around the table. We fill our ready bellies with potato, turnip, onion and beef wrapped tightly inside golden pastry. There is nothing like a freshly baked, Joy Tamryn pasty. If anyone says differently, administer a hearty slapping to their upper section, in order to put the liar straight.

The Pullman pilfering would be Grandad's final act of deviltry. No more would the old man venture into the removal business, any business. The favourite man in my life would never again take us boys out on the tractor. Never again be in a position of a parent that isn't. The man Dusty and I looked up to as a father and mentor passed away that same evening. It was a departure of the strangest kind. I can hardly bring myself to talk of it. It is only right I do.

Grandad, having disposed of a jug full of his own home brewed cider in order to wash down the last morsels of the pasty, had decided to downgrade to the crap with the same name at our nearest hostelry; The Maltsters Arms.

The tiny Maltsters Arms is tucked away in the next hamlet, Little Petrock. If twenty folks are in attendance at the bar it would resemble an almost full sardine can.

Grandad Tamryn had stumbled from the ramshackle Maltsters and it seems he'd taken a shortcut through a small wood to get home before daylight. It was on this return journey that the mishap must have occurred.

The wheels of fate, like the wheels of the two aged carriages, must have rumbled into action. The old feller, in his misty brained forgetfulness must have climbed the stile to oblivion.

Less than a hundred yards from home lays the great tree encircled pit. A quarry of ancient times where Cornishman of the past must have hacked, chipped and drilled the grey-blue slate from Mother Earths' bowels to fashion roof tiles and cold, hard flooring for the two roomed hovels they must have called home.

The great pit is still in use even in this twentieth century. There is a chance it will last even into the next. Slowly, but unfortunately not fast enough to have saved Grandad, it is being filled. You name it, it's down there, except now my beloved relative.

The old man might have climbed the stile to nowhere or could just have tripped. 'Is it physically possible to stumble and trip when legless?' It would seem so!

Whatever; Dusty and I had been sent out in search and somehow it had taken just a few minutes to find his cold, broken remains. The peculiar thing about our discovery was a battered peak cap that remained clutched in his death grasp. A peak cap bearing a rusted badge and its dulling inscribed message: Great Western Railway! There was a hint of a smile etched on the old man's weather-beaten face as we reached him. The cap did not belong to him I'm certain.

What happened? Did the old chap find the battered headgear here as he rolled and tumbled down the slope? Did he snatch at it as he came to a halt after the fall?

Perhaps some mist enshrouded apparition had waylaid him. A spectre dressed in the old olive-green uniform of the GWR might have approached demanding the return of the rusting rolling stock so recently dislodged and removed. Did the old station master appear? Did the two fight to the death; one of them at least? Grandad would have been dead drunk, nothing more. The other would have already been promoted to station master in the sky. Could the battered hat have been snatched while the two fought; man, against spectre? It's a mystery and forever will be. I took that battered cap from his chilled bony fingers. I knew just what to do with it, where it should be laid to rest.

Grandad was extracted from a junk filled hole, one side of the main coastal road that slices through our village and put into another, much smaller and relatively empty one, on the other side. It had been a good thing Dusty and I had found him: Rest in Peace has a nicer ring to it than Rust in Peace.

The whole village turned out for the funeral. The Methy Minister from Padstow spoke some words about him. To be fair his long speech wasn't all good, but our local vicar was satisfyingly determined to even things up!

Ma, Dusty and me rightfully cried; but not for long. I do believe she thought in me she had a readymade replacement. The three of us and others so inclined, everyone, proceeded solemnly around the bend and over the tiny, ancient bridge that spans Little Petrock Creek. We'd entered the Maltsters and as far as I know that old peaked cap can still be seen hanging on a nail above the bar as a warning to all. 'Don't go down in the woods at night!' Nasty surprises are never the best.

The storm that had threatened had exploded into life, flourished and just as surely expired in much the same way Grandad might have. It had blown up from the West about the time he shambled down to the Maltsters and was diminishing as Dusty and I tripped over the cold, wet remains. It had been a shock to the pair of us to find him lying broken amongst all the broken crap in the hole. In the short ferociousness of the storm, Grandad had at least gone out with a heavenly crescendo, without any angels hanging around and making a musical racket.

None of us knew what the old feller wanted those old train carriages for, none of us ever would. Slowly, they would fill with unwanted junk and rubbish, which would have been better off down the pit. My Grandad was a collector of anything useful or useless. He never did get the chance to make his own donations to their interior.

Those coaches quickly became useful for our vagrant, multibreed chicken flock and half dozen, half wild cats. They would make their homes inside and underneath. On summer days foxes would laze on the ancient curved roofs.

There was one unfortunate hen that got in the way of Ma's erratic driving. It was a mess and there was no way it could be sorted out by vet nor oven.

Another time, Ma flattened a poor orphaned kitten. I'd watched helplessly a day or two before as its mother had been whisked away by a sharp-eyed Sparrow hawk.

The sad little bugger had been blind from birth and had somehow decided to sleep in the shade beside the wheel of her car. As they say, whoever they are: 'life's a bitch', 'shit happens', 'Que Sera Sera'. Grandad was a great fan of Doris Day.

It is our hope that one day, Ma will even take her driving test.

To say we three got over the loss of Grandad with ease would be wrong somehow. He'd hardly had a day's illness, so his departure was totally unexpected. Anyway, we Tamryns blew our chests out. Ma didn't need to obviously. We got on with our lives. We were sure it's what he would have wanted. I hadn't been one to hang on to his coattails. With the old man's sudden absence, I made some plans to move my own young life on.

It is time for me to earn some money, get a job. I didn't need to. I could stay around what is fast becoming a financial success, the Magic Mushroom Farm. Mixing concrete isn't my idea of fun. I should explain. Ma has her own cottage industry; she produces concrete garden ornaments, mushrooms to be precise. They are everywhere, all over the country. She churns them out and away they go. There's one in Downing Street apparently That's what Ma says when she has a reluctant buyer. It could be true?

Anyway, there's always Dusty. It's about time he did his bit about the place. Ma knows she can call on me if she is pushed. For now, I'd taken enough of her money. If by chance, Hollywood did call to say they are making a Mushroom blockbuster I will roll up my sleeves again. Somehow, for me, Day of the Mushrooms doesn't hold the same latent threat as 'Day of the Triffids'.

I determined to find something different to do. I'm not sure I shouldn't have stayed where I was. I'd been in the Mermaid before of course. Mostly I was thrown out by the landlady. There is no disgrace in that.

Known to almost every local as The Granite Goddess, Blencathra could not only be described as a shock for sore eyes, she would be apt to supply them to any agitator. I'd say she was twenty-five stone but if I said it at all it would be under my breath and from a fair distance. Twenty-five stone of muscle and somehow one gets the impression her head is as wide as her girth.

If out on the town for an evening, Blencathra would look splendid in a funnel from the Titanic, so long as folks are careful of flying rivets.

Bligh is the husband. Oh yes Blen' is married; to a man with a facial waterfall. The old feller could put out moorland fires for a pastime. On a good day, small boats could be launched from Bligh's top lip. In a water shortage, he could run a bath.

I found myself idling outside the creaking inn and then I found myself inside the interior where the creaking grew in strength. I looked up ominously for a second at the thickly cobwebbed ceiling and expected something nasty to come through.

"Don't worry lad, that be my Blen', she 'ave gone to the bathroom to wash her feet."

"Wouldn't 'er find it easier to take off her steel toe cap boots matey?" I suggested.

"Shhhh, Jesus Christ boy, if she 'ears 'e, you'll be wishing this was a bleddy hospital. You idn't gonna live long in here boy, no sir!"

I couldn't help myself. "You seem to be doing okay."

"Look boy I'm bleddy busy. What the hell do you want to go with the thick ear you're gonna get drekly?"

"I wanna job here." What was I saying? I might just as easily have climbed back up the church tower and hung myself with the rope on the flagpole. I'd only get covered in seagull shit or some half-witted holidaymaker would

28

come and try and talk me out of it. There's no future in trying to do away with yourself in Padstow. Even when I wasn't inclined to, some tosser thought I was.

"I dunno about a job. I do all the work about the place."

Bligh gave me enough time to decide what 'all' was that he did about the place. Nothing, apart from pouring the occasional beer sprang to mind. I waited, watched and listened patiently for further information.

I study the old geezer going through his facial motions. The old git's nose is twitching, I see what might be the beginning of an eventual downpour forming at the tip of that marvellously revolting centrepiece.

Nervously, I take a step backwards in fear and anticipation and something soft and foul-smelling on the floor. It is discarded food of some description. I shake most of it from my trainer and return my eyes to Bligh's potential facial cloudburst.

I don't know why I am so worried; the Captain has it all under control. He completes the drying process with a bar towel advertising Dry Cider; I am fascinated to watch the old feller's next move. The old sod is using the soggy cloth to wipe dry a pint glass. I am almost for running right there and then. A good job I'm made of sterner stuff.

"Oozat you're talking to down there, Bligh?"

This is the unmistakable booming voice of the Mermaid's landlady. I'd heard it many times before and have no doubt it will resonate about me on numerous occasions in the future. It isn't so much frightening. Maybe it is.

"Bleddy hell, the cannons on the Victory couldn't make that much noise." I venture.

"It's young Maccy Tamryn, says he be looking for a part-time job my lover. He's likely to get a fat lip if he doesn't shut his gob!"

"Send the little bugger up here to me. Let me see what I can do with him."

Its possible Blencathra is confusing me with someone else. Last time I looked my age was just a single digit different from my weight. As I'm seventeen, 'little' hardly applies to me anywhere. I break my silence and go for broke.

"Now look here Cap'n, you tell your Blen' I don't do heavy lifting. Beer barrels, stroppy customers, no problem, that's all."

"You cheeky bugger. You can 'ave a fair trial lad. We'll see if you're any good drekly."

A 'trial'. I haven't done anything wrong apart from step willingly into Padstow's own hell. What if I was found guilty: The Ducking Stool over the quayside, a nasty burning at the stake?

"You bring yourself back here later this evening lad and I'll find you something to do. I can't promise no bleddy wages mind."

"No wages? I don't believe I mentioned money, Cap'n. A couple of pints in lieu should do well enough."

"In Looe, if you're in Looe you can't be working here. You'll have to make your mind up boy. Either you want a job, or you'd rather be waltzing all about the county. You can't be in both places at once."

Bligh is fully aware of my meaning. The old geezer is as sharp as a tack and will use any available tool to avoid the subject of handing over money.

I may be only seventeen but I'm a willing learner. Bligh, if nothing else, is a first-class teacher; a third-class pub landlord but a first-class teacher.

"If you're here later I'll show you how to pull a pint lad, if you're not I won't bother, choice is yours."

"Listen Cap'n; how about if I don't go away; then you'll know I'll be here and you won't be disappointed. I'll work for a couple of pints a night and tips."

"Tips, what bleddy tips?"

I would sort the tips out myself, I decided.

"It's a deal. You watch the bar for me while I make my Blen' her damn tea."

"But what about training?"

"You're being lippy again lad. I know what I'm doin', now get yourself back behind here, sharpish and find me a clean glass."

"I reckon I can pull a pint Cap'n. I can't do bleddy miracles."

Somehow, I didn't quite think it was all going to happen this way. I saw myself as humping barrels, scrubbing the cellar floor, cleaning beer lines and putting out the rubbish; which could still happen, only the 'rubbish' looks like it will be pulling pints for a while.

Well, I suppose I feel as though I'm looking a gift horse in the face. I shouldn't be complaining.

Imagine my face at the sudden attendance of Alice Copestick as my first customer of that evening. Alice is alone. She looks different tonight. Clothes will do that to a woman I suppose. The golden halo is still in place, just a little dimmer than at our earlier meeting, but that is mainly due to the poor lighting in the Mermaid Bar. It does my heart good to see her but not as much as the morning's vision did.

"Alice, what can I do you for?"

"Hmm, I wonder Maccy Tamryn. What are you doing behind there, are you old enough?"

"Old enough for you my lover. You just tell me what you want and I'll do my best to satisfy your every need."

"Will you now?"

"Yes, I won't disappoint you my lover."

"What about my Mervyn, he can get real jealous."

"Well seeing as I saw the bugger pulling away in his boat nigh on half an hour ago I don't expect I'll worry much. 'Have Mervyn gone out night fishing, Alice?"

"Naw, he have gone across the estuary for his tea at home with his mother."

"Don't you cook for him then Alice?"

"Mervyn says I idn't much good in the kitchen."

"And is he right my lover?"

"Just half right Maccy, just half right." Alice winks at me and I believe right then I can read her mind.

31

"Mervyn is gonna have a long wait to get back, Alice. Didn't the bugger check the tides, they be going out and he will have to walk miles across the mudflats to get back before we close up for the night."

"Tidn't nothin' to worry about Maccy. You just told me you'd look after my needs."

"And I will too but I gotta watch the bar for the Blighs right now. Blen' is having a bath and the Cap'n is scrubbing her back. Wire brush or Brillo pad I shouldn't wonder. And then he is preparing a banquet of some sort. A pig-roast I believe."

"Maccy Tamryn, I can hear you down there boy, watch your bleddy mouth." It is Blencathra.

"Bleddy hell and there is me thinkin' only whales and dolphins have sonar bleddy hearing." Maybe it's a water thing.

I didn't set eyes on the Captain again until closing time; methinks he and Blencathra had some sort of early night effort before he got back up from his bed again at closing time.

I earned myself a couple of quid and three pints of Todger's Droop for my trouble. One pint had belonged to One-Armed Frank Pendrake. He forgot to drink it, so I helped him out. I don't understand why folk come out to the pub, buy a drink and go to sleep for two hours; it doesn't make sense. The old bugger only awoke to have a smoke and was straight off again.

Frank and Lil the Tart were my only customers other than Alice. Dear old Lil with her Gin and Tonic would smile crookedly as she made up Frank's rollies. It isn't an easy task for him with just the one arm.

After closing for the night, Alice walked me home. Not to my own of course. Well if she had walked me to mine she would have to turn right around and walk back again. There'd be no time for anything else.

I did have to spend a while canoodling with her at the end of the quay. The two of us stared romantically at the moon as it kissed the Atlantic millpond, but you must

32

expect that sort of thing where the ladies are concerned. It was all pleasant enough. We two eventually went up to the penthouse. I wasn't downhearted that Alice didn't go through her fitness routine again but she is obviously the better for her morning exertions. No sign of a dead moggy anywhere.

I got myself out and away just before daylight. I never did see Mervyn again during the evening which was a blessing. He may only have the one eye, but I wouldn't want the bugger keeping it on me. I have heard he's pretty nifty with a gutting knife.

The sacred Alice even hinted at the possibility of my nudging big Mervyn out of his side of the bed permanently. I had to tell her I was just too young and inexperienced to take on such responsibility although I took her offer as a compliment, which at the time it surely was.

"Suit your bleddy self." She had said in a mild strop at our predawn parting.

I did. Dear Lenny, as I have already explained, is the best friend anyone can have but my late evening dalliance with his elder sister would put a smidgen of strain on our friendship. Lenny is touchy about the females in his life. It's the one reason I never returned the advances from his mother the one time I stayed overnight at his. Lenny would have gone ballistic.

I just wish I had taken the lovable Alice's self-confession about her cooking prowess a tad more seriously! Other than that, Alice could best be described as having fire. Chances are I'll be back in the frying pan in the near future.

Chapter Four

Storm and a Teacup

Later that same morning I had my first proper verbal encounter with PC Twotrees. Twotrees, despite his name, is a strange one and no mistake. The copper shone his torch into the side window of a quayside café at just before six a.m. and there was I, beaming right back at him.

After my earlier exertions, I'd decided not to bother walking all the way home. I would wait for old Bert the cleaner to arrive and let him know I was there. I did, he did, and he wasn't surprised to be greeted with a mug of steaming tea.

I know my way about Padstow like no other, its back alleys and buildings better than anyone. As for breaking and entering? I didn't break anything and as far as I know stealing a mug full of hot water and a teabag is not an offence punishable by anything resembling death.

Talltrees, unknowing that Bert, the old geezer and I were on friendly terms, decided to lay down the law in my direction.

Tell me I'm wrong but if you ask me, he's out of his tree. The following is the conversation we had after I let Twotrees in with old Bert's keys. I idly spun the heavy bunch around my finger as the copper questioned me in the manner of Kojak, minus a lollipop, only he sounded more serious than Telly Savalas. He would do, Savalas was an actor.

"Is this your property…? Sir"

"Not as far as I know." I got the feeling 'Sir' was something of an afterthought.

"Are you employed here?"

"No." I wanted to say; 'no comment'.

"Did you break into these premises?"

34

"No."

"Did you enter the premises with the intention to steal?"

"No."

"Did you secrete yourself about the property while it was still operating yesterday?"

"No."

"As far as you're aware, does the owner know you're here?"

"I doubt it."

"And what do you think he would say to me if I told him?"

"No idea."

"Does anyone know you're here?"

"Yes."

"And who might that be?"

"There's you." I was almost disappointed in the lack of effort in my replies by now.

"Shout when you want a top-up Bert." Bert was out of sight; mopping ketchup stained floors and pocketing any small change he might find.

"I will Maccy, thanks lad, you're a good boy. Put some more bread in the toaster lad and bacon, put some bacon on for us boy."

"What do e want with n Bert?"

"Just more bacon Maccy, good lad."

"Goodbye officer, have a nice day, eventually."

"But, but, what about a mug of tea?"

"No thanks, I already have one."

See what I mean? Two trees only wanted a free tea.

Bert reappeared beside me as Talltrees left in a confused huff. "You shouldn't antagonise the tosser Maccy!"

"He started it Bert."

"Ais, he did."

This is the copper who thinks he can catch speeding drivers in his sleep!

A little later as I gazed over the quayside, I notice Mervyn returning from Rock, the lumpy posh place across the water. I wait while he steps off the early ferry. He climbs the worn and slippery ancient steps.

"Morning Maccy, you're up and about early lad."

"Ais Mervyn, old Bert and me have been having breakfast in the café. You have just got back from your Ma's, have you?"

"I 'ave Maccy, 'ow the bleddy 'ell could you knaw that?"

"Lucky guess pard'. Say good morning to Alice for me when you see her."

"I will Maccy, I'm on my way there for my own breakfast."

"I thought as much. Does she cook well matey?"

"Nah, she does her best but it idn't good. Between you and I lad, I'm not with her for her skills with a frying pan. Do you know what I mean?"

"Yes, I believe I do Mervyn, I believe I do."

As for me settling in with a woman, Alice anyway, I'm far too young and have too much to do for the next five years. I prefer to see my woman across the roof tops and chimney pots. From that day on, it was the only time and place we two ever spoke about our star counting night together. We would most likely chat a lot but not about that. A hundred plastic luminous stars had shone down on us from her bedroom ceiling.

Not that I got into the habit of settling on the tower regularly. Just occasionally I'll pop up there with the blind box, for a chat with the governor and Alice of course. There's no harm in looking. Talking to Alice in this way is rather like having a long-distance conversation without the electronic stuff.

I hear from Alice. She and Mervyn are to be married soon. They're much too young but I wish them all the best for the future. Mervyn will need all the help he can get.

It was the strangest thing that happened as I left the café after chewing the bacon fat with Bert. I had pulled the side door shut after me and noticed something on the ground. I bent and picked the item up. It was a wallet and without looking inside, I could feel it was pretty much loaded.

The meeting with Mervyn had made me temporarily forget the bulge in my back pocket.

I take it out again as I walk and turn it over and over before eventually opening it. The name on the driving license means nothing to me. P. Calhoun. This is not the property of a local. I am certain no one of the name lives in Padstow. I know all the newcomers. I know all the old timers though they don't all know me. There is a thick wad of twenty-pound notes inside the wallet. I'm not interested enough to take them out and count them. I am not about to go in search of Twotrees with my recent find. I have other ideas.

At the completion of my interview and intensive one-minute induction course, Bligh had given me a key for the cellar door at the back of the pub. I could come and go when the beer lines needed cleaning, or the empty barrels putting out for the draymen.

I use my key to let myself into the cold, damp area. I pass through another door that leads into the Mermaid Bar, another cold damp area. Even in summer the Mermaid is like the interior of a coffin after a burial at sea. I settle myself on a bar stool and with a tall, chilled orange juice and wait for signs of life. I fingered the thick wallet and wondered who P. Calhoun might be. It is a strange find as I'm positive the wallet wasn't present when I let myself into the café. It could have been.

Rather than go chasing Talltrees who more than likely was already tucked up in bed with a cuddly toy or an inflatable doll, I propose to tell the Cap'n of my discovery. I would ask him what my best course of action might be. Once more I flip the wallet open. I try to find out more about the owner. It couldn't do any harm to look.

Some coins fall out. A photograph rests behind the plastic shield; a baby. So, he, or she, the owner, is a parent or grandparent. Lastly, I pull out the thick wad of crisp notes. They amount to almost two thousand pounds. I am a tad shocked at my find.

I should explain here that the money, although an impressive amount, has no interest to me whatsoever. I could pocket the lot and probably sell the license on for a tidy sum; that isn't me, not my way at all.

If I am skint which I mostly am, thanks to Dusty, I would only need to ask Ma for a sub. My one and only parent would scold, lecture and scowl at me but any needed cash would be forthcoming. Dusty and I hardly ever went cap-in-hand to Ma. Somehow, we both made money when we needed it. As you now know, Dusty makes his out of me.

Stealing is just not my thing; the odd teabag, bacon sandwich perhaps, nothing more. Scavenging, I can do scavenging; the odd roadside skip or the quarry when I could be in need of something I might discover down there.

I slide the large notes, all twenties, back inside before closing it up, I take one last look at the photograph. A cute curly headed blonde lad had smiled willingly at the photographer. I drop the overloaded leather case onto the bar, as Bligh yawns his way in behind it.

The old bloke takes just a fleeting glance at me as he blindly searches below the top for a glass. A grubby tumbler is shoved under the Scotch optic twice. In one go, Bligh downs its contents. The old landlord shivers in satisfaction and pulls another double; he sets the glass down leaving the contents so far undisturbed.

"What's all this Maccy lad?" Snotty snatched up the wallet and turned it around in his hand in the same way I had.

"It's a wallet Cap'n."

"I knaw it's a bleddy wallet. I seen one before but not as thick as this'n. I got one myself but there's bugger all in it."

"I found it, down at the back of the café on the quay."
Why did he ask what it was?

"Found it, you found it?"

"Well I never had it with me before I picked it up offen the ground, so I must have."

"And all this was in it?" The old git didn't take all the cash out. I'm sure he has an inkling as to how much there is.

"Well, I haven't put any in there and I've taken none out. It's all there, as I found it."

"I believe e lad. I wasn't suggestin" you'd 'elped yourself to some, like you 'ave my bleddy orange juice. What are us gonna do with it boy?"

"I dunno, that's why I"m here, to see what you thought about it."

"'Ave e looked inside for a name lad?"

"Yes, tis P. Calhoun."

"I don't know anyone called P. Calhoun." The landlord pushed a hand through the sparse scrubland that hardly covers his head. "Foreign by the sounds of things. Irish I bet. Bugger won't be Scots or he wouldn't have lost it, would 'e?"

"Wouldn't know myself, expect you're right. What would you do iffen you'd found the bleddy thing?"

"Me? I'd get around to the bookmakers sharpish and pay the bugger what I owe, mebbe."

Somehow, almost impossibly to all that know her, Blencathra has appeared in the bar. She had arrived downstairs in silence. Now I'm no small fry but she towers over both the Cap'n and I. I felt like I was at the toddler's school with the biggest teacher available looming over me. I almost held out a hand out to receive six whacks of a cane. Thank God she zoomed in on the shaky husband like a heat-seeking missile. 'Shock and awe' might describe her arrival.

"What's goin" on down 'ere? I could 'ear you buggers whispering from in the bath."

Blencathra is wearing a dressing gown that would make Lennox Lewis look like a midget. Thank goodness it isn't too small for her, that the belt seems to be holding fast. I wouldn't want it coming loose for fear of being buried in an avalanche of quivering, pulsating flesh.

Bligh belatedly attempts to hide the whiskey filled glass from Blencathra's view; he is too late, she has already seen it. Her look is one of stone production; thankfully it is thrown in the old feller's direction.

The Cap'n spoke up for himself. It was the weakest of excuses.

"I 'ad the bleddy toothache my lover, t'was givin" me gip something bleddy awful. Whiskey be good for toothache, they do say."

"You go and tell 'they, whoever they be to come and tell me. Wait, tell them to come and tell me, 'ow the bleddy 'ell you can 'ave bleddy toothache when all your bleddy teeth be on the bleddy bedside table! Mebbe you should take that glass of bleddy whiskey upstairs and let your bleddy teeth 'ave breakfast in bed."

Now I could see the old geezer feels like he is in with the headmistress. It is a wonder to me that he doesn't go to the back of the room.

"Now then Maccy do you have something to say, my bird?"

"Not me Blen, nope, I"m happy to listen and learn from you my 'ansome."

"So you should be. What's this wallet doin' there, who does it belong to?"

"It belongs to P. Calhoun, we think, that's the name on the driving licence inside." I didn't know if I should have been replying to her but as Bligh didn't look as though he would be doing so any time soon, I think it best to speak up.

"What about all this cash in here? Pretty little nipper, bless n!"

"I suppose that do too, Blen', what do you think?"

"Who's this P. Calhoun when he's at 'ome?"

"Us don't know Blen, see that's the problem. I don't think he is at home. If he'd been home, he might not have lost it!"

"I think it should be me that should take hold and look after this until we can find the rightful owner."

"I was about to suggest that very solution Blen'. I think the Cap'n said something along those lines before you flew down here."

"Flew, flew down here, what do you mean Maccy bleddy Tamryn, you best take your bleddy words out and take a good look at them before you send them in my direction, my lad."

"Tis easy Blen', you must have floated down here like a lost butterfly as we two never even heard a dainty footfall from you, isn't that right Cap'n?"

"Maccy's right my lover, he's right. Us didn't know you was 'ere, 'til you were 'ere."

And so for now, the mystery of the wallet is taken from my hands, snatched away by Padstow's own Sphinx. I'm glad. I have other things on my mind.

I also have the feeling Blen' is about to embark on firing a broadside at the poor old geezer for his midmorning withdrawal from the Bank of Scotch Whiskey. It is something I didn't feel the need to witness. I leave the old geezer floundering helplessly, not unlike a recently landed flounder. I am in search of calmer waters and bigger fish.

I stand outside for a minute or two and the silence from inside is deafening. The lull before the storm I think. I decide I would take cover from any fallout. I would make a visit to some old and dear friends. I would have to put to sea for the purpose.

Lady Alma and Admiral Birdsall live in the quay. Don't get me wrong, they aren't members of some aquatic nation and related, albeit distantly to Patrick Duffy, nor leftovers from the mud larks of nineteenth century fame. The Birdsalls, known to us locals as the Birdseyes, live on their own little floating home. A small, expensive cabin cruiser. I had noticed a flurry of activity about the boat in the last few days and was interested enough to ask.

"Come aboard Maccy lad, come aboard."

The voice belongs to Alma. Lady Alma as we mostly call her but only behind her back. She is something of an enigma, there are a lot of folk around here who can claim to be such. Alma hails from East London and is a true cockney whereas the Admiral doesn't and isn't. I love to listen to her talk as she just adds a smidgen of airs to her cockney speech and graces to her well pronounced movements.

The Admiral appears at her shouted words. He repeats her friendly invitation. "Morning Maccy, welcome aboard my lad. What brings you out to our humble little home?"

Like I said, I had to put to sea. I accomplished this by stepping into nowhere for a split second and then by nervously landing my foot onto the Birdseye's pine decking. I'm not a regular seafaring man.

"Nothing Admiral. I was just interested in what you have been doing. Poking my nose is all."

"You shall have to come back when it's all completed lad, can't take you inside right now as there's wet varnish everywhere. Isn't that right darling?"

"Oh yes Maccy, everywhere and in any case my dear boy, the bar isn't complete yet. That's why the Admiral and I are out here for our elevenses. What would you like to drink young Maccy?"

Well the bar may not be finished but it isn't something that would stop the Birdseyes. There is a good array of spirit bottles on a crystal platter and matching glasses stand alongside.

Now I knew these two liked their gin and tonic. I rather fancy sitting on the plush little deck with a drink in my hand. I accept the invitation without hesitation and ask for my G&T. There was a slice of lemon deftly dropped in beside the ice cubes by the old man, without my having to ask for it.

"I hear you are working in the Mermaid, Maccy."

"That's right Alma darlin', apparently I'm filling in for the barman Bligh didn't even know he needed."

"We shall be in to see you when we get the chance and see what kind of job you're making of it my lad."

"Tis only until I leave for college Alma."

"So, you're going to college Maccy, good lad and what will you be learning at college?"

"I'm gonna be learning to cook Admiral. When I have done that, I'll be learning how to make it pay."

"That's the spirit lad. Have a top up."

"Have you noticed any strangers about the quay?" From their vantage point, the Birdseyes would likely see anything or anyone unusual about the quayside.

"Can't say I have. What about you Alma dear?"

"Not that I recall. Why do you ask Maccy?"

I tell the Birdseyes about my find and what had become of it since. They promise to keep all eyes open for the unfortunate and so far, faceless P. Calhoun. I glance at my watch and decide I have nothing better to do and even if I had, the Admiral had already taken hold of my glass and is replenishing it. I believe I will be settled in for a while. The Birdseyes are a little eccentric but well, who isn't in Padstow? The main thing is they are excellent company and I make the most of my time here. Just once or twice, I felt Alma was being a tad provocative and not a little suggestive. Normal really. I managed, as any invited guest should, to fend off her none too subtle attentions. Not that Alma is in any way unattractive, even though I suspect she is already well past sixty; far from it and the Admiral is by now asleep on his lounger. At some other time, I might have showed some encouragement.

It seems the Tamryn menfolk have always been burdened with some magnetic attraction to the fairer sex.

I leave the pair to soak in their gin and the soft, late autumn sunshine. I am rather pleased with myself. In amongst the debris that had been removed from the boat's interior were the miniaturised bathroom fittings, common to such craft. Before his eyes fully closed the Admiral had with raised eyebrows promised the tiny bath, bidet and bijou toilet pan would be mine. I had no idea why I wanted them; just didn't like to see the semi-elegant pieces go to waste. At some time soon, Lenny and I would need to get them transferred to the Tamryn farm. The spirit of Grandad lives on.

That very night Ma told me and the kid all about our great, great, I'm not certain how great he was, grandfather. It was an unusually cold frostbiting night and the three of us were confined by the ice crusted Cornish lanes, to the house. Ma was dispensing with a second bottle of Cabernet Sauvignon. Dusty and I were making do with lager that might have been extracted from a Hedgehog's bladder. Bad as it was, we drank it; Ma drank her dark red wine and we got onto the subject of our ancestors. This is how Ma's telling of the story went:

"Henry McCarthy lived in Cork, Ireland. He had the wanderlust. When he was in his early twenties, not much older than you boys, he took a ship from Cork to New York; from there he travelled to the Kansas Plains. Along the way he met and befriended his future business partner, Tafflyn Edwards. Don't forget this was all in the eighteen seventies. A hundred years or more ago. Anyway, he and Tafflyn jumped from the train somewhere in the back of beyond and somehow, while gambling, the pair of them won a saloon in a card game, in the middle of nowhere. As far as I know it's still there today."

"What's it called Ma?"

Dusty and myself were mightily interested in this tale and he asked the question before I did.

"The pub, the saloon was called The Plainsman, I'm sure it was. As far as I know Henry and Taffy virtually built the place themselves. They had to rebuild it more than once as it was almost blown over by a tornado on at least one occasion."

"It seems Henry and the woman that had been running the place married. She already had a son, Joey. Henry and the woman had two children of their own, two girls I think.

44

One daughter was my grandmother, Patricia! Patricia, for some reason returned to her roots in Cork and that's how I came about. That's it, near enough."

"No, there must be more." Dusty questioned Ma again before I could manage one of my own.

"Not much, but Henry eventually became the mayor of the town and Taffy was the police chief. Henry killed a man with a revolver, so did Taffy when he was the Town Marshal."

"Why Ma, why did Henry kill someone, who was it?"

"The man who owned the saloon and lost it in the card game. In a temper, he attacked the woman and Henry shot him to death."

"They were cowboys. My great, great grandad was a cowboy?"

"Yes, I suppose he was. But that's not all. The town was named after him. McCarthy. It's empty now and mostly derelict from what I hear. It's what the yanks call a ghost town I believe."

"How do you know so much about it?"

"I hear from Ireland sometimes."

Chapter Five

Home Sweet Home

"Lenny, I'm gonna move outta the farmhouse." I announce proudly to my buddy.

"You leaving home Maccy, bugger that old buddy, you'll starve. You'll look like a bleddy tramp in quick time?" Lenny suggests.

"No pard, I idn't goin' far, I'm gonna build my own gaff at the farm. Remember them old railway carriages that we helped Grandad Tamryn steal that are full of crap and stuff? It's time they were put to good use."

"Yeah, I know we put most of the crap in them didn't we."

"One man's crap can just as easily be another man's crap. They're what I'm gonna move into. They're gonna be my new gaff. First we have to get rid of all the junk."

"Why did we collect it in the first place?"

"No idea. Why does anyone?"

"I don't know Maccy. Thought you did knaw, it's mostly your'n."

"Nope. If we hadn't, we wouldn't have anything to do."

"That's true mucker. Fair enough. I didn't think of that."

I'd spent the occasional night sleeping inside one of them before. They were quite useful whenever I'd got into some minor trouble and had wanted to keep out of the way of Ma. Her glare can occasionally be a tad vicious.

"You've slept in them too mate."

"That's so. Anyway, you'll need my help old buddy to get the crap back out. That's too big a job for one man." Lenny replied helpfully. I knew he would.

"Ais it is, I reckon I will Len, so you up for it?" I ask.

The two carriages are nestled in a corner of a field on our farm, just about invisible from anywhere but from the air. They have been there since the day Grandad passed away. They stand as a kind of silent monument to him.

The old station at Camel's Halt closed back in nineteen sixty-four. A government minister going by the name of Doctor something had wantonly decided the Wadebridge to Padstow line was no longer financially viable. All because less than five thousand Cornish chose to ride on it to England each week. A half million English come to the Duchy for their yearly vacations and long weekends. What's the point of us going there? If the Duchy's good enough for the emmets, it should be good enough for us.

No one bothered much about the rusting remains left behind after the major surgery, until the old man swiped the coaches. It was the beginning. I noticed later the disappearance of several long sections of rails and other bits and bobs. The rails probably wound up with the local scrap metal merchant and fetched a tidy reward. The farm next to ours has a signal tower in one of its fields. It reminds me of a mechanical scarecrow effort. Someone else stole the gates from the Mellingey Mill crossing. It still doesn't stop you looking both ways when you approach. Silence now prevails. I'm sure they're in a railway enthusiast's garden somewhere, doing nothing. There are still some strips of rail in the main street at Wadebridge. More at Helland on Bodmin Moor!

Since the day the coaches arrived, they had only been used as store sheds for useless farm tools and rusting bicycle frames. I have no idea where most of the items came from. Dusty might know. We had no idea why Grandad wanted the carriages, he never did say. He didn't get the chance what with expiring so suddenly.

Lenny and I would empty the first coach and make a start at leveling it off properly. I wouldn't want to accidentally roll out of bed, especially if I wasn't alone. When the first is level we could pull the other closer, facing the two end to end.

47

"I'll see thee in the morning then Lenny, don't be late boy. Breakfast at ours and we'll get on with it drekly."

"I'll be there. Remind your Ma I like my bacon crispy and fried bread not bleddy toasted and spaghetti not bleddy baked beans, they play bleddy havoc with my guts."

"Yes, they do, as if I'd forget. Tell her yourself when you get there Lenny. Just don't leave your chin sticking out too far, Ma might just take a swing at it when she gets your order." To be fair, Ma wouldn't take a swing at anything. She is placid physically. She can talk worth a fight mind if one gets on the wrong side of her.

"Okay mate, I'll see you in the morning. What about mushrooms, and grilled tomatoes?"

"Steady now Lenny, you're starting to sound like a bleddy emmet lad. It's a kitchen, not a bleddy café!" My friend likes his breakfast far too much. Truthfully, he likes any food too much!

Lenny would keep his promise once he knew he'd be eating some of Ma's good old fashioned, farmhouse cooking. He'd stuff himself at his leisure. We wouldn't get on to our task until midmorning. I know my mate of old, he'll be late. Lenny doesn't do early!

Ma is fond of Lenny, she treats him like a family member. Our AWOL father hadn't been seen since Maggie entered her residence at 10 Downing Street, which coincidentally, was about the same time Dusty was conceived and I was a two-year old pain in the arse. Grandad Tamryn filled the wayward father's shoes nicely. I'd like the chance to one day tell the bastard he was rendered unnecessary the day he departed. I still live in hope. We did alright without him. It will continue that way.

We got started early. Dusty mucked in to help. Like grandad, we'd used a tractor to accomplish the feat. It took us the best part of the day to maneuver the carriages into place. The tractor reared up on its back legs more than once. We finally got it done with a small amount of effing and blinding and the occasional drop of spilled blood.

Every bit of unwanted scrap is now deposited in the bottom of the quarry. I just hoped there was no one down there looking for something useful.

By the time we had the coaches sitting pretty, Dusty happened to notice a herd of grazing cattle in our neighbours' pasture. A certain look of devilment came over him. He was instantly up and running with a yell that sounded like the trail boss in Rawhide, or a marauding member of the Comanche Nation. Comanches wouldn't ride cattle of course. They were known to be superior horsemen, all the same.

Like myself, Dusty can't resist a ride. He was over the hedge like shit off a tin miner's shovel. Lenny and I were close behind. We three had worked our nuts off today. It was time for some fun.

Speaking of 'nuts,' it would be ideal for the male gender to not possess these anatomical necessities when attempting to ride a member of the bovine tribe. Horses are much less bony and can be saddled of course. Saddling a cow doesn't seem right somehow. Cows are inoffensive as a rule, but they are uncomfortable to sit astride. It's not intentional. Can't be helped!

For those who've never ridden a cow, they haven't lived. The beasts are so unpredictable; they do have a sense of humour, just absolutely no sense of direction. The only way to get three cows in a straight line is at the slaughter house in Wadebridge. Even if you could successfully line them up for a race, there'd be no winner; they'd all go straight off in different directions.

Cow to other cow: 'I'm bored. Think I might go see what happens at the Abattoir.'

'Can I come with you please?'

'Yeah, go on then, follow me and no dawdling.'

Anyway, we were having a great time until the farmer came yelling and squawking from his place, wildly waving what looked pretty much like a twelve bore shotgun. The fact he didn't fire the weapon was probably due to the value of our mounts. His language was a tad choice. We replied in a similar vein obviously. It didn't seem to placate him much.

He'd made quite a fuss. I don't believe the bugger went off in the best of moods, which was puzzling. I mean, let's be fair, we had given his beasts some exercise, which can only be a good thing. I've never seen him ride them. I have seen him chasing sheep though. That's another story.

I am pleased with our day's toil. We seemed to have worked miracles in just a few hours. With the aid of some of Ma's cement pallets, I'd be sleeping in the first carriage by the end of the week hopefully. The second is bound to be easier now we had shifted most of the crap to the hole in the ground.

Ma has a mountain of pallets from her concrete mushroom business. I am amazed at how well she'd done the last few years. For just a few quid she'd bought a secondhand cement mixer and made her own moulds. The dowdy grey ornaments are in garden centres everywhere. The mushroom profits would see me through college. From the start, you could say her business had mushroomed. It continues to do so.

My brother wouldn't be moving in with me. He much prefers the comforts of home, and Ma's fussing. Dusty is a year or so my junior. The kid is a lazy sod when it comes to mundane household tasks. He doesn't do housework. Ma claims she doesn't need our help.

Ma is an independent sort. She prefers to do everything herself. We two would bend our backs without complaint if she has a gamut of orders to fill. She wouldn't need to ask twice. She wouldn't have to ask. Even Lenny will help occasionally. My mate always works for three or four meals a day without complaint. We consider him an honorary member of the family. I once made a solemn vow I'd never tell anyone about my one-night affair with his sister. I know the golden-haired Alice will also be discreet. It would upset Lenny deeply and ruin our friendship. As I might have said before, he can be a tad touchy about the women in his life.

Not to mention Lenny's mother, and again I won't!

The following day, Lenny is at our door later than we agreed, which is no surprise. He eats everything which had not been claimed, before we go about the business of getting my digs closer to up and running. In time, we will construct a solid floor between the two coaches. This will conceal the coupling gear and connect both cars. After a few cold beers our interest waned somewhat. I decide to call a halt for the day.

Later that same afternoon in the Mermaid Bar, I overhear someone mention a cheap caravan for sale; I can hardly believe my luck! The van is mine for fifty quid. The owner is good enough to tow it back to the farm. He places it as close as possible to the two coaches and is on his way back to his pint with his cash. I now possess a miniature kitchen sink, gas stove and refrigerator, plus the posh bathroom and toilet fittings promised me by the Admiral. By the time I am through, the caravan will be a skeleton. Ninety percent of its contents were useful. Fifty quid well spent. Caravan now resting easy in quarry.

As for day three, I am on my own. Lenny fails to show, which doesn't surprise me. Dusty is in Wadebridge for a fancy haircut I wouldn't fancy. Better him than me. I spend the morning poking through the house. I find some soft floor covering and lay it in the first carriage. I'm chuffed with my resourcefulness. My future home is taking shape. The farmhouse is shrinking inside. I'm not sure if Ma knows I've been 'lifting' stuff from the house. If she does, it isn't mentioned. Ma never worries over the small stuff. She is basically still a hippy at heart. There's a lot of Ma in me!

On day four, I complete the construction of my bed which stretches across the entire eight feet width of the coach. There is ample storage space beneath. I have no mattress, so I use the abundance of cushions I had rescued from the caravan. They slot together perfectly to form a workable double sized bed. Nearly there!

For the next few days I concentrate on building a roof where the coaches connect. The cars are solid oak which makes it easy to join them both together. Once the doors are off, I'd have dry and easy access to both carriages. One thing I did notice while making the roof fixings was that I could see Rock from my vantage point.

In all honesty the posh place across the estuary is known better by other names, like the lumpy place, snobby cove, that sort of thing. Apart from one or two council houses it is well moneyed. A bit of an effluent, affluent society; well healed. I make a mental note that whenever I'm up on my roof, to look in the opposite direction. That too brings problems. I would be staring at Padstow Town. That would suggest me being between Rock and a hard place. It sort of reminds me of Clint Eastwood a tad. The Good, The Bad and the downright Ugly! As a Padstonian, I am trying not to be too affectionate towards the overly wealthy Rockites. One last mention about the outcrop should be this; the wealthy socialites are antisocial and the dozen or so social tenants of the Social Housing estate might be on the Social. It really is a funny old world!

My biggest problem is electricity. I am no electrician. I'm still breathing anyway. I do eventually manage to join enough coloured wires together correctly. I bring my power in from the old milking shed a few yards away. We don't have dairy products on legs like the bloke next door and so the shed is now redundant. I do have plans for it in the future. With the aid of a transformer, half a dozen tiny light bulbs glow proudly once more. It all looks pretty good. I have no idea where to get replacement bulbs when the time comes. I might need to take a look down the quarry.

I somehow manage to get things the way I like. I will at some point need to lay a gangplank. Mud is my enemy. The ladies won't want to venture here in high heels for fear of slipping on their arses! No one wants to see a woman crawl. Neither would I. The odd one might. Best of all, I have no address other than 'Train Carriages in a Field.' No address. No Poll Tax. No annoying and annoyed husbands!

I now have light, thanks to an old fashioned standpipe I also have water; the plumbing is scant. I would have to be content with 'bucket and chuck it' for the time being. Last, but not least, I add my stereo, a portable TV and a telephone. I'm not too keen on the TV or the phone, but I might get visitors. As for the caravan skeleton? It's down the pit, waiting for someone.

Although I have kept myself busy, thoughts of the Plainsman keep sliding themselves into the back of my mind. The subject won't go away. I must nag Dusty. I could go on my own. I believe this is something we must do together. My brother, despite his juvenile antics, is good company. That's how he tells it anyway.

Chapter Six

Birthday Suits

Little of what Ma related to Dusty and I on that cold night had come as a great surprise apart from the fact that Ma is a complete and total pacifist, though occasionally she has a glare that might cause a minor injury.

She has never raised a hand to either Dusty or me though I guess there would have been times when a good clip around the ear would be just reward for some teenage transgression. I'm admitting to nothing.

For a day or two now a section of my mind had been busily planning for the time when I would be making a transatlantic journey, to discover for myself what my great, great grandfather had discovered for himself; McCarthy City, the town and what might or might not be left of The Plainsman, a hotel. I need to see it for myself. I suspect Dusty would want to do the same. That's for another day, hopefully not too far in the future.

I decide I would linger and catch a quick pint at the Maypole Inn before tackling the hill. I must pass by the place and it would be unsociable if I didn't pop my head around the door.

I know, I'm still not eighteen but the landlady is easy going. One way or another, most ways from what I hear about town. I would be pleased with my decision. Eventually, I would almost regret it; it was a close thing!

As I enter, my memory suddenly provides a weird combination of a fast forward flashback effort. Thinking about my still being seventeen suddenly reminds me I am very soon to be eighteen. My social life planning department has been rather underworked recently.

I sip at my pint of Wrecker's Revenge and consider what I would have to do to organise my eighteenth bash.

Maybe Ma might already have plans, perhaps Dusty. No, Dusty doesn't do anything unless he's doing it with a young maid or for cash.

It is at this point my eyes focus on the Maypole's buxom landlady, Queenie. Fortunately for us but unfortunately for her husband, she returns my stare. I believe I will be staying longer than planned.

Perhaps Queenie knew of my soon to be elevation in age and has decided to give me an early birthday present. A kind thought you have to say!

At just after eleven she turns out all but me. It is immediately obvious she doesn't want my help in the glass washing or ashtray emptying department.

Queenie is lively and well-rounded but not everywhere, which is nice. Once again, I am in possession of a large gin. Queenie imitates me by doing the same, for a second or two and then the glass is put down and I find myself grappling with Mama Octopus. She is all arms and legs. I hardly know which is which. I have no time to complain as she throws me into the task. Her tentacles recede. She smokes a cigarette and I don't. I never have partaken apart from the occasional cigar and as far as I can tell at this early stage of my life, I never will. We talk, Queenie talks. She talks about a regular replay on a sort of season ticket basis but without the ticket or payment. I talk myself out of it.

"I'm honoured Queenie. Sadly I have to decline. I'm far too young to be settled. I have to go to college in a few weeks and god knows what I'll be doing after that and for how long or where."

"Well Maccy, just don't be a stranger when you're home my 'ansome. Pop in when you can," she pleaded.

After tonight, I'm never likely to be a stranger to dear Queenie again. 'Popping in' won't be on a regular basis, quite the reverse. Why is it that every woman I meet wants me to settle down with them? I'm eighteenish, not eighty! Some time in my future I might feel the need of a full-figured, mature, boisterous woman but that's a while away. I am contemplating an age limit on those I closely fraternise with.

Dear Queenie won't be seeing fifty-five again. Death by flesh just does not appeal. Our late night, early morning chit-chat is short lived. The mood is suddenly broken. I hear a key turn in the lock of the door. It could only mean one thing; the old man is home early. From the look on Queenie's face, he is unexpectedly present. At Queenie's barked order, I drop myself into a large, but hardly large enough blanket box at the foot of the wildly distributed bed. I quietly pull the lid down above me. It is a good thing there are no blankets inside or I would have to sit on the top which would be rather pointless. I settle in for what I think might be an uncomfortable night. I have no idea what Queenie did. I had to endure half a night of the old man's snoring.

My escape is completed in the early hours at a time when the old man must have suddenly become somewhat fruity. Similar noises to those made earlier by Queenie and to a lesser extent myself, echo around the bedroom. I can take no more. At some minor increase in volume I lift the lid of what might have become my coffin and am out of the Maypole's confines like liquid shit off a tin miner's shovel, minus my trainers, which I believe to be somewhere under the bed. I think about going back for them. They are wearing a bit thin anyway. Another consideration would be my dislike of riding in an ambulance.

Queenie's old man is something of a brute. I'm sure he would want to book me into the do-it-yourself ward at the county hospital if he were to discover I had spent half a night in his blanket box. More of a worry would be the difficult task of finding an available ambulance; they tend to be few and far between in this neck of the woods. It could be the drivers are averse to coming to Padstow in the early hours.

So once again I find myself in place, waiting for old Bert to arrive at the café.

By now Bert is becoming less surprised by my appearances behind the tea urn and catering sized toaster. The liquid is poured. The inevitable questioning begins.

"I believe you 'ave been up to no good again, Maccy lad."

"Whatever makes you think that Bert, are you psychic matey?"

"Tidn't six o'clock yet boy. You look like you 'aven't slept proper and you don't have anything on your feet neither."

"That would be mostly correct Bert."

"Like I said; you 'ave been up to no good!"

"I wouldn't say that Bert, she was rather complimentary as a matter of fact."

"Who was she this time lad?"

"Aw come on Bert, you wouldn't expect me to divulge information of that kind, would you?" The tittle-tattle will be all around the quayside by eight o'clock if Bert knew.

"I don't know, Maccy, how can I tell iffen you idn't giving away any bleddy clues?"

"Toast and tea?"

"No, let's us have us some hot bacon sarnies lad. You'll find good back bacon in that fridge back there." Bert points, but there is no need. I'd had a Saturday job here once, a year or two ago. Just the one Saturday. It was more than enough. I don't mind hard graft, but I like to get a fair reward. Fair reward isn't uppermost in the minds of the local Padstow business folk when making up employee's wage packets in these parts.

"I know where the bacon is kept Bert. You go and do some of what they pay you peanuts for and leave the breakfast cooking to me."

"Right enough, lad. Brown sauce with mine. The good stuff, not the watered down squirtings they do put out for the bleddy tourists. Another thing, don't scrape the marge off after you put it on. It's a bleddy bad habit!"

I get to work, and Bert gets to work. Fifteen minutes later with the restaurant floor now sparkling, the old geezer and I eat our leaking sandwiches. I had slipped runny yolked fried eggs in on top of the bacon to give us both an early morning treat.

This is no sudden transgression by me into petty pilfering of catering goodies. On such occasions as this, I would help Bert with his chores and even some that weren't his. At different times, I have taken in the bakery delivery, the milk delivery and the fish delivery. I've put the rubbish out for the council men, who, on arrival, would immediately tip some of the contents back out onto the pavement in readiness for when they next called. I cleaned the cooker after my bout of culinary exploits. I've often wondered if the café owners know yet of my secret existence, which of course would no longer be a secret if they did. I somehow doubt Bert would divulge any information to his employers concerning my efforts. I do make his life a tad easier.

I wash down the remains of my sandwich with more tea and sit in the café window watching the sun come up over the waking town. There's something about sunrise, sweet tea and a fried breakfast. The way to start a day! For one thing, tea just does not taste the same after any other meal. It's a sweet and sour thing. I tap my teaspoon as I lounge and listen intently at the incessant crying of the now wide-awake gull population. I also use the time to try and count the splodges of seagull shit on the café's large picture windows. Before you ask, I have no idea why!

I think some more about my upcoming but so far unplanned birthday celebrations. I don't immediately come to any definite conclusions. My time has not been totally useless. What begins as a smidgen of an idea has now completely formed. I have two ideas, so two smidgens. I never have done well with one thing at a time.

First idea: Party at the Mermaid. Second idea: A plane ticket. I rather fancy the trip now. The McCarthy story has taken a good grip of my imagination. I want to know more. I want to see something of my past before continuing further with my future. I have four weeks before having to take up my place in the West London catering college and just one week before my big day. In between, I have three weeks to do bugger all or something useful. For once I would settle for useful. I would make Dusty do the same. I wasn't going to America alone. I needed to hold someone's hand!

Dusty hadn't thought twice. I knew he wouldn't. Ma wasn't overly chuffed and refused any chance of coming along with us. Her mind firmly made up.

"Dusty's too young. I'm far too busy." She had said it with a motherly firmness. She relented in Dusty's case as I was certain she would. She knew the kid and I would look out for each other and rocket science wouldn't be required to get through Heathrow and out the other side. Dusty has GCE's anyway. Can't say much about the Yank side of things. I know they can be a funny lot of buggers.

The kid and I outlined our strategy; we pored over maps in search of this supposed city that nestles somewhere deep in the Kansas Grasslands. At some time in history, McCarthy City had come into being. Right now, I have an idea that 'village' may have been more apt, but if city it is then city it should be. McCarthy must be left off every map of the United States that has ever been topographed, all those maps we could get our hands on anyway. I have a smidgen of doubt that my tasty word - it's a mouthful for anyone - for mapmaking, might be missing from every English dictionary in a similar way.

Ma made calls to the 'old country' and after much scouring and magnifying by thick glass, we never did find it at all.

There is only one thing for it; Dusty and I would have to go empty-handed and trip over the place whenever, wherever, if ever it appears before us. Henry had found the place in the same way by all accounts, so it might work!

First and foremost there is a birthday bash to, well, bash. There are invitations to be made, catering to be organised. I need to tell Bligh he can let me have the Mermaid and the Mermaid Bar for an evening. Knowing the Cap'n as I do, he would have me working behind the bar and serving myself.

I spend some time over the next few days inviting half of Padstow, the Birdseyes, Lil the Tart and One-Armed Frank. All my favourite oldies and all my old favourites. Lenny and guest, Michael and guest. Dusty will invite himself and will surely be accompanied by a handful of sixteen-year-old giggling females. I ask one or two females of my own age, well, they will be tomorrow.

Bligh's first words at my entry into the Mermaid on my big night are something of a surprise. "Bloke was here earlier Maccy, P. Calhoun. He has got his wallet back now. He said to thank you and left some money behind the bar for a round of drinks. Hundred bleddy quid!"

"Hundred bleddy quid? How did he know it's my birthday?"

"I told the bugger."

"Bleddy 'ell," It's going to be a long night.

I am proved right. I tend the bar for half an hour while Bligh and Blen' eat some sacrificial offering. Thankfully the old bloke was true to his word, half an hour it was. I had every opportunity to enter into the spirit, spirits and of course the free beer, for the final hours of my seventeenth year. Bligh bought me my first legal pint, having many times previously served me the other variety. Come to think of it, I hardly had to put my hand into my pocket for the whole evening. For a short while I would have no visible pockets to dig into.

Despite the lure of Buddy Holly and Wild Bill Haley from Noah's jukebox, not a one of us danced. Dusty had the best chance to get physical and I dare say he did, after chucking out time.

We eat well, thanks to Ma. We drink well, somehow thanks to Bligh's cellar. We yak. I should say, Frank yakked, mostly about Padstows' long and colourful history. The rest of us listen intently. I never heard the one-armed old feller talk so much. I learn stuff I would never have known about my 'outpost'. I learn to keep my mouth shut until Frank has completed his history lesson of the long forgotten Padstow Chase! I should have kept it shut.

It seems in days long since passed, an annual race had been held between the younger males of each Padstow hostelry. The race is started from one end of the quay and the runners must get to the other end and back again. Easy enough but for one thing: each runner will hold onto a full beer tankard of ale in each hand. Not so difficult either but our challenge was to be a little different. Lenny, Michael and I are about to run the 'Chase' completely starkers. Stark bollock naked! This is to be the Padstow Streak! We three are gonna 'streak' the length of the quay, twice! There would have been more of us but Dusty is invisibly busy and the Admiral is told, in no uncertain terms, 'No' by Alma. If you ask me, she doesn't want the old man getting in her line of sight. I'm not certain he was really up for it in any case. One-eyed Mervyn was too embarrassed to participate, probably because he is afraid of running in the opposite direction. Mervyn is chosen as race starter. Thankfully he just waves his arm for us to begin. Frank would have done it, but with only having the one he decided against it, after admitting he might be tempted to wave the wrong one.

Alice, like Alma just wants a front row seat. She gets her wish. I get a sly wink as we line up. Needless to say, our hands aren't down at our sides, mine aren't anyway. It is all I can do not to spill my beer. I make life easier for myself by supping an inch from each tankard. I don't check on the other pair obviously.

Even Blencathra isn't to be left out. It is she who makes the most encouraging noises as the three of us shiver on the starting line. Lil the Tart waits impatiently, perhaps with thoughts of some late-night custom. She is going to be disappointed. It is a chilly night. I notice a solitary watcher standing to one side of proceedings, wrapped in a heavy and obviously expensive overcoat. The bloke nods and smiles as he produces the recovered wallet and waves it at me. P Calhoun! I nod back.

Ma isn't too happy about our naked intentions but there is no stopping us once the decision has been made.

The race is run. The end becomes a shambles with Lenny falling and bringing Michael and I down with him. The glass tankards somehow stay in one piece. The beer is spread far and wide. The Chase is over. If there is a winner, I don't get to hear about it.

The next and most important contest is to get some clothing back on before the hovering Alma and Lil can move in. I notice the lonely watcher has gone now as we three dress where we had undressed, in the shelter, after turfing Dusty and two maids out of it first. There is just time for another hour's partying. Actually, this isn't entirely true. It is already way past the legal drinking up time, but we do it anyway.

It is almost daylight when I begin to crush and squeeze my pillow into shapelessness.

As for birthday presents, Ma gave me a cheque to pay for our flights to the States. There would be quite a bit over for other expenses. Dusty gave me a wrinkled packet of out of date condoms. Alice gave me hope! Lil gave me the shivers.

One last thing: later in the week, the local paper offered a reward for the names of those that partook of the race. As far as I know, no one has been forthcoming with the required information; perhaps in the hope it would become an annual event. That's for others, I've run my first and last Padstow Chase!

Chapter Seven

Gunfire and Ghosts

It is obvious from the condition of the ancient road that few cars have driven along McCarthy City's main street. I believe ours to be one of the very few, maybe the first, most likely the last?

I would bet the last time a vehicle passed through here it would have had the Wells Fargo logo emblazoned on its sides, a shotgun rider spitting tobacco streams of black fluid and calling everyone 'pardner'! Dusty and I are a tad nervous at being here in Kansas surrounded by our family's ancient history. Though to be honest we can't wait to get out of the truck and walk the streets our great grandparent had walked, explore the remains of the buildings. We are in silent awe as I pull the truck to a halt outside the largest of these remaining buildings.

McCarthy City! It is smaller than Little Petrock. The window frames of the old buildings are almost all broken or boarded. One can feel the history behind the boards. McCarthy might have moved on from Henry's time but not by much I'm guessing.

I assume the last people had lived here at the beginning of the twentieth century. What do I know, I could be wrong? My brother and I are about to find out how wrong. It looks like McCarthy is a ghost town. The impression didn't last long.

What comes as our first surprise is the little dust cloud that suddenly scoots up in front of my right foot. Another follows a second later. It can mean only one thing! I'm guessing someone has a gun. Whoever they are know which end the bullets come out from, which in effect isn't useful. Two more dust clouds have us hopping from one foot to another. My buttocks clench themselves, voluntarily. Whoever is shooting at us has an easy target; two! The shooting stops as suddenly as it had begun.

"Maccy, somebody in this miserable town has a gun. Someone is shooting at us."

"Now kid, ain't you glad we made you stay on at school?"

"Very funny brother, what are we gonna do?"

"How the bleddy hell should I know. You stayed on at school. You're the one with the 'O' level in something. I've never been shot at before!"

"Nor me, I know we should have stayed at home! There's some nutter here trying to kill us and there's me thinking I'd live until I was a hundred. I'm gonna miss out some."

"Dusty stop your bleddy whining. Let me think. Just keep flat, be still boy. I'm a bigger target than you. Did you notice which way the bullets came from?"

"I never saw any bullets. I wasn't looking for any."

"Me neither. They're bleddy hard to see when they're moving, easier to find when they hit you, I suppose."

"I thought you were supposed to be thinking, do it faster! I can't be lying in this dust much longer, I got an itch."

"Best you scratch them now kid, while they're still where they're supposed to be. You might wish you had done Biology instead."

From out of nowhere comes a voice like a paper bag. "You two can get back in that there vehicle and git your arses outta my town, git movin' or bleed, I'm warnin' ya."

"Was that you kid."

"Was what me?"

"Farted, one of us did."

"It was me. That's all it was as far as I can tell. I'll update you when the time comes."

I realise something must be done. Since I am the oldest, it is up to me. With my voice trembling, I shout at the so far, invisible sharpshooter.

"Where are you?" I'm not certain I want to know but can't think of anything else to say. It's difficult talking to someone you can't see, unless it's by telephone.

Again, the paper bag speaks. "I told you to git your arses outta here. I got more of the same iffen you decide against it. Now move yourselves unless you wanna be able to crap from more than one place at a time."

"Suits me, we're going old feller. Just point that bleddy thing somewhere else for a minute or two."

"Git out of my town. Git out of McCarthy."

"Hurry up Dusty, let's back off before the old git changes his mind and keeps his promise. I got all the holes in me I need right now. One of the buggers is about ready to act up. Let's go." As for 'McCarthy? I didn't have time to think about it.

We retreated as far as the railway lines a quarter of a mile from the town. The kid continues to whine like a schoolgirl. I consider it myself.

"What a waste of time, we came five thousand miles just to be told to piss off by a gun-crazy crank. We could have gone to Birmingham or Plymouth and saved the plane fare."

"I'm not leaving kid, not yet. I'm made of sterner stuff."

"What do you mean, not leaving?"

"Guess."

"I don't wanna guess. You go back if you want. I don't have any clean shorts."

I ignore the kid's continued complaining. Carefully, I get out of the truck again and walk back toward the sun bleached remains. I hear Dusty slam his door in anger. I knew he wouldn't let me go alone. I didn't want to go alone. I hear his footsteps behind me. I stop at the nearest building that has not yet become firewood. Maybe it will later. I am careful not to lean on it. I wait for the kid to catch up. From where we stand, we can both see the spot where we had parked before the ambush. It is at this point

I can make out the remaining faded letters on the decaying building.

The Pla nsman Hotel

A single letter has disappeared. It is ironic that we have been lying on the ground counting bullets in front of the place we had been in search of. We never made a complete plan either.

"Dusty, it's the hotel, Henry's place, there look."

"I can see it nicely from here Maccy. Can we go home now?"

"Not on your life!"

"Don't bleddy say that."

"Don't say what?"

"What you said. It's tempting unnecessary fate, mine."

"Come on, we'll go around the back of the buildings and see if we can get closer."

"I don't wanna get closer, this is closer. I'm close enough. Closer is open-ended."

"Okay stay, see you later."

"Do you want flowers or donations?"

"I wanna see the inside of that bleddy hotel, don't you? No flowers, they make me sneeze!"

"I'll wait for the film to come out. "Death by Ventilation", "Idiots Killed by Idiot." "The Thing from the Black Lagoon without the Lagoon bit."

I step away from the building. I can hear the kid padding along behind me again and it makes me feel a tad safer. At least for now Dusty has stopped predicting our lack of a future. I am certain whoever had shot at us was inside the Plainsman. I am scared right now but not enough to make me change my mind. The weathered hotel is pulling me like a magnet. From behind the building, it looks sad and dilapidated, which of course it is. A small lean-to has begun to collapse in on itself. There is a back door at least, I creep forward. I try to push it open. The door won't budge although it looks ready to fall off.

"Only one thing for it Dusty."

"What might that be?"

"We gotta go around the front again."

"Not me, I've gotta do some shopping, I'm off to the closest gun shop."

"You can't kill the bleddy bloke, boy."

"Wasn't gonna shoot the bloke. I thought if I shot you now, it would save him the job drekly. That way he might let me off for good behaviour. I could join his gang!"

I ignore the kid's whining threats as I creep around to the front via an alleyway. It is now or never. I walk straight in the front door and stop in front of the oldest living person I've ever seen. The bloke is a hundred, more. I try the pleading approach.

"Don't shoot me!"

"Why the hell shouldn't I?"

"It'll hurt. I don't like pain."

The rifle is lowered fractionally at my pathetic confession. I don't trust the old geezer. One good thing I notice straightaway is my tormentor doesn't seem to have great eyesight which isn't surprising considering his age. I don't mention it in case it might be my own that is faulty.

"What do you kids want here? This is my hotel, my town, you ain't getting' it and you ain't getting' me out neither. You best get that straight, afore you leave."

"We, my brother, Dusty and I are visitors. We're here to see where our great grandfather lived. We haven't come to take you away. Didn't even know anyone was here still living. We thought McCarthy was a ghost town." 'It still could be, I think.' From the looks of this old geezer, we've met one of its original occupants. If he's a ghost, I hope there aren't more. They could all be armed.

"Who's Dusty? Looks like you're on your own youngster. I ain't no frickin' ghost, boy. Think on."

The kid has simply chickened out and not followed me inside. It is only now at the sound of his name that he half, less than half in all honesty, appears inside the doorway. The long barrel of the rifle rises up again for a second before the old geezer allows it to once again drop. He doesn't let go of the weapon completely. I glance around at the inside of the building. It is dark, cool with just a single shaft of bright sunlight searching through a grubby window. The large room smells of dust and age and of course Dusty, my brother. In a way, it looks almost on a par with the Mermaid. It is hardly any worse.

"Your great great, grandaddy lived here in McCarthy? I don't believe you. You're English kids, ain't you, what do ya want here? I ain't got nuthin' you want."

"Near enough, pard, my brother and I are from Cornwall, we're Cornish. That's something entirely different."

"What was your great grandaddy's name boy?"

"Henry, Henry McCarthy. Henry was from Cork, it's in Ireland."

"I know where Cork is boy. I should do. So, what are ya'll poking around out here for, what do you want to know about us McCarthys?"

"I'm Maccy, Macdonald Tamryn, and this is my only brother, as far as I know. What do we call you old feller?" I notice the rifle twitch sharply in the old man's hands. I might have stepped back a tad. Further would be pointless under the circumstances. He could still shoot me in the back while I'm running away. I suppose it would be preferable.

"Word of warning to you boy, you call me old feller just one more frickin' time and I'll blow your balls clean off. Then neither of us will have any, 'ceptin' the youngster out there, I can work on him later!"

"So, what should we call you pard'?" Somehow, I miss the subtle hint the rifleman is now in fact a riflewoman. Maybe my eyesight isn't so good after all.

Dusty has stepped inside the broken door. I'm relieved he has taken the attention away from my treasured share of the family jewels. For a moment or two it feels they have left for calmer waters. It is all I can do to stop myself checking for their whereabouts. I don't think the old lady

68

would be too pleased with me rummaging about in my shorts. I manage to refrain from engaging in that most manly pastime. A pointless pastime for a woman of any age.

"Pard's fine but don't you get to mixing me up with the menfolk of our family youngster. My daddy, your great, great granddaddy had me christened after my mother, Renee. I'm Renee McCarthy, my hair's falling out, my looks ain't what they were, and my titties have gone someplace I can't find them. A bit like your balls son. I'm a damned woman and don't you pair forget it none."

"Shit!" I couldn't help myself!

"I thought your little brother already had Maccy, he don't smell so good."

"Dusty never has Renee. I mean, sorry for my language. You're our aunt! You're our great aunt?"

"Might be, iffen you are who you say you be. Henry McCarthy was my daddy anyways."

"Bleddy hell Dusty, Renee here is your aunt, great aunt, might be more." I know it is rude to point but she had started it. At least my finger isn't loaded.

"I knaw that Maccy, I got the 'O' level."

"Pity you didn't do better in bleddy Biology kid. You thought we were chit-chatting with our great great uncle."

"Me?"

This is all unexpected, Dusty and I hadn't expected anybody would be living in McCarthy when we left Heathrow. The two of us had wanted to see some of our roots, take a look at our rotting family history. The history is standing in front of us, drying out at least. Her voice resembles the opening of a family packet of potato crisps. I begin to wish Ma had come with us. Women tend to get on better with women. It had been a short argument and Ma had won. "I've got too much to do here." she'd said, and that was that.

Dusty, almost seventeen and myself not much more, had flown from Newquay airport to the big one in the smoke, where we embarked on the long-haul flight. We

69

had a reasonably unentertaining flight, only disturbed by the kid requesting copious amounts of lager and being refused each time. We touched down at Dulles, Washington, where we rented the truck. I drove fifteen hundred miles in three or four days and McCarthy is suddenly before us, as is Great Aunt Renee. Weird, really weird! To call her 'great' is something of an overstatement. She is minute.

"Where are you boys staying? I don't have no fancy sleeping arrangements here. Don't get visitors much, never have."

I thought about asking Renee how she practiced her shooting skills with a lack of tourists arriving but decide against it. Her gnarled hands still have a firm grip of the rifle and I sensibly hold back.

"It says Hotel outside, Aunt Renee." Dusty is persistent.

"There's a building down yonder that says Undertakers youngster. You wanna sleep here or there?"

Dusty becomes silently thoughtful at the old lady's reply. I quickly change the subject.

"Saw a motel about fifty miles back. "The Cactus Flow?"

"It's the Cactus Flower boy, the letters have fallen off. Place is a shithole, you don't wanna be staying in that outhouse. You'd be better sleeping in your truck out there. The snakes and varmints won't get ya. Buzzards might take your eyes out, best you sleep with one open!"

I am puzzled at the old girl's reluctance to let us stay now that she knows who we are and hopefully our lives are no longer in immediate danger. One shithole is the same as any other. I look at my surroundings once again. Yes, this is a hotel, is a dump. It's tidier down the quarry. Letters have a habit of falling off in Kansas it seems. I don't want to stay here. Dusty has other ideas.

"We don't need anything fancy, aunt. We have sleeping bags and can make do with anything. Us have slept in worse places, Maccy has."

The kid is right. My recent night at the Maypole is proof enough. Not that the Maypole is falling down and in an advanced state of decay but the hours I had spent in the coffin at the end of Queenie's bed might have given me a slight curvature of the spine. Dusty has a question for the old girl and for some reason I'm glad I hadn't asked it.

"All this talk of crapping and outhouses has got my bowels in thinking mode. Can I use your bathroom Aunt Renee, I gotta go?"

She spat. "Thought you'd already done gone, boy. The crapper's out back." She points to what I decided was the door I couldn't open earlier. "Through there. There ain't no bath boy. There's a creek over yonder. Use that."

"Thanks, Aunt Renee."

"If I let you boys stay here in the hotel, don't you go thinking I'll be waiting on you. You two can sleep where you feel most comfortable which doesn't allow you a whole lot of choice."

I'm not listening to Renee. I'm far too busy watching Dusty dismantle the remains of the door from its doorframe while cleverly attempting to contain any advancement from his inner workings. Dusty is a natural entertainer. I can't help smiling at my brother. Renee sees the funny side and cackles to herself.

"You lost an I, darlin!"

"Not me boy, I still got both though they ain't as good as they were, I'd have shot your damn toenail off at one time."

The old lady emits a giggle. The sound resembles the opening of a potato crisp packet. I still am not convinced she didn't mean to separate parts of us earlier.

"On your sign on the front of the building Renee, you got a letter 'I' missing sweetheart."

"I do? I don't get out much Maccy, I never noticed."

The kid returns. The old lady mellows. The three of us come to an agreement about the sleeping arrangements and I promise to buy some supplies.

We are out on the open road again. Only this time we have an extra passenger. I jump every time the rifle twitches in the old lady's hand as she sits in the back of the pick-up. We manage to get to our destination and back without bloodshed. It has been a long day, a long four days since our departure from the airport. Now we are on a shopping spree. I am anyway. The kid isn't old enough to drink here or at home. Even now I didn't realise we were both in the same boat. I only notice the warning poster barring under twenty-one year-olds from drinking alcohol as we are leaving the Circle K store, Kansas' version of Spar. I am in possession of two dozen bottles of Pilsner. Renee clutches a large bottle of Jack Daniels in each hand and is sat on a full case. One bottle is already open. The rifle rests between her scrawny thighs.

The kid and I sleep in sleeping bags in the old saloon. We awake to the unmistakable smell of burning food. As we eat the burnt offerings, Renee crackles relentlessly on about the 'good old days' of McCarthy City. She explains more about the ups and downs of the place. She makes a promise to take us to the cemetery later and show us where her parents and our loved and soon to be no longer lost are buried.

"That there is where Henry was saved from a burning hell, boys." Renee points at a patch of open ground. "The hotel that stood there caught fire. Henry rescued everyone from inside. Taffy Edwards had to go in and bring Henry out after he collapsed. My father recalled Taffy toted him over his shoulders; the stairway had already burnt away. The big Welshman threw himself and my daddy clear through the upstairs wall."

"Over there is where my half brother Joey killed a Kiowa. The brave was about to scalp old George Benford. George published the newspaper here, Joey helped out, learned the business. Joey was just a twelve-year-old kid then, shot the Kiowa brave between the eyes. You can see the hunting knife hanging on the wall inside the hotel. You already seen Joey's rifle. Wild Bill Hickok gave it to the kid one time when he was here visiting just before he was shot by a back-shooting arsehole."

The three of us stroll slowly along the straight main street until we are standing inside the tiny, neat cemetery full of battered wooden crosses. Most are bleached white and broken.

"Somebody must keep this place neat and tidy, Renee?"

"I do, only time I ever come out of the hotel."

"That water trough is where Soul Broadbent drowned. That burn there is where a murdering bastard got speared by Tungsaw, the hotel's cook."

I looked at the charred trough with no bottom. It must have been a while since it held water.

On our final day in Kansas, I awoke early and decided to take a dip in the deeper section of the stream. Renee's bathroom facilities were sparse to say the least. I was in up to my waist, it didn't go any deeper. I didn't expect anyone else to be around and so was surprised to hear a sound on the far bank. A horse came into view carrying a rider. I dipped lower in the water. Not sure why as I had run around Padstow naked in the past, with an audience.

The girl allowed the horse to stretch down and drink. At that moment I didn't think she had seen me. Once the horse had quenched its thirst, she allowed rein and let it walk away. At the top of the bank she looked directly at me and I shrank down even further. There was a thin smile, she fingered a star on a chain that hung around her neck. Then she was gone.

Our time in McCarthy ends far too soon. Renee has talked incessantly. As if she was making up for all the years she must has spent alone here. It was fascinating listening to her recall stories of hardships, love affairs, births and deaths and baseball games. Her story of nineteenth century Kansas. The kid and I hardly managed a word edgeways. We had nothing useful to say.

Dusty and I had so little of interest to tell this old woman. We did make her laugh occasionally. We left with all sorts of promises ringing in her ears but thankfully we

73

left with no threats ringing in ours if we ever returned to McCarthy City. I was almost tempted to roll the old lady up, shove her under my arm and carry her home to the Duchy.

Our return was almost identical to our departure from Heathrow only this time Dusty somehow managed to look eighteen.

A week later I am once again travelling. I'm gonna be an emmet for a while. London finally calls! It didn't call. I got a letter!

Authors note: The 'Yellow boy' Winchester rifle, so called as the firing mechanism of the rifle / Carbine was made from brass. The model was first manufactured in 1866 at The Winchester Repeating Rifle Co. Calibre 44-40 cartridge. It weighed 9.5 lbs – 4.3 kgs barrel length thirty inches.

Chapter Eight

The Padstow Pirate!

Almost too quickly, my first term at college came and went. I spent my spare time and my cash in and around Fulham and Chelsea's lowlier standard of pubs and of course their football grounds; sometimes not completely certain which I was in.

I returned home to some sad but not totally unexpected news. The old sharpshooter, great Aunt Renee, had passed away. Her toenail shooting days are finally over. The promises of a return visit might now be broken. McCarthy City might now fade back into the Kansas Grasslands where it belongs. With no one left to tend it, the neat prairie cemetery could, like its occupants, now turn to dust. Dusty and I were grateful we had taken the opportunity to meet the fine old lady. It felt like we had made the visit for a purpose what with her passing so soon.

It was an odd coincidence, I had always set my heart on entering the catering trade. It's in my blood I suppose. Perhaps it is all due to Renee and Henry McCarthy. There is nothing in Kansas for any of us now. A shame, the past must stay just that, the past! Thoughts of the girl on the horse receded from my mind, I had to think about my future.

A college break; the summer had witnessed me traveling back home to receive the news. I did not return alone. There were four of us, it might have been five. It's still a tad hazy, in a mini cooper. Small parts of us may have travelled on the outside.

The early summer is promising a scorcher. There are few places one should be under the circumstances, on the beach or on the way to the beach. We are on our way. After my quick visit home to collect the clothes I might or might not need, we headed for sun, sea and sand. My new muckers and I spent half the time at the railway carriages and the other half at the beach where we established something of a non-working commune. That's to say, the commune worked with little or no input from any of us.

I put in the occasional evening shift at the Mermaid. I did enough to make my pockets rattle. I guess there's a lot of Ma in me in some respects though I can't be called musical. She never worried where the next meal was coming from when dossing in St. Ives and singing for her supper in the shadow of the Knill Monument.

There were just five or six of us out at 'The Well' in the beginning. Soon others come at the news of our tenancy. There was Lenny and Michael, who, like me, were home from college. Can you guess what kind of college Michael was attending? Michael was intent on following in his dad's footsteps and becoming a man of the cloth. I was all for it. I gave my pal my full support. 'Friends in high places and all that.' It can't do any harm to have connections and from Mike's point of view he'd know exactly the kind of temptations his eventual flocks would be wrestling with. He and I had invented one or two in our murky past. Bloody hypocrite!

At times, there were a dozen or more of us at St George's Well. It was all very casual. It was all heavily alcoholic. We built a lean-to shelter out of anything we could lay our hands on. It served as shade from the sun during the day and as sleeping quarters at night, though most of our resting was done by day. We didn't indulge in full-scale orgies or anything of that sort. However, it was a carefree environment.

Anyone or everyone who came to our exotic enclave carried as much beer, wine and food as they could, and we existed on barbecued Mackerel and Fish and Chip takeaways, usually without the fish. If the weather turned bad it was back to the Tamryn farm and the bone-dry interior of the two sturdy train carriages. They could have been renamed: 'Bodies are us!'

76

It would be a great and glorious summer of non-restriction and freedom of movement. None of us bothered to dress in more than shorts and t-shirt. At times, even those items of clothing were discarded which possibly led to our one and only nasty incident in all the weeks we were out there.

One afternoon, two or three of the girls had come over yelling and shouting. They were visibly upset. An offshore peeping Tom had been sighted. It wasn't surprising I suppose, they had been lying naked on the tiny sand bar, resembling enormous underfed Lemon Sole.

"He's in a rowing boat around there." She and the other two had pointed at a small jutting promontory at the edge of the tiny beach.

"The dirty bugger has got binoculars. Do something about 'n Maccy, my bird." This girl was insistent. She had jabbed my shoulder with a hard, determined finger. Her insistence gave me and the lads little choice.

"Yeah Jennifer's right, you blokes should go and sort the dirty little sod out Maccy." Another had said.

A quick glance at the trio made me wonder why the pervert was wasting his time. They weren't what might be called buxom beach beauties. All three were a tad on the scrawny side. It didn't matter, we were the 'men of the house' so to speak and their appeal should not have to fall on deaf ears. Somebody was violating our space. We would need to show him the error of his ways. Lenny, Michael and I and the other lads grabbed any available beach debris, of which there was quite a selection as we raced to the area the semi-naked and part grilled girls had pointed out to us. The dinghy is still there, bobbing about some fifty yards distant. Its owner seemingly scouring the beach with trusty steamed up binoculars. I instantly recognize the lone sailor. It is Bessie.

Soul Beswetherick is a local and a tad on the weird side, our village idiot, though he lives in town. He was about to receive a heavy and continuous bombardment of anything we could lay our hands on. Bessie didn't expect our aerial attack and was soon in complete disarray as he lost his hold on an oar while feebly attempting to get out of range. Eventually on retrieving the errant oar, Bessie managed to get away. It was the end of the only bit of 'aggro' we had all summer. I did catch up with the pirate in town some time later and was able to push home our earlier point a tad more personally. I hadn't made physical contact as most of my scrapping was done for fun. Bessie's actions weren't funny. I made it clear any repetition would result in a good smacking.

That evening we had a party and more than twenty of us celebrated the dismissal of the pervy Padstow Pirate. Most of my friends didn't know his name, I did of course, he gained a few new ones the day he decided to come visiting at St Georges Well!

The long roasting summer continued as did the party, with some short breaks in between for shopping and sleeping. In mid-September, it ended abruptly and although I returned occasionally from Chiswick, when I managed to drag myself kicking and screaming out of the pub, to see Ma and Dusty and to improve my living quarters in some small and useful way, there was no repeat of that fine summer we had on the beach. There was just one other memorable break. It was the beginning of the end of any friendship between PC Twotrees and me. Not exactly heartbreaking.

Mrs Twotrees has an allotment up along the back of the town and she and I had a bit of a dalliance in short, salacious meetings. She had given me a nod and a wink one day when I was home. I returned the signs, naturally. Apparently one of the other green-fingered bunch of oldies on the allotment committee was a tad jealous of my achievements and dropped us both in the manure with the copper, who spent most of his time playing with a Rubik cube in his patrol car parked up in an overgrown lay-by on the Winnard's Perch road, whilst pretending to catch speeding motorists. Everyone knew he was there and would be indulging in something of the kind. I never heard of anyone caught speeding in the vicinity.

Twotrees had little evidence but the bugger knew for sure Mrs. Twotrees and I were raising something more than Pansies in the toolshed. It was hardly my fault. Too much indulgence in childish games. Not enough attention to family matters. The important thing was Twotrees never actually caught us red-handed or green-fingered. Somebody once said there's nothing worse than being caught by the fuzz. I wasn't!

There were just a couple of occasions when the landlady at the Maypole Inn collared me with lewd invitations to renew our old acquaintance and to stay for 'afters', which I did once or twice, when her husband was away night fishing, which is another name for poaching. Apart from that, I was well behaved. I was a small disappointment to myself.

Now, just over two and a half years later and I am about to return permanently and armed with qualifications. I have my bits of beer stained paper; a celebration of receipt being inevitable. I would return to Cornwall in search of my fortune, which was just as well right now, as I hadn't quite got all the train fare, none of it. I came home flat broke. For over five hours and two hundred and fifty miles I lived on my wits. Most of this was achieved in the pokey British Rail toilet where I had to endure numerous selfish and annoying interruptions from passers by shouting 'how bloody long are you gonna be in there'? 'How the hell should I know? I'm not a bleddy train driver.' 'Shit and shove it under the door. 'Better still, stick your arse out the bleddy window, but don't do it in the front carriage!'

So now I am home. I'm back where I belong, my beloved home town, Padstow. I would soon, thanks mainly to Lenny, be quickly rewarded with that wonderful cozy feeling of never having been away. West London and more particularly 'rough as a dog's guts' Chiswick, 'Poncey Fulham' and 'Champagne Chelsea' bare not even the tiniest of comparisons to what some might affectionately call the 'arsehole of Cornwall'. Of course, there are parts of the Duchy that deserve the title much more than Padstow!

To me the hustle and bustle of cosmopolitan West London would not and could never be mistaken for the relative deserted January silence of my home town. After my long and mostly boring tenancy of the smallest room available to rail passengers, I am back. Nothing much has changed. Lenny and I would soon be providing convincing proof.

I was back in the Mermaid, The Mermaid Bar! Some say the old inn had been built from the timbers of some smashed ship that had run afoul of the treacherous sandbank, also known as the Mermaid Bar. When the Mermaid first came into being it would have been nameless. Just an ale house, a beer shop. Right now, the Mermaid of today isn't. It's the Mermaid of yesterday, maybe the day before. The place is entrenched in the past, at a standstill, it gives the impression it'll stay that way. Time might never catch up with it. The Mermaid and its peculiar sitting tenants are right now futureless. If some time traveller were to arrive here, he'd think his machine would need a full service and an MOT.

Just a short walk from the inn was for years, a long wooden bench now replaced by a soulless stone shelter. The old ones will have wallowed there for hours with their tankards and their tall stories of extremely tall ships. Like a high council, they would have idled their time away and barked orders and suggestions at passers-by, be they locals or not. In their way, these councilors would have put the world to rights. If they were present on their bench today, they would offer to persuade emmets they would be better off somewhere else. The Long Lugger is still talked about with great affection and rightly so!

Instead now, the space is invaded by families that might be digesting congealing fish and chips from yesterday's newspaper or overheated Cornish pasties from greasy paper bags. Both newspaper and bags will be conveniently stuffed down the back of the seat where they would eventually be pulled out and shredded by insistent, local gulls; those that remain alive. The shelter has many times been utilised by us boys for other nocturnal pastimes, mostly when accompanied by young females.

Dustbins are provided close by, but these are only to be used for empty beer cans, wine bottles and disposable nappies that somehow have the capacity – no pun intended - to make themselves open up and display their tepid, oozing contents once again.

I can only imagine how the old port might differ now from those long gone days when scruffy, ragged-arsed tackers would have stood in awed silence as they listened in to the bewhiskered old timers recalling tales of death and destruction, of terrifying Atlantic storms and broken backed wrecks that, like many of their Cornish and often foreign crewmen, have long disappeared to rot beneath the shifting graveyard that occasionally, even now, seals the narrow navigation channel into the safety of the old harbour. I guess that, at the very least, large doses of exaggeration are employed by these old deckhands in their constant retelling. There's no doubting many of the stories of bravery and daring rescues, always attempted but not always successfully, of those brave boys that manned the lifeboats of the past and those that still do, even today.

In these more modern days a powerful and fast diesel engined craft waits for the inevitable call. Big as I am and strong as I'm rumoured, I could never hope to be a member of that illustrious group that would drop everything and dash for dear life when the emergency rockets are fired from Stepper Point. I suppose one day, I might volunteer to become a fully paid up crew member. Right now I value my existence too much and it all somehow makes me feel a tad inadequate.

God only knows how the men of old managed with oars only when they took out the Helen Peele or the most famous of all the Padstow lifeboats, the Arab. The infamous and

81

treacherous Doom Bar forever shifts in the expansive Camel estuary. It is at its most frightening when it cannot be seen, when it is invisible to the eye. Even the very name is a sinister threat, and no one knows when it was christened so. It is common knowledge the Doom has claimed many hundreds of lives, maybe thousands and still occasionally does, even with today's advancing technology.

For at least one thousand years now they say Padstow has existed as a harbour. Recent evidence suggests an even more ancient harbour existed a little further out from the existing one. The Camel estuary, if it is reached, is a natural haven for ships of all shapes and sizes that have endeavored to seek it out at the threatened advent of great Atlantic storms. For those that manage to safely traverse the Doom, they would be at anchorage in the safest port on the North Cornish coast. In midsummer, the Doom Bar is a kiddy's playground. The bucket and spade brigade will wander about out there for hours without a care in the world, under a hot August sun. Midwinter can see it at its worst.

A South Westerly blast from a foaming Atlantic can turn hightide on the Doom Bar into a playground of death and destruction, a churning, grinding place. No longer a playground, but a cemetery! The Doom Bar has a wicked voice of its own, but god help those who are ever close enough to hear it!

Chapter Nine

Maccy's back in Town!

They, whoever they are, say that Saint Petrock the legendary Saint the town takes one of its names from, came here just before the Dark Ages, which I suppose could have been lighter but more likely the even Darker Ages. Whatever they were, the great one is said to have turned up here in some shell-like craft after leaving Wales to go to the Emerald Isle for higher education. A forerunner of the Open University perhaps? Once better equipped, the old feller arrived here to pass on his new-found wisdom. Obviously, Saint Pet' had no trouble with the Doom Bar on his arrival. It does seem a shame his teachings must have gone in one ear of my forefathers and out the other.

Why on earth anyone would listen seriously to a total stranger who'd supposedly travelled across the Irish Sea at least twice, in something that might have resembled a teacup without the saucer, is beyond me. At least he had tried and deserves this short acknowledgement, if not my thanks for not improving the Tamryn genes. There's me forgetting my Ma came from around the same place. I would never ask her how she travelled!

The men of the town today use more appropriate means to enter and exit the harbour through the deep channel that passes the Doom. They fish and pot for crab or lobster for the local markets. Few of them make a full-time living.

Others operate pleasure boats for sightseers or high-powered speed boats for the younger thrill-seeking visitors. There are those who like to poach Salmon. No, they don't go around cooking them in a shallow pan. They catch them, sell them and celebrate with a few beers.

In high season the centuries old sail lofts and quayside cottages masquerade as ice cream kiosks, pasty shops, boutiques, restaurants and takeaways. Others sell postcards, trinkets or toys that won't last twenty-four hours. In the winter, they harbour countless dead wasps. Died in captivity! The tiny shops that only have floor space for just one family must endure two or three at once. They are choked with squabbling parents and moody teenagers. Snotty nosed whining kids and sunstroke victims in the making, throng and complain when their parents say, 'shut up and enjoy yourself you little sod, you're on bleedin' holiday'. The flat of a hand might collide with a cheek. Crocodile tears would suddenly become real. The parched parents will head for the nearest pub with grub and fruit machine. Why they are called fruit machines is beyond me. I've never seen a banana come out of one yet.

Other emmets, as we locals like to call them, at least when we're in an amiable mood, will just to and fro or lean over the rusty, flimsy railings with no fear of dropping any personal possessions in the quay, but they do. The harbour mud must be full of wallets, sunglasses, false teeth and huge mobile phones.

If the erstwhile Saint Pet' could make a return visit one August Bank Holiday in a cut down Guinness barrel and see the state of the place, he'd turn right around, probably moaning 'I'm a Saint, for Christ's sake; get me out of here!'

It was never my intention to ply my newly gained trade here in Padstow. My qualifications had been sought for other climes. I'd worked in the backstreet cafés and chippys and even behind the bar at the Mermaid when I was a lad. I still do the occasional stint for the aging Blighs. I'd gone to Chiswick with the intention on my return of getting a position in some better class restaurant or hotel in Truro, eventually opening my own eatery. I did well at college, I got my papers. I increased my vocabulary. The Queen's English still has not taken me over completely. I can converse with the best of them but not perfectly. I can talk with the worst particularly well.

I'm almost twenty. I am ready to let myself loose on an unsuspecting, hungry, ever changing population. Somebody once told me: 'Folk will always need to eat and drink'. That statement had lodged itself in a large part of the rear section of my mind.

When the time came to choose a way of earning my living, I dragged the stored thought forward and got on with it in the knowledge catering is a sound trade. It's hard work, long hours but most importantly, financially rewarding, unless you're not self-employed.

The kid had made himself scarce before my return. Ma says he's in Loret de Mar, an awful place in Spain full of British holidaymakers. A bit like Padstow only louder! He is working for a holiday company on the entertainment side. Oh, sure he is. He'll be entertaining females, nothing more. Dusty might as well have stayed at home and continued as before.

As the last few days of my term were dwindling away, I couldn't wait to get home. I could smell the Mermaid. I might have smelt Blen's well forested armpits. I've smelt my own on occasion, I wouldn't recommend it. I don't think Blencathra Bligh knows what lurks inside a deodorant can. I did hear she owned one at one time but instead of spraying it, she squeezed the can. The top blew off, the deodorant came out all in one go and didn't make a difference.

On my return, I caught up a little with that I had missed most, sleep. A couple of good early nights and late mornings followed by the odd afternoon. Being followed by an 'odd afternoon' should be frowned upon.

I am ready to set sail in my local. I am set for a gallon. I now had thoughts for nothing but downing eight pints of the latest ridiculously named brew to be marketed by the Saint Piran Brewery. I am ready to announce my return in the right and proper way, before I would venture out into the world of Cornish cuisine.

My attendance at the Mermaid is not of the disappointing variety. I haven't even reached the halfway mark of my quest. My fourth pint is no longer a pint but there is still a couple of mouthfuls of something called 'Virgin's Despair' in my glass as Lenny and I got to 'it'. It was inevitable, it always is. 'Getting to it' in our quaint, homespun language usually means a party of the knuckle-swapping variety. Lenny and I had a disagreement of the sexual sort. Don't misunderstand me it was more a suitor's tiff rather than a lover's tiff. I can do cheerful, I can do happy, I can't do gay, although I believe they mean the same thing in some quarters.

Lenny and I had been desk-mates all through our schooling years. We had turned up at the institution at the same time as five-year-old's. We had both become tearstained at our first attendance. A fight not fear, of education. Lenny and I have done everything together ever since. Not quite everything as some maids can be quite straight laced about that sort of thing. Lenny has never been one for sharing. The two of us have only really been separated by my three-year foray into the brighter world of the capital, made brighter by streetlights.

The beginning of the evening is used to catch up with what we both have done since our parting. What Lenny had got up to wouldn't bare thinking about. Most of what he did and what he said he did but didn't - Lenny likes to exaggerate - would have been at the horizontal. It was a while ago now that the two of us had stood at this very bar where we both contemplated something we should have done. Our greedy young eyes had been directed towards a cavorting hot-panted daughter of a coal miner from Nottingham. She may have been an offcut of a carpenter from Carlisle or the apple of an eye of a Kentish fruit farmer. Whatever she was, wherever she was from, she had been on show. She had known two panting local lads were frothing more so than the St Piran Best Bitter as she kept us entertained with her lower adjustments and movements.

Cap'n Bligh, with support from others who had no interest in the little tart's squashed buttocks by way of advancing age, dabbed cigar ash into our foaming glasses.

Bligh and One-Armed Frank both knew the girl would be put off by our throwing up just about everywhere apart from over her shorts. It was close. There may have been a splash or two. She made a great fuss while continuing her adjustments. Blencathra dragged me outside into the back yard to complete what we had started.

Instead of a sixteen-year old temptress tonight, this one is sixty-plus. Alma is making a play for one of us. There's nothing wrong with it of course. What's that old saying about tunes and fiddles? I'm not in the mood for music and rather slyly, while Lenny is out the back signing his name on a wall without the aid of a pencil, I return her nods and winks. I get the impression from Lady Alma that when the Admiral is past his halfway mark, he would have no interest in what his wife might be doing with me behind the towers of empty barrels in the Mermaid's rear yard. It turns out Alma has already nodded and winked at Lenny.

The thing is that Alma is a fair bit younger than the Admiral and I believe this is the reason for her occasional search for a young bit of rough. Lenny and I firmly believe we can do rough. Obviously in this case, we couldn't both be doing it at the same time.

I am in a fix. I brag quite innocently and tell Lenny what is on my menu. He is peeved. Lenny gets rough first. A finger jabs at my eye as he proclaims it is he that would be looking after Alma's carnal interests tonight. Talk's cheap I think, and my reply comes in the form of action as I counter his opening with a long reaching left that just connects with my friend's hair.

It has been a while since my last bout of quayside scrapping. Suddenly I am fully prepared. It is a signal, a confirmation of my homecoming. When Lenny and I fight it is never a case of handbags or Pat-a-Cake. We would always put everything in to it. This is no exception. I am like John Wayne, eager to get back in the saddle. Lenny comes back at me and tries to gouge at my good eye. I stoop but my grab misses that which Lenny hopes to share with Alma. Lenny catches the scruff of my neck. We two are one. We topple, furniture is scattered. We are too close for punching as we fight to get a better grip and then some other greater, invisible force enters the fray.

I can't see what it is. I doubt Lenny can either but the pair of us are being dragged over the cold slate by something immensely more powerful than ourselves. We hold on to each other as we squawk like an old married couple. I suddenly feel something hard hitting the side of my head. It is the massive doorframe. We are leaving. I twist my head around and catch sight of that which is prevailing.

Blencathra has decided it is time for her intervention. Her massive hands grip on the pair of us as she powers us into the open space above the concrete steps that lead to the waterside. The female Sasquatch lets go. She employs a foot to roll us out over the doorstop where Lenny and I are left to continue.

It is a small relief knowing Blen' isn't prepared to fully participate. For one thing, I don't fancy getting any closer to her. For another, she would likely emerge victorious against the pair of us. Blen' has won previous bouts in times past; I don't want her winning this one. Her short physical interjection was an honour for us both. My eye is shut and stinging now. A procession of unwanted tears run down my face as I stretch out almost blindly to get a grip of Lenny. I am partially successful and catch my fingers in his mouth. He gnaws sharply as I try to tug my hand away.

It is unfortunate for my mate as the small manufactured plate comes away in my hand. Lenny pulls his legs around and twists them about my neck. He tightens them as I bite his earlobe. It isn't intentional. Just a light nibble, something like a baby crab on a kid's hand-line but as Lenny tightens his thighs my mouth naturally clenches shut on the head handle. My mate screeches as a miniscule

88

piece of the gristle comes away. It is like having a soggy crisp in my mouth. I spit it out.

It is at this point my good eye focuses itself on Lady Alma and her look of sheer excitement at our fighting over her dubious favours. I notice everyone else from inside the Mermaid has emerged. A rough ring forms around us. They back away to allow the space we need to continue.

My attention is snatched back to the task in hand as Lenny pushes two fingers inside my nose, causing my eyes to water again. We roll over again. I put my hand over Lenny's mouth. It slips inside. Lenny has few permanent teeth. Some of the originals are lying in a field full of Meadow Muffins near Wadebridge. Lenny lost them in a grudge match when playing for the Wadebridge Camels against the tear-arse Kilkhampton Kickers, or Killers as they might prefer to be known. Anyway, they're scattered around a rugby pitch somewhere north of here.

Lenny cannot have realised; I held the mouth-piece as he smashes my arm on to the damp granite. The plate shakes loose. It hops out and rattles silently as it comes to a halt on the wet stone. I won't deprive my mate of the expensive molars, though I'm happy to crush the knuckles of his outstretched fingers.

For a second, I think I am scrapping with Lenny's gorgeous sister Alice, as he emits a high-pitched scream before I've even made contact. Actually Alice isn't a screamer. On reflection, I would prefer the physical attentions of Alice. I'm not suggesting I would have made less effort. It's possible I would have been a tad gentler, I have been on the odd occasion. Lenny, certain of my intention, pulls his hand away a fraction of a second before my foot slams down. I can't stop my stomping attempt. Jarring pain shoots through my leg as the foot meets the unforgiving granite. Lenny's hand is closed over my mouth and stifles my own agonised scream.

Unfortunately for Lenny, I don't have a sister, at least not one I know of. My Ma is the nearest thing I have to a sister and she fights no one. Twisting, we edge closer to

89

the errant teeth. Leonard sees another chance to scoop them up. He snatches out; the movement causes another complete roll. My superior heft allows me to get on top. Leonard looks up at me. For a split second, we two have perfect eye contact. We exchange crooked smiles. I do my bit, I can't be certain Lenny is smiling. Lenny's face changes, suddenly fearful he knows another half turn will take us both into the watery gloom, which, I should add, will not be the first time. It won't be the last. It is too late.

Lenny's grasping hand has missed his nestling gnashers as the pair of us slip over the edge of the granite and enter the water some ten feet below. The dislodged teeth had obviously followed we were soon to find out.

Deep below the surface the pair of us disentangle in the gloom. I resurface. Leonard must have stayed below searching for the lost item. It seems those molars must have been grinning brightly at my mate on the harbour floor as his head bobs up above the water. A hand held high in cheerful, dripping triumph.

I breathe easier now as I stand on the top slippery step of the ancient stairway and watch satisfied as my buddy Lenny climbs the worn, slimy-green stone steps, finally emerging onto the crowded quayside. The rest of the crew stand shivering, wondering, perhaps hopefully, the battle might recommence. Clasping their half filled glasses, Admiral Birdseye, Lady Birdseye, Lil, the Tart and One-armed Frank, Bligh and Blencathra, along with nameless others - I'm sure they have names, I just don't know them all - cheer and toast our lively performance.

Lenny wipes the mud from the mouthpiece and once satisfied attempts to pop the piece back in place. They don't settle. His cheek bulges outwards in proof. For a second Charles Laughton as the hunch-backed gargoyle stands in front of me. Lenny tries again; still the piece will not sit evenly.

"They don't bleddy fit Leonard, there be too many teeth for e lad?"

"Try the buggers the other way around." Bligh comments uselessly.

"Them ain't your'n Lenny!" Come on boy; we'll 'ave us another look for the buggers!" Lenny and I disappear once again into the murk.

In no time at all we return topside and my mate is again familiar with all that is necessary to eat cod chips and oozing curry sauce. Having returned to the Mermaid to take up space on a wooden bench just inside the great door we sit, shiver and continue our friendship without further ado. Lady Alma would have to wait. Our ardor is dampened.

As Lenny and I are counting and recalling our injuries, the blood on his ear formed a crust. I would hold my hand up to inflicting the molar marks in the back of his calf in the same way he would admit to having become momentarily intimate with my share of the family jewels, the very items I had intended to acquaint with the semi-elegant Alma.

As they say and if they don't, they should, all's fair in love and war and crushing your best mate's nuts in the palm of your hand whilst gleefully scrapping inside and outside of your preferred local hostelry, I still spared a thought for Alice. There would be no further outbreak of hostilities and the evening broke up at Bligh's unnecessarily shouted midnight question of: "Ain't you buggers got no bleddy 'omes to go to?" So original.

The request is drowned out by the chilling sound of Blencathra's heavy footsteps pounding across the upstairs landing. The yomping feet help us to decide discretion is the better part of valour. We begin our homeward trek.

"What are you doing tomorrow Maccy?"

"More of the same Lenny, I shouldn't wonder, you?"

"Sounds good!"

Lenny and I begin our alcohol induced shamble around the now almost silent quayside, all the time fighting off the spasmodic dive bombing of some nocturnal and persistent members of the local seagull population; should that be;

Stuka population? The gulls as one, hold to the belief in a divine right to attack any wandering human foolish enough to be carrying food laden newspaper.

It's possible these night flyers were orphaned by we two some time in the past and they're out in numbers with revenge on their tiny minds. We stop abruptly near to the creaking bandstand where we peer unsteadily down at the small cruiser rocking and bobbing on its permanent moorings.

It is still mid-January and nippy as nippy goes, especially if most of your clothes are blood spattered and still a tad on the damp side. It is cold but not particularly windy; just a light breeze was flicking up the water's surface. The nearest boat's lurching movements are a tad guilty.

"I do reckon the Admiral's in dock Maccy."

"Looks like it Lenny, bleddy typical! Can you see anything through the curtain?"

"Me? I ain't bleddy looking!"

I nudge Lenny aside and peer through the slightly parted curtain at the cabin window. A low light from a tabletop lantern illuminates the cabin's interior.

"Got me a birds eye view Len. They're at full sail."

Like two schoolkids who'd just laid our greedy, beedy eyes on our first dirty mag', we giggle and trip our way towards and up Padstow Hill. We part with the required promise of an early Saturday evening rendezvous at the Sailmaker's Arms, where Lenny insists, they have a pretty looking barmaid with an unusually attractive upper section. It's probably an exaggeration!

Lenny and I walk onwards and upwards as we'd done a thousand times before.

"What'll I do with these bleddy things Maccy?"

I look down at Lenny's outstretched hand and its contents. I have only one ready answer for my friend. We are both lucky not to wet our pants at my words. "Give 'em to your Ma. She can use 'em for crimping her pasties!"

My first night back in town and my dearest and oldest friend and I have somehow completed a brawl without result. Lenny has come away with more teeth than when it had begun, which is quite an achievement. I suppose in all fairness my mucker had won the contest in extra time. He had punched me on the way down to the water. My return from the capital has been just perfect. I wouldn't have had it any other way!

Lenny and I parted at the top of Padstow Hill. On arriving home two hours later, which for me is two cleverly converted wooden railway carriages, now with hot and cold running; though the cold is outside, I had slid into my pit and slept like a bump on a log for most of the following morning. I hate being followed by anything at any time of the day.

Chapter Ten

Ye Olde Seadog!

On waking, not a little sorely, I shower and dress. I step over the crossbar of the rust-caked bike I hadn't ridden for almost three years. I quickly dispense with it. Both tyres are flat. I leave the bike leaning against the grass.

I follow the path of the long-gone railway lines that had been torn up at the supreme orders of a sixties arsehole going by the name of Doctor Beeching. There's me thinking doctors are supposed to mend stuff. I suppose on thinking about it, it is easy for me to forget that without the skilled surgery performed, I would have no roof over my head.

Nearly an hour and a half later, I am tapping a coin on the bar top at the Mermaid Bar, ready to face my favourite liquidising landlord once again. Like others before me, I have made it my business to inform old Bligh many times that the Mermaid does not literally have to live up to the meaning of its name. Mermaids can bring bad luck!

The Cap'n would just shrug his bony shoulders and grin, forgetful of the time One Armed Frank had wantonly smashed a barstool on the slate floor, before scooping up all the pieces. With his huge, one good hand, he had chucked the pieces in the empty fireplace and set it all alight with a rolled-up copy of the Padstow Rocket. It was possible Frank was aware of the sealed-up chimney. More likely he just didn't give a toss and did it in the desperate hope of raising the room temperature a degree or two above below freezing.

Blencathra had arrived before Frank had time to dismantle the only other barstool, or I wouldn't be perched up here now. Frank's sentence for the crime was to be banned from the Mermaid for a week. He didn't take any notice and still turned up every day. Not another word was said about Frank's days as a celebrated Cornish wrecker.

In support of Bligh, he will light the old gas heater on occasion and indeed he had done so just the night before, after Lenny's and I had completed our stint of flesh eating and Morris dancing.

As for One Armed Frank? I realise that had Frank still owned two complete and fully working arms and accessories, he would have no nickname. He'd just be plain old Frank the Firestarter.

It is a freezing night. I am the lone customer, maybe I am the last. The Mermaid can give one the impression of sitting in the waiting room just before taking the driverless bus to the end of the world. Like waiting in a queue at the housing department, you know you might or might not get something. You can't be certain what it is, when or if it will arrive. I wait in a line of one for the un-inevitable. I am at the front and back of the queue of guess what happens next. I don't have to wait long.

Bligh made the decision to come around the bar and yak to, at me. I don't invite him. He is self invited. I am trapped, there is no escape as I know Queenie's old man is at home at the Maypole. Even he wouldn't go out on a night like this. It is a fair walk to the Sailmakers, better known to us locals as the 'Saw Pit'. I am in for the duration.

I think briefly about Steve McQueen and motorbikes, obviously he only had the one. I accept two can ride on one motorbike, can one ride on two? I'm doubtful, what do I know? I have a feeling it could be a painful exercise, a bit like being hung, drawn and quartered I'd guess. Physiology isn't my thing. I am certain my personal pain won't last indefinitely as Leonard with all his teeth, hopefully in their rightful place and now with a spare set that won't fit, will arrive soon, late but soon. Lenny doesn't do early!

"Now then Maccy, this is for your ears only mind, don't tell a soul." Bligh drawls in a low voice reminiscent of Q in a Bond movie. I wait for some new-fangled death ray to appear, a bag of exploding peanuts. The beer pumps are in fact machine guns and the bar top will suddenly become a high-powered raft. It is like facing Groucho Marx, I just don't know what to expect as he leans into my face so closely. I'm sure I can feel the long whiskers that sparsely dot his lower nasal area. I am face to face with an anorexic Walrus.

I resist the ancient Groucho joke 'I like your nose did you pick it yourself?' Bligh may be seventy-ish, but I wouldn't mind betting he could still throw a decent punch. One fight a week is plenty, even for me.

Two kids and Old Lil arrive. I endure a short wait while the landlord pours their chosen poisons. Wishful thinking on my part. The youngsters disappear into the gloom at the back of the room. Lil retreats to her usual table to wait patiently for One Armed Frank's arrival. Frank will keep her occupied; rolling his ciggies as and when.

"Listen 'ere Maccy, you know I was on the water fishin' and such before me and Blen' took this bleddy place on."

I am given no time to do anything but remember, Bligh had a reputation as a damn good Salmon poacher in his younger days. I nod. I know what 'such' is.

"Well t'was a night somewhat like this'n, shitty and misty. I was out there tuther side of the blasted Doom Bar. T'wer getting late, I remember. T'was colder than a Witch's tit in a freezer. My nose was bleddy froze."

I was glad I wouldn't be about when it defrosted.

"We was jest skiffing in slow like, just the two of us, me and the fat old bitch. The mist was 'anging low over the water and the Camel was flatter than a witch's chest, not a bleddy ripple. I said ripple boy."

I hadn't even sniggered! My third eye did click into automatic and conjure up a hideous, portrait of a half-clothed Blencathra huddled on a salt-encrusted blanket. A seaweed covered bone wedged firmly in her snarling, slathering jaws. I stay silent trying not to smile in recognition of my overactive imagination. I'm not sure this is a true story. When you're facing this old geezer, nothing can be taken for granted. I find it amusing Bligh has such an interest in the non-existence of Witches' mammary glands.

"You remember ol' Span' don't ya Maccy?"

At last! I squeeze out an excited answer. "Spaniard?" I reply with self admiration. It is short lived. I instantly regret my thoughtless, unintelligent reply. I stop myself from receiving a self-inflicted slap.

"No ya bleddy tosser; Span' my ol' bleddy dog gawd bless 'er. We called her Span cos 'er was a Spaniel. We couldn't think of another name for 'er. We did use the one she already 'ad. Anyway listen I'm tryin' to tell 'e somethin' boy."

I seal my mouth tighter than a Padstonian restaurateur's wallet, to allow the commentary to continue, in the happy realisation that if I keep quiet the tale will be completed quicker. I wonder about the possibilities that might have occurred had Bligh owned a Shitzu instead of a waterlogged Spaniel. The great door swings open again.

One-Armed Frank halts the tale for a moment. Bligh and I wait while the three-cornered regular trips and sways a path to a table next to Lil's. There is so much of his beer on the floor he might consider buying two pints at a time in future. Frank's arrival is the last intermission for a while.

"Like I was sayin', we was coming in on a maiden's breath as I calls it. I could see Stepper Point across to port, knaw t'was starboard. I always get that wrong! Padsta was winking 'er lights at me at the front. I couldn't 'ear nuthin but ol' Span grating her teeth. She were sleepin'."

I nod, unable to disperse the image of the drooling, growling landlady instead of a flea-bitten mutt. There might be little to choose from both if legs don't count. I recall a story I was told by a student at Chiswick that Lincolnshire was so flat you could watch your dog run off for three days. I doubt Blen' could run for three seconds!

"Now c'm 'ere an' listen to me careful young Maccy."

For some stupid, unknown reason; I move my beer and myself closer in anticipation. Bligh's nose is ripe. I watch mesmerised as the nasal whiskers quiver and a clear liquid bubbles and starts a slow elongation of warm snot. Tiny circles appear and spread around the inside of my glass. I stay silent, struggling to keep myself from smacking the disgusting facial protrusion that has polluted my beer. I wonder if Bligh has done it on purpose in the same way he had when flicking cigar ash into my glass a while or two ago. The consequences were fatal, to my love life.

I can't help wondering if Bligh and even Blencathra too are the hideous results of too much interbreeding out on Bodmin Moor. Are they in fact forgotten members of the Cardinham Clampitts or the Pensilva Pikeys, maybe the Upton Cross Dressers. Turned out by even more revolting parents to fend for themselves or to rot away in some lonely Moorland cave, next door to Daniel Gumbs' ghost! I'm wondering if 'Alice' lives there now? Apparently, 'she is living next door to someone'.

Don't get me wrong, I love the old geezer to bits. Love isn't always enough. I hold my temper in the knowledge that if I thump my tormentor Blencathra would be looking for me like Clint Eastwood looking for a runaway bank robber. This 'punk' isn't about to make her day.

Bligh continues. "This bleddy great 'and appeared out of the water! Like that there Liberty tart; er with the big torch and the spikey hair! Bugger me iffen she ain't got the biggest bleddy mackerel you ever seen. T'was longer n my ol bleddy todger; near as long as my arm t'was. I grabbed right at n!"

"The woman?" I ask, sounding ridiculous. I am particularly careful not to produce a mental picture of Bligh's 'bleddy old todger'.

"T'wernt a woman come up yer bleddy fool, t'was a bleddy mermaid. She were stark nekid. Part of 'er were nekid anyway. Why should I bleddy grab 'er? I was fishing."

98

Who am I to question what might be the difference between nekid and part stark nekid? "What happened then Cap'n?" Bugger, I never learn!

"I got a right back 'ander from Blencathra! She kicked me out of bed. I had to sleep with Span' on the bleddy sofa."

And there it is, an anti-climax all in the last sentence.

Once more I contemplate a violent reaction towards my cackling compare. I am itching to imitate the brutish Blencathra.

For some strange reason, Bligh, with his wondrous tale now complete, takes the opportunity to wipe a grubby shirt cuff across his completely dry nose.

I begin to wonder what that early day tourist Saint Pet' would think of Cap'n Bligh. The poor sod would grind his teeth in the certainty his works had all been in vain. Thoughts of violence towards the old geezer are soon dispelled as my senses are suddenly attacked from another, louder quarter. Just when I believe the night couldn't get any worse. I should have stayed outside and talked to myself!

Suddenly there is a sound unlike anything I have ever heard and one no one should have to endure. It is like some prat has drilled a live squawking gull into my eardrum. Even though, after a few seconds, I am certain the squealing has stopped, it still echoes inside my head like a runaway dentist's drill. It is as if an alien visitor has arrived and is unsuccessfully attempting to tune itself in to our language! It was like listening to the Eastenders theme tune, speeded up. Maybe somebody upstairs has a pneumatic road drill and they're using it to get rid of earwax, belly button fluff, perhaps a decaying tusk?

Bligh looks to me in a silent appeal, his mouth opening and closing like a freshly landed Haddock lying on a marble slab, gasping uselessly for one last breath before the arrival of the gutting and beheading knife. A bit like Mel Gibson in Braveheart, with a bit less gore! Ok, the same amount.

"Jeezus Christ Cap'n, what the friggin' hell is that?" I ask, for fear that whatever it is might suddenly materialise violently here in the Texas Chainsaw Mermaid Bar.

"T'wern't me Maccy lad!"

"I know it weren't you Cap'n."

"Reckon it was Blen, 'er bein'' upstairs on 'er own like. Don't knaw what's got into 'er; shouting and yellin' that way!" Bligh's voice trembles without control.

So, there isn't a mad dentist up there after all. If there is, if there was, I wouldn't want to be in his shoes. I take another gulp from my glass, forgetful of the recent free top up, an unsolicited gift and wonder at the old bloke's shivering reply and his lack of interest in finding out what might be wrong with his stricken wife. I knew it was her all along. I doubt she has a chainsaw or an oral hygienist in her bedroom, but she might.

"Why don't you go up there and find out Cap'n? She could be dying, maybe worse. Go and see to her."

"Me? I ain't goin', you bleddy go! What's worse?"

"She's your bleddy wife! I've no idea and don't need to know."

"Tidn't fair. You don't have to remind me. Er's gone quiet now. I'll go up drekly. It might get busy in here soon. I'd best stay put."

I follow the Cap'ns hopeful gaze around the bar. It had better. There are other customers but only the four that are visible in this age infested place. There is the young local couple checking out each other's palates by way of tongue exploration. I can't quite see where the two pairs of hands are. Probably they are just in pockets keeping warm. The two seem to be well acquainted.

One Armed Frank is asleep, despite the recent howling from above. Lil, the Tart stares at an empty glass. She is no longer a tart as far as I know. Age has taken toll of her looks, I suppose. I'm quite certain she must have looked different at one time otherwise she would have starved to death some fifty years ago. As far as I know she's retired from horizontal pleasuring. It could be I'm assuming too

100

much. Lil may still be self employed. She might have always been eightyish and ugly. From some of what I've heard, her services weren't always horizontal and not always that pleasurable. She just needed to be in position. Dear old Lil is what we call a two-sack job. One to be placed over her head and another to be carefully placed over the client's pate in case hers falls off before completion of intimacy.

I avert my disinterested gaze quickly as Lil smiles at me in a way that makes me think she has ideas of dispelling any doubts she is still active in the knee trembling department. To be selected as her first customer of the decade is not on my wish list.

I wait for Bligh to pull me another pint. Stupidly I try to imagine what Lil' might have looked like in her prime, which to be fair, would have been sometime after our little fallout with the Kaiser and just before the Wall Street crash.

I come to my senses and give up. It is a little like playing I Spy without a partner. Like playing tennis on your own. I glance around the nicotine stained walls. Thickening cobwebs are beginning to take the place over.

Large spiders are gradually making the Mermaid Bar smaller. Decorating the place for All Hallows Eve seemingly. I can see a mouse. It might be a dwarf rat, in a semi dark corner, chomping at what looks like a hardened sandwich dropped by god only knows who or when. I wonder how long ago it had been lost. I don't want to know the answer. I can't hear the rodent sawing through the crust, I suspect it is.

"You doing food now Cap'n?" I ask with a gentle hint of sarcasm.

"Knaw there ain't any call for it, what with all them other eating places all over town. Why do you ask, young Maccy?"

"Just wondered me ol' matey. Have you thought about having another barbecue night?"

It is Bligh's turn now to follow my gaze. "That there bleddy sandwich ain't from here. Some bleddy walkers in here at the weekend dropped it. Don't know what the hell they was doing walking at this time of the year. At least it idn't bein' wasted young Maccy."

Bligh pauses. "It's too bleddy cold outside to do a barbecue Maccy."

"Not outside me old mate, in here!"

"That'd be stupid lad; we don't have enough folks come in here."

Bligh misses my point. A lighted barbecue should at least allow the temperature to rise by a half a degree. I'm not even thinking about my stomach thanks to the little furry creature that is now trying to drag its partly crystallized supper away. Probably hoping the rest of the family will soon come out and help. At the sudden sound of the wide heavy door opening, the mouse lets go of its weekly shopping and scurries away towards the toilet area. I look up with some relief to see Leonard's smiling face.

"Leonard my boy, what ya' drinking? T.D or V.D.? I see you got your mouth back in working order."

"Not keen on bleddy V.D. Maccy, ta! I've heard the food at the clinic isn't too clever." Lenny grins just wide enough to confirm my stating of the obvious.

"Todgers then!"

"Aye!"

That last isn't the beer's real name, but Lenny tells me it does have the stated effect, after having downed eight or nine pints of the stuff.

The Cap'n 'tops off' Lenny's 'Todger's' and takes coins from the little stack where I'd placed them on the bar top just as the heavy front door opens fully and just as quickly slams shut again. Bligh grunts something I don't understand. I can't be bothered to ask him to repeat it. Almost at once the door is shoved open again.

This latest newcomer is four legged. It has what can only be described as half a face. The Alsatian squeezes itself inside and makes straight for the half-eaten sandwich which is immediately sucked up.

Almost to a second the hungry mouse reappears. The ravenous dog makes a dart at the rodent and within seconds a wriggling tail is hanging from the one good side of its deformed snout. I turn away. I can just hear faint squeaks as the rodent fights heroically against its impending death by canine cannibalism.

"That's handy boys!" Bligh bursts into excited conversation suddenly. "Saves my Blen having to clean up when that bleddy ugly dog comes in here."

Just as the last words are being completed by the Mermaids' landlord, I am wondering just how thorough the landlady's cleaning habits are. The mouse wins its fight for freedom. It slips out of the damaged side of the dog's mouth. So, almost but not quite 'a dog's dinner'. Seemingly unhurt it scurries up the stairs that lead to the accommodation area. I make up my mind right there and then never to eat sandwiches with meat in, especially if the meat is still wriggling and is still a whole animal, which the dog isn't.

"Didn't you ought to go see if she's alright Cap'n?"

"It's a bleddy mouse Maccy."

"Not the friggin' mouse, your bleddy wife for Christ's sake!"

"Listen 'ere you boys. If I was that bleddy mouse, I'd be bleddy worried. Wouldn't you? He's had one lucky bleddy escape tonight."

I consider Bligh resembles a six-foot mouse as the whiskers on his nose begin to quiver once again. The surround sound increases in volume.

The Alsatian whimpers softly and looks appealingly from Lil's puzzled face and back at us. I glance at the old landlord and wait for his reaction to this new outbreak. The hairs on the bulbous section of the old boy's nose twitch multi-directionally for a second. At the same time a tiny tidal wave of clear, warm liquid begins to form into a balloon just below the tip.

We are treated to the crescendo! I deftly snatch away my glass. I don't intend getting caught twice in one day!

There are inaudible sounds followed by crunching footsteps that remind me of the Maroons. The Maroons are the distress rockets that boom off Stepper Point to call up the crew members of the lifeboat, so they might launch their craft and assist some storm ravaged vessel that might be heading for the dangers of the Doom Bar. A similar warning for anyone heading towards this place might be useful. Glasses rattle an out of tune chorus on the head high shelves. I feel Lil smiling cautiously behind me.

The dog begins to howl in the only way a half-faced dog can. Suddenly it is gone. The mutt abandons ship through cowardice and a partly broken sash window. I remember it was in the same condition before I went to college.

It's a puzzle to me why the rockets are called Maroons, their colour is unimportant I would think. The noisy bit holds higher importance surely. They could just call them bangers!

Bligh quivers. Lenny wears a startled look, he had been absent at the first outbreak of Blencathra's earsplitting cries.

Lenny can hold back no longer. "She's afraid of mice then Cap'n?"

"Naw, she's got bleddy gut's ache and the backdoor trots! She'll be in the bog crappin' through the eye of a needle if I idn't mistaken."

"What about the bleddy mouse?" I couldn't help myself. I should have resisted another stupid question which was near enough identical to an earlier one.

"Well now young Maccy. I don't knaw! I suppose it could 'ave the same! My own guts idn't too clever tonight."

Bligh rubs at his stomach with this latest admission. It is a final warning sign for Lenny and I too hastily relocate. I feel its time to leave. If Blen' is about to blow like a half-sized Krakatoa, I don't want to be around for the fallout.

Pyroclastic clouds aren't really my thing, nobody's I suppose. I have never heard of Pyroclastic Cloud chasers. Mind you, some folk will do anything in front of a camera!

My mate has already drained his glass. His hand is on the brass door handle. I pull the great door tightly shut behind me as we leave in search of the Maypole and hopefully calmer waters. The dog follows us up Padstow hill, it probably feels safer with Lenny and I.

Chapter Eleven

George and the Dragon

My Ma has asked me a hundred times or more, why I spend so much of my time and money at the Mermaid Bar. The secret lies in the last two days, and nights. You just don't get this kind of stuff on TV! Soap operas are not made of this. They can't compete.

Ma has no room to shout. If she can't be found, she'll be holding court in the Maltsters Arms every night, at Little Petrock, a bit like Barbara Windsor, minus the jutting out bits, not completely obviously.

The Maltsters is fractionally more appealing than the Queen Vic'. It's a Cider house. Cider imbibers don't look for comfort, they just look for more cider. Not everybody drinks the Apple juice, but the remainder seem to be a minority, so I heard!

According to Bligh, Blencathra has improved during the night. Today she is away somewhere in England, as that lady will call any place that exists on the other side of the Tamar River that separates us from the English. She is right.

England can only be reached via the huge, ugly, concrete bridge that has, since nineteen sixty-five, dominated the Saltash landscape. It will earn it's keep one of these days. It's still being paid for nearly fifty years after it was completed. To listen to Blencathra anyone could easily believe Scotland, Wales, Ireland and every other land do not exist at all. There's just Cornwall, 'over there' and 'up country'. There is another bridge at Gunnislake, but we try not to acknowledge its existence. There are strange folk thereabouts.

As for other foreign countries? In all my time, man and boy, I never once heard our landlady mention the name of another country. I might be guilty of a tad of exaggeration. Blencathra has very little knowledge of elsewhere. This place, some water, another place, a lumpy bit. Forget the O level in Geography.

Dusty and I should have taken her to Kansas with us. She would have got on well with Aunt Renee, for a short while. I can see the two of them now in the middle of the street, pacing off for a stand-up gunfight. Renee difficult to hit because she is so small and skinny. Blen' wearing a funnel, bullets ricocheting everywhere, reminding us of that great Australian; Ned Kelly!

One Armed Frank and I enter the Mermaid at the same time. I allow the elder crew member to get served first. I listen with a smile as he attempts to wind up Bligh. The Alsatian appears through the broken window. It's come in for a wash apparently.

"Usual Frank?"

"Is it clear?"

"Course it bleddy is!"

"Look Bligh, your clear and my clear aren't always the same!"

"Do you want n, Yes or bleddy naw?"

"I'm here, aren't I? I haven't come to help you decorate the bleddy place, 'ave I?"

"Good at decorating, are you Frank?"

"One more crack from you Bligh and I'll take you outside."

"Then what will you do Frank, wave at me?"

"Where's that old Dragon of yours tonight. I'll get a better conversation from her, than you."

"You might lose more body parts if she ever hears you talking about her that way."

"She doesn't frighten me mister."

"She doesn't frighten me neither Frank but like I said, you'll be counting your remaining limbs if she was here. I'd take you outside and make a start myself, but we might get busy drekly. Count yourself bleddy lucky."

"Do you knaw your way?"

107

"How would you like to be try supping your pint with a broken arm, Frank?"

"How would you like a new set of teeth?"

"You're gonna be needing a straw with this iffen you don't button your bleddy lip. I don't have time to put you straight. I'll get the missus down here herself."

Frank loses the verbal battle but offers a single V sign as he admits defeat. He couldn't offer a double obviously. He takes his beer and stumbles his way to his usual table, next to Lil. Which is only right as she has to roll his cigarettes. Bligh pulls my pint of T.D, it is indeed perfectly clear. A much clearer pint than one would get in the Sailmakers Arms. One mustn't forget the Sailmaker's has other, earthier attractions, almost as important, to counterbalance the inconsistencies of their cellar.

"Decorate the place? What the bleddy hell would I wanna be doing that for? What's the matter with it?" Bligh conjures up a final fusillade to the forlorn Frank.

"Come on Cap'n, don't kick him while he's down."

"Well, he started it, Maccy lad!"

I just want some peace and quiet. Frank is already down and out, disinterested. He drops his baccy tin and papers in front of Lil. She will keep him supplied with rollies while they are in attendance. Without giving Bligh at least one of a dozen replies I personally have in mind, I keep quiet and study my pint.

I'd paid my money. It is time to make a start. With my glass firmly clutched, I glance around the room. One old painting of a ship in distress is hanging upside down, which is appropriate. It has been that way since the fight between Lenny and I. It'll stay that way no doubt!

"Bligh, what did appen to the bloke that lost his wallet I found. I never saw him again after the 'Chase', did you?"

"No, he's long gone I expect. Irish bloke he was. What was his name, I can't remember?"

"Paddy?"

"That were it, Paddy something, Irish I believe."

"Padraig Calhoun!"

"Bleddy 'ell Maccy. How did you knaw that?"

"It was me that found the bleddy wallet?"

"Aye, but "ow did you knaw it was Paddy?"

"No idea, a lucky guess I reckon. It's pronounced Porrag."

"Porridge?"

"Porrag!"

"That's what I bleddy said you bugger!"

Even I've had enough now. The conversation breaks down before it gets too far out of hand.

The Alsatian seemed unaware of the insult trading. Now underneath the pool table, it continues its work. The two kids are once again at it in the corner. Frank is already beginning to doze. Lil' smiles at me. She produces a half wink as I take in the far too familiar surroundings.

I'm hoping she knows I haven't been anywhere near her. She has an annoying habit, or so I'm told, of winking at all customers from her horizontal past. At her advancing age, she might somehow believe that I have at one time been on her client list, a regular. I shiver with sound effects! On thinking about it, I suppose there have been times on waking that I can't fully remember who the lucky woman was last night. I'm ninety-nine percent certain Lil was never her. One percent is a worry I'll have to live with. I return her cross-eyed wink out of nothing more than politeness.

I look back to the grimy shelves behind the bar, where small, dusty jars of cockles, mussels, Bryant and May matches and bags of Pork Cracklers sit patiently in the thickness of ever deepening dust. My grin widens somewhat at what I see next. Bligh, at this very moment is opening a bag of what I'd bet are out of date Cracklers. He peers into the opening as a ripe, drip of wayward nostril juice falls into the bag and disperses amongst its doubtful contents. Bligh's excitement knows no bounds.

I am chuffed to bits. I feel that in some way this is justice and fitting, for the times Bligh has allowed similar leakages to disgorge into my glass whilst leaning over to

109

tell me some gossipy titbit, perhaps something about the lusty landlady at the Maypole Inn.; titbit I have already been party to a couple of times. I should admit to nothing! It seems to me for a second or two that Bligh is taking the piss. After extracting a couple of pieces of the soggy monosodium glutamate encrusted rinds and shoving them into his hardworking mouth the old bugger makes me an offer I can and will, easily refuse.

"Want one Maccy?" I'm certain it is a serious question. I am prepared for it.

"Er, no thanks all the same. I'll have a bag of my own please!" I have no idea why I say that. Temporary insanity may be to blame!

I shove some small change across the bar as Bligh grabs at the last but one bag from the shelf. He is about to tear it open for me when I reach out and snatch the bag from his hand. Bligh means well. It is a close thing!

"So, why's Blencathra gone across the bridge Bligh?" I am playing one for me, two for you with the ugly Alsatian, while I wait for my answer. The Cracklers taste like corrugated cardboard. I feel it only right the mentally disturbed, facially disfigured dog should have the larger share. He doesn't know what cardboard is.

"'Er's gone to get 'erself some of what they call breast implants you knaw, to make 'er titties look bigger and firmer like!" Bligh allows his guessing hands to give me an idea of the size of Blencathra's possible mamorial improvements.

"Yeah?" I ask incredulously. I feel myself cringe at the thought of Blencathra's enlarged breasts looming into view and allowing themselves to sprawl menacingly across the breadth of the bar top. I think they are already bigger than he realises, I don't mention it.

Two miniature Zeppelins in the same bar would surely necessitate an entry in the big Guinness Book. Bligh must think they are pillows. Of course, it is all a wind up. I should have known straightaway. I don't. The old boy does me almost every time; in the same way that he does

110

just about everyone that dares to enter the Mermaid Bar, allowing this old geezer to insult their hearing and dissect their dodgy intelligence.

"Knaw, I'm pullin' your leg young Maccy lad. She 'ave gone over to Plymouth to start up a nudist colony on Drake's Island."

I can see it, it's gross. I won't believe it. I wait calmly for the real reason Blen is away. I do admire the persistent old sod.

"She 'ave gone to her sister's in Devonport, on a visit."

"Sister, English?" No, no, I don't doubt this one. Bligh couldn't make this up.

"That's right! Er be one of three twins. My Blen" dropped out over to Bodmin. The others were extracted in Plymouth on account, they were so damn big they couldn't get them out over here. I suppose they got stronger doctors over there. They should have taken her mother to a garage and hauled the poor little tackers out with a block and tackle."

Bligh cackles loudly at his own mischievous insult, safe in the knowledge he is safe, for now. Frank opens an evil eye. Maybe Bligh is making this up. I am just half listening by now and I shut my third eye quickly as it begins to conjure up a vision of the horrendous workshop birth of Blencathra's sister. I see a broken down ambulance at a lonely mist-enshrouded Dartmoor roadside. A saluting, peak capped AA man stands in attendance fully equipped with tyre levers and a tow rope. Worst of all, if Blen 'dropped out' how big are the other two?

I give a passing thought to Bligh's reference to a third twin. We all get confused from time to time, some of us more than others. Right now, I might be one of the latter. It is exactly at this point the huge solid front door blows open for a second and just as suddenly slams shut again. I feel this a little strange as it isn't particularly windy. There is no physical evidence of anyone having entered or departed the Mermaid. Bligh has my answer and it swiftly leaves the tip of his tongue, unfortunately.

111

"That'll be George come in I do reckon! He was about 'ere last night too, I believe."

"George, George who, who the bleddy hell is George?" I turn my head to find the answer to my own question. I scan the room and can just see the two kids tentatively groping each other in the darkness. Lil' is still smiling in her way and Frank's eyes are once again closed. His glass is half empty, or if you prefer half full. I could be exaggerating. His baccy packet is neatly folded over with a heavy Zippo lighter holding it down. I don't know anyone called George. As far as I am concerned, he just isn't here. Bligh is losing it.

"George, he's a bleddy ghost. He belongs here, sorta!"

"First I've heard of it." Unfortunately, I believe it won't be the last. 'I don't know anyone called George, alive, dead or even as he might be in this case, George the Zombie who likes a fag.'

"That's because he isn't here an awful lot!"

"Right, let me get this straight Bligh. The Mermaid has a ghost, but not very often. Just turns up when it feels like it? Sort of part time. On a spirit level."

I am pleased with my little joke, but it is obvious Bligh does not immediately catch on. I leave it hanging in the air, rather like the remains of poor George might be. Ah well, at least I know someone called George now, almost. Did I need to?

I scan the room again in case the dead man might fully materialise. Nothing else that could be called supernatural occurs, as far as I know. It's a pity, I am hoping to see Frank levitate and Lil's head spin around; maybe another night. I consider the possibility she might have a crucifix in her handbag. I snap myself out of such a horrendous thought. I wish now I hadn't seen that film. I didn't see the whole of the Exorcist, I sneaked out and went to the pub. I was underage in the cinema anyway!

"Naw, it ain't as simple as that Maccy. There be two reasons why George visits; one is, when Frank's here, on account we do reckon George is Frank's old man cos

112

Frank's old man was called George. We think he's Frank's dad see."

"And the other, what's the other bleddy reason?"

"Now that is simple Maccy lad! George don't like Blencathra, they never did get on! "Fraid of her see! Iffen Blen idn't 'ere, George do come and visit. He has been here a lot lately. He was up the stairs and outside the bog door a day or two ago when Blen' was still at 'ome. Blen' do always keep the door open when 'ers squattin' in the lavvy. I do reckon the bugger did it to frighten her. It worked too. She went off to Plymouth and 'aven't come back yet."

So, George and Blen' are scared of each other. That puts everything into context. My mind is playing terrible tricks on me by this time. I see Blen' perched on the wooden seat knitting; George appears before her and says, 'you dropped one'. I imagine Blen' running down the landing trying to haul her billowing knickers up. She is screaming blue murder with Jack Nicholson suddenly appearing, brandishing a large chopper, axe to you and I. There's no sign of the red-headed twin sisters.

My imagination shuts down suddenly. It is all too much. My mind slowly returns to something near normality as I would call it. Right now, I can see why George, Frank or any one of us might be afraid of Blen'. I'd be a tad frightened myself if I saw the landlady on the bog. Who wouldn't?

I just don't see myself qualified to disagree with Bligh telling me that Blencathra is feared not only by the living but the undead also and it is reciprocated. I should think about that one. Maybe I've done enough thinking for one night. And then I wonder, am I once again being taken in by this wrinkled story teller extraordinaire. I ponder the odds for a while and as Bligh, with a grin of his own, pushes a damp rag along the sticky bar top, I come to the decision the old geezer is once again pulling my plonker. I can't be certain, I don't want to be certain.

"That was proper Maccy boy! A spirit level! That was good. That'll be the college education you got. If anyone was asking me, I'd have to say I don't believe in such things."

"Spirit levels?" I'm not certain what day it is. Maybe I should smoke something that might return me to normality.

"Naw, bleddy ghosts. Try and keep up lad."

Bligh's sleeve brushes at his nasal orifices as he begins to cackle like the head witch in a one witch coven. Although the reply has taken a while, I am pleased it isn't a complete waste of effort. Bligh's own reply leaves me in further doubt, as to his sanity and my own.

Somehow this evening's episode will become a small, defining moment in my so far young life. I am now a firmly convinced believer in the world of the supernatural, as almost instantly the massive door again opens of its own accord. Again, it slams shut. Open again, another slam instantly follows.

I don't see George. I do feel I am getting to know him better with every passing minute. The dog has departed, I'm not sure how it opened the door.

Chapter Twelve

Death and Destruction

I don't see it, I do hear it. I had turned my face to the grimy shelves after checking on the old tart. A sudden crash, splintering of wood and breaking glass signaled Frank demising as he, his chair and table topple over behind me. It might have been worse had Frank still owned two arms, there's no telling how much more damage he could have done. I now think I know why the door opened and shut twice.

"I could be wrong, but my guess is you got yourself another ghost Bligh." I had glanced around at the crunching. Frank isn't taking a quick horizontal nap. He isn't trying to get more comfortable or looking for a recently dropped coin.

Frank's eyes are wide open. I have the feeling two old pennies will be far more useful now. No point in using the decimalised version, they would just fall out, Lil would pick them up and shove them into her bra, from where they would just fall out again. Frank hardly knew where he was going half the time. We were alike in some respects.

"Could be young Maccy, who the hell is this come now? We're getting busy in here tonight, lad? A pity Frank has gone so early. He usually has a short last thing."

I am thinking about the wasted firewood as two men appear somewhat in the manner of grim reapers having come to drag Frank to the next phase. The two are a second or two late. Who's counting? Like Bligh, I wait impatiently for official identification. I just have time to wonder if they have been respectfully waiting outside. Maybe checking their notes on whose time has come and if they are in the right place. 'How might their conversation have gone,' I wonder?

"That's him behind the bar. He looks about ready."

"Where, no, I bet it's the one sitting at the table and leaning on one elbow."

"Could be, neither look too good. Move over, I can't see through all this dirt on the glass. Hey, he's been careless, he's only got one elbow. Shall we go in now or wait until he drops."

"No, it's not allowed, we have to wait. We have to be respectful."

"Just think it will save time if we pretend we are tourists."

"Emmets, they call them emmets 'round here."

"Do they? Not me. It might be the woman, she doesn't look too grand. Then I don't suppose she ever has."

"No, a male, between seventy-five and eighty-five, it says on the collection chit. Not all there."

"Could be the landlord then?"

"I don't think so. Says here eight thirty-five. There he goes. Oh, he's spilled his beer. I hate it when that happens, such a waste."

"Me too, this must be the right place, let's go and get him."

"Do we need to take these in with us?"

"Nah, we'll leave them out here. Don't want any nasty accidents and they are bloody sharp."

"After you then."

"No, after you."

"Do you think we might get a free pint?"

"No chance, they're Cornish. In any case, we have another pick up at nine forty-five across the river. We can't go over there half pissed."

"I forgot that. Some rich bastard I suppose. Go on then. I thought it was the Scots who were tight."

"You go. I hate being first. The Cornish came from Scotland. Moved to Wales, didn't like it. It was too wet, so they came here."

"Are you sure you're cut out for this kind of work?"

The first reaper does not resemble the average emmet, nor is his companion carrying a long handled scythe with a wicked curved blade. Neither are wearing long, dark flowing robes, or pointing accusing fingers, but it's early days. The odd couple look like off duty coppers. I can tell a copper. Shifty eyed buggers. Something about the way they carry themselves; maybe these two are off duty or out of uniform. Plain clothes reapers. No, here is something different, something I cannot pin down. I wait. The stocky reaper ignores Bligh and me. I fancy he throws a quick wink at Lil who hasn't budged an inch since the fall of Frank. I hope he won't live to regret the attempt at friendliness.

The newcomer crosses directly to the now unmoving, three-limbed carcass. "The guys bought it, I guess."

And here it is; the answer to the question that has begun to slowly bulge in a central section of my brain. America, the cavalry has arrived. That one first sentence is enough. 'I guess 'bought it', gives it away.

"Bought what?" Came Bligh's brusque answer.

"He's gonna be a DOA Sir."

"Bought it, DOA? What the frig does the bloke mean Maccy lad?"

"Says Frank's dead. Bloke's a yank. They all talk like that except the women, they're worse! DOA, Dead on arrival."

"Dead on arrival, dead on arrival bleddy where? He was alive when he arrived, you know he was. He was alive, so he couldn't have been dead on arrival, he drank half a pint. The bugger couldn't have done that if he was dead!"

"Treliske Hospital." I didn't want to get involved in this foolishness. It just happened.

"What the buggary is the point in taking Frank down to Treliske bleddy hospital. If he's dead, he's dead. What's the point of taking him to the bleddy hospital? Nothing

117

they can do for him. DOA? DOD I'd say. Dead on departure! Bloody nuisance him dying in here."

"I could tie some weights around his feet and drop him in the quay or toss him into Lost Soul's Creek out the back if it helps."

"Listen up feller you need to inform the authorities, sudden death like this. It was sudden, wasn't it?"

Yep, American. If I was asking that question, I would have a smile on my face. 'Just as sudden as your arrival,' I thought to myself. "I'd say so."

Its possible bodies lie around in bars all over America for no reason. We do things differently on this side of the pond. We have decorum.

"Do you know Maccy, Frank's bleddy father died in here once?"

"Just once? Sort of a family tradition then Bligh?" That's how it's done. Decorum, a tad short on respect.

Bligh pulls himself together at the clear and precise but well-meant advice.

"Ais, I reckon you're right Mr." I notice Bligh is eyeing the shorter yank a tad strangely. So am I, both. My nose isn't twitching.

"Name's Virgil, Virgil O'Colligan, recently of the Catskill O'Colligans out of the County of Cork O'Colligans from Ireland. This feller here, he's from some goddam one dog town in West Texas. Ain't that right Hardin?"

"Sure is!"

"Hardin can get real talkative when he has a mind, best you remember that!"

Somehow the atmosphere has now taken on a surreal feel. I am quietly sipping at my pint of Todger's, Frank's invisible father has wandered in; Frank expires amongst a pile of firewood and broken glass and if that isn't enough the two kids are still tackling each other's tonsils over in the corner, completely disinterested or more likely unaware of the Mermaid's sudden loss. Ireland has somehow become the topic of conversation. My head is preparing to spin. We are also entertaining at least one American cousin minus half his mind.

Maybe he never had a complete one to start with! Blencathra has a sister, two sisters and that is a frightening thought. Quincy has just arrived. I enjoy Quincy. I watched it once while I was in a Chinese takeaway. I was waiting for my brown paper carrier bag full of King Prawns and Egg Fried rice with a delicious sweet and sour sauce, best tasted by sucking at a bottom corner of the carrier bag. No need for foil trays. Just ask for the food to be tipped straight in the bag. Virgil O'Colligan Quincy is spot on.

We are just waiting for the Oriental laboratory assistant to arrive with further information and proof that Frank has naturally died of natural causes. Shouldn't be a problem, I couldn't see any holes in Frank and there is no traffic in the Mermaid tonight. There is nothing sticking out of him other than three remaining limbs and the other usual bits and bobs I'm sure are still in situ. It must be natural causes.

One thing is certain. Frank is deader than a Dodo, whatever that might look like. I thought they were all dead but what do I know, they could just be dormant? 'As dormant as a Dodo!' Thinking of things dormant, I feel obliged to check on dear old Lil. Well you never know. The old girl is sitting bolt upright. I watch with mild interest as she raises her half-filled glass in a silent salute to the very recently deceased, as yet, undeparted, Frank.

"Damn, er's gonna be right shitty when she sees the mess Frank has done Maccy. Bleddy man's forever breaking the bleddy furniture and now I can't get the bugger to pay for the damage. Is that his change down there?"

"If I was asked, I would say that Frank's firewood providing days are well and truly over matey. Shouldn't you be phoning someone?"

I ignore the monetary query. Unlike Lil. She snatches at the few coins that have spilled down from the tabletop and pockets them without a word.

"Who?" Bligh scratches roughly at some imaginary itch at the back of his head.

"I'm not sure but you can't leave Frank where he is, it'll look bad if you get a nice family in here drekly."

A family? To be honest I was thinking more along the lines of Elvis and Napoleon, maybe a London busload of alien abductees might appear looking for bed and breakfast. They would think they'd been brought back to the wrong time era. My own choice if I was allowed one, would be the Addams family. They will feel right at home here with their not so distant relatives.

"Ais, I suppose. I wish my Blen' was here. She'd know what to do!"

I can see it all. Blencathra will shoulder Frank by his one stiffening arm and walk the eight miles to the Wadebridge undertakers without visibly breaking sweat. Let me make it clear. That that can't be seen or smelled is best left that way.

"What happened Maccy?"

Intelligent life! Thank god for Leonard! "It's poor old Frank, Len. He's demised. He and his old man just left. You might have passed them on your way here. Oi Bligh, does that mean Blencathra must be on her way home?"

"Dunno young Maccy. Tis a worry! There'll be a heap of trouble when she gets here mind. It will all be my fault!"

"Why? It wasn't your fault Frank had to go. If you hadn't been here, he would still have gone, pard."

"Tidn't that boy. What worries me is the Yank there. She isn't gonna be best pleased when she sees him drekly, no sir. She'll be in a nasty bleddy mood. She'll be spitting nails."

Believable "Why?"

"Oh god Maccy, she'll be fit to bust a gut! That there yakky, short-arsed yank is one of her twins. He's her

120

brother. I recognise him. I know why the bugger is here too. Oh, bleddy hell Maccy. I dunnaw what we are gonna do."

"Spit it out Bligh!" It is a foolish suggestion on my part. Instinctively I step back. Bligh doesn't usually need an invitation. Luckily, the old bloke speaks with hardly a dribble. She isn't here. There's no need to worry about the threat of a large exploding torso just yet. So Bligh had been telling the truth all the time.

"He'll be wanting this place! Lessen I'm mistaken. See my Blen' borrowed the money from his bit of the family to get this place. That were nigh on twenty-five years ago. We haven't never paid them any back yet. I guess that's why he's here. That yank bastard wants the bleddy Mermaid."

As unlikely as it seems, I believe this latest story completely and can see Bligh is genuinely fretting about the future of his and Blencathra's living conditions.

"I didn't know Frank's old man was still alive."

"He isn't Lenny."

"But you said…."

"Leave it Lenny, it's a long story. How's your ear?"

"Brave thanks mate, only a scratch. How's your Goolies?"

"More or less in the right place, no thanks to you. A tad swollen. Not a bad thing! Hope they don't go down too quick. It's like having mumps without the swollen glands bit."

The yakky Yank has taken control of the Frank situation. Bligh, at the insistence of his long-lost brother in law, has telephoned to inform the relevant authorities as to the death of Frank.

We wait in anticipation for the arrival of the doctor, the police, the undertaker and any other that might have an interest in an incomplete, non-breathing body in possession of a pile of firewood and an unlit roll-up. At least we won't be requiring the attendance of the fire brigade. If they do turn up, it might be nice.

"So, Bligh, just how did One Armed Frank become One Armed Frank?" I am idly looking for conversation while we wait, if only to bring respite to the icy silence that has blended itself so easily into the already normal chilly atmosphere of the Mermaid, with the arrival of Blen's big brother and the Pecos River. A long streak of West Texan water.

While we wait, Lil strolls across and deftly takes the unlit 'rolly' from Frank's still warm fingers. On returning to her chair, she flips the Zippo and lights the end. She sits contentedly blowing perfect smoke rings as the silver lighter is replaced carefully on top of the now damp packet. I suppose this is only fair, as Lil does, or did roll Frank's ciggies for him. Someone had to do it and Audie Murphy never seems to be around when he's needed. Frank would lose half of his baccy on the floor every time he tried. The old sod couldn't smoke at all until Lil arrived at the Mermaid. If Lil had bitten the dust first, Frank would have had to give up smoking before he started. Come to think of it, I never saw Lil smoke before anyway.

Bligh opened with an explanation. "Frank'd be best telling you. Shame you didn't ask him before. There's some would tell he was a pilot up down over at St Merryn airdrome and was shot down in a dogfight."

"Some would say he was in an accident with a bad-tempered tractor and others would have it Lil's old man come home and found George warming his side of the bed."

"So, which was it Bligh for Christ's sake?" Lenny asked.

"I don't know if I should let on young Leonard. It isn't respectful. Frank might be here listening."

"He isn't 'ere Bligh. He did leave with George remember, where does this George go when he isn't here anyway?"

"Ais Maccy, so he did. Anyways, I'll tell you some of what happened when they have took Frank away. I hear

George is over at the chippy mostly. I believe that's where he is when he isn't here.

"Why? Why would the old man be at the chippy?"

"He can't be in two places at once I reckon."

"I thought he was passed over Maccy, you just said so."

My mucker has a fluctuating IQ.

"Well now young Maccy, the chippy wasn't always a chippy. It was a sail loft in the old days. The story goes that Frank was apprentice to George. George was a tradesman making sails and the like for the old boats that did come into the harbour one time."

I resist the impulse to grab Lenny's collar and drag us both away from what I'm certain will become verbal torture, but I am interested to know how Frank had become one armed. Although Bligh had already said he wouldn't tell us while Frank was still warm, and wet due to the spilled beer, it is obvious he intends to impart his knowledge of the mishap at some point. Just as he is about to spill the beans all the officials and their dog arrive.

None of the newcomers did bring a dog but the half-faced Alsatian had taken the opportunity to wander back in alongside the Admiral and Lady Birdseye.

For now, we would have to wait for Bligh's recollections. We are treated to the sight of the mutilated mutt splashing contentedly at Frank's spilled beer. Obviously, Padstow dogs don't do decorum. We pass the time watching and commenting on Frank's removal. Once officialdom had completed its duty, the two Americans, after having partaken of small cold beers also made their exit, not without informing Bligh that they were staying locally for some while and intended to revisit. I noticed the old landlord had shuddered involuntarily at the promise.

Bligh continues. "Like I was telling, Frank apprenticed for old George and that was around the time part of him went missing. They tell me George weren't just teaching Frank his trade. He was teaching the boy everything. Frank and George had been drinking. Could be they'd both been in here. It would have been different in them days."

The Birdseyes, Lenny, Lil and even the kids at the back seemed to have forsaken their physical explorations for a moment. All now appear to be listening to Bligh's tale. It seems to me the old landlord is for once telling a story that might be true. Not one that he has produced in a moment of boredom. Just one thing and I know some frown on nit picking, but Bligh's statement regarding the condition of the Mermaid: 'it would have been different back then!' No! Not unless the place has deteriorated from some pre-war grandeur. The old geezer continued his story of the three-quartered corpse.

"What happened was this: George having like Frank, taken on a skin full, decided that the lad should become acquainted with other human pleasures, you knaw! George took Frank to the Candlemakers' shop up on the Drang. It was known there was a lady working up there. It was the place to go for such as Frank needed. Unfortunately, this was the very night when the woman's' husband discovered what she got up to when he was away night fishing. He did catch her and the boy at it and he'd brought his hunting gun. Poor young Frank had his arm blown clean off. Twadn't really clean, but it was gone."

"That's bleddy bullshit Bligh!"

This sudden shouted interruption comes from behind me. All eyes turn to Lil. She is on her feet looking blood dripping daggers.

"You bleddy liar Bligh. That isn't what happened you bleddy knaw it! It was bleddy George that was having his pleasure with my Ma that night. Young Frank was waitin' his bleddy turn."

Lil continued. "Young Frank was keeping watch outside the door. He wouldn't let my dad in when he turned up and the two of them went to scrapping. Dad shot the boy accidental in the fight. That's how it happened and that's why George won't go off to where he should. He's feeling guilty about the lad's arm. You should be careful what you say Bligh. Could be there are things come out here tonight you'd rather didn't."

124

Lil's statement quiets things down somewhat at the Mermaid. Lenny and I glance at each other. The two kids slowly re-engage in what they do best. The Admiral, which is most unlike the Admiral, orders drinks for everyone. The subject of Frank's arm is discreetly dropped. Lenny and I don't budge. Time is getting on and it doesn't seem worth the while to move on to the Sailmaker's now. The added physical attractions that I'm informed it now possesses would again have to wait.

I chuck some coins into the Jukebox and search the yellowed name cards under the glass. House of the Rising Sun seems to give some poignancy. I am known to be in possession of a sick sense of humour. I draw the line at Jake the Peg, leaving that particular ditty unplayed. I choose the only tune on the box that has any reference to the oldest profession.

It seems Lil's new-found voice and dire warnings have the desired effect on our host. Bligh becomes subdued and content for the remainder of the late evening to pour drinks as and when requested. I get the impression he would much rather be somewhere else; anywhere else, even England. It would surely be a last resort.

With no visible means of traveling anywhere he discovers a zealousness for cleanliness, deciding to wipe and polish away long ignored dust from the back shelves.

An hour later Lenny and I amble along the quayside, this time giving no thought to the Birdseye's nocturnal nuptials. As we begin the steep climb towards the top of Padstow Hill, Lenny cannot help himself as he mouths a question.

"Maccy what was all that about?"

"Lenny, I dunno. Old Bligh is bleddy worried up."

It is a slow ascent. I explain the events of the early evening as best I can and with Lenny's occasional nods and post-midnight eye stretching exercises, I am certain he doesn't have a clue what I am telling him. We part at the top of the hill and I make my way across the fields and along the disused railway line. I am in my pit in less than two hours. I need a good night's sleep. I am required to play a pool match tomorrow night at the Sailmakers Arms. A quieter night!

Chapter Thirteen

Just the Ticket

With twelve hours unbroken sleep recently completed, I am back in place. Before making my official appraisal of the recently installed barmaid at the Sailmakers I have checked into the Mermaid Bar for half an hour to partake of a livener.

"You don't look so bleddy good tonight Bligh. What have happened now old feller?" Of course, I remembered perfectly the happenings of the previous night. I think it better than to just bring the subject straight into the conversation and just as well by the looks of Cap'n Bligh.

I do my best not to mention Frank's departure and the sudden arrival of the two American visitors, who resemble a twentieth century version of Laurel and Hardy, minus the bowlers! I needn't have worried. Bligh changes the subject before it is begun.

"Nor would you, young Maccy, if you'd gone and done what I'd not gone and done, on account I forgot. Tis 'er own fault for bein' away. She have given me what for on the bleddy telephone. Made my bleddy ears burn, she did."

"I don't reckon I ever did Bligh but being uncertain as to what it was you didn't do, I can't be bleddy certain that I haven't. In any case Blen' isn't here is she, so surely you can put whatever's wrong, right, drekly."

"Shut up and listen boy. Believe me, young Maccy, you didn't not do what I didn't. You wouldn't want to. Put it right? It be too bleddy late, they already had it last night!"

"Gotta go matey, I have a Pool match at the Sailmaker's drekly." I've heard enough. I see a faint chance to get away with a goodly portion of my slowly diminishing stock of sanity intact. To be fair, that invisible section of my personality is being sorely tested right now.

Bligh keeps a decent pint, most of the time at least and that's about it really. As for the company, 'the crew' as we call ourselves? There's dear old Lil. She keeps herself to herself mostly; though there was a time, as you know, when she was apt not to. In fact, she put herself about a fair bit by all accounts. Though Lil flashes what passes for a cheery smile on occasions, she is what you might call pretty unpretty. Lil makes ugly an art form. I'm beginning to wonder if there is a Nobel Prize for hideousness. If I was told she'd been smacked in the face with the flat side of a long handled Cornish shovel it would be believable. The zigzag of dark red lipstick adds to the vision of her having a head on collision with the cubicle door in the lady's powder room. It gives the impression of the stuff being applied during an eight pointer on the Richter scale. One could be forgiven for believing the dearly departed Frank applied the stuff for her, with his missing arm. Funny thing is, I never had what you would call a real conversation with Lil. She does chatter at times, but in the main only to herself and the late Frank. The previous night's sudden outburst was very different.

My curiosity gets the better of me and I have to ask. The old git will tell me anyway. Might as well get it over with. "Let's be having it Bligh, what did you not do?"

"I dunno young Maccy! Oh ais, I do remember; I did forget to get her bleddy lottery ticket and guess what did happen?"

"She won?"

"Er bleddy numbers did come up! Ers never won nothing afore and she haven't now neither. She isn't best pleased with me. I'll be for it when she gets back home drekly. 'Ere, how the hell did you know?"

"Lucky guess." Against my better judgment I shove my grubby glass towards the miserable looking landlord that makes hangdog sound like some bugger did just that to his four-legged friend.

The old feller shoves the glass under the tap and pulls on the long handle as he continues his explanation as to why he isn't in Blencathra's best books. I take little further notice until he changes the subject.

"Thought you were supposed to be playing Pool, Maccy lad? You'll be pissed as a fart before you get your stick in your hand!"

Bligh is cheering up. His grin spreads wider at his feeble attempt at hilarity. I have no idea it will end as suddenly and awfully as it does. Bligh is shaking himself out of his misery. Laughing full mouthed he loses what little control he has of his top set. I have a psychic interlude. I'm not quick enough to reposition my glass. The inevitable happens. I watch incredulously as the manufactured piece of face furniture vacates the cackling chasm and plops with an untidy splash into my refilled pot. My biggest worry is the old boy seems not to notice his sudden loss, perhaps due to temporary lower face paralysis. I am beginning to wonder which of them is the ugliest; Lil, Blencathra or Bligh with his teeth on the loose and seemingly supping contentedly at what remains of my pint.

"I dunno why your lot don't play your bleddy Pool 'ere in the Mermaid. Blen' would likely put some food out for you boys and the other team when you do have a match here."

"I wouldn't mind Bligh, honestly I wouldn't, though there are some drawbacks to be considered. First one, your pool table, as it is, it isn't a lot of good on account one leg is gone." A vision of Frank pops into my third eye. I didn't know I had one. It must have been mine or I wouldn't have seen it. I see Frank fully equipped. One leg is beautifully carved and rolled.

"Fair do's Bligh, she's propped up near enough level with the beer crate, but it idn't really legal for playing serious matches on. Secondly, half the bleddy town knows it was used for sexual purposes last New Year's Eve. Thirdly, there was a replay on New Year's Day." I don't think Lil was involved but I wasn't about at the time. I must have had a premonition.

"Fourthly, er, fourthly, oh yeah, there's no friggin' light over the table, and fifthly, well fifthly, Blen' don't 'do' food, on account, she doesn't do food as you can vouch for. I suppose what I'm trying to say is this: your table was used as a prop in an orgy, it's dark over there and Blen' can't cook. See what I mean? Oh yeah, and one other thing." I might as well go for broke!

"What bleddy other thing be that lad, go on?"

"You don't 'ave any bleddy balls!"

"That's a bleddy lie. I'll bleddy sue you, cheeky bastard, see if I don't. You ask Lil there, she'll put you straight!" Suddenly the old landlord realises he might have let a certain cat out of a bag. He is swift in changing the subject.

"I could help her do some sandwiches."

Bligh has slipped up. He is trying to change the subject. I'm not for letting him off easily. Why should I?

"You dirty git! You didn't? Pool balls, I meant there aren't any balls in that bleddy table. They're in the quay, remember? I dunno how Lenny and me didn't come across any of them the other night when we were having a dip. Mind you I couldn't find my own when I got out!" I said that last bit sotto voce, I didn't want to get Lil excited!

I ignore Bligh's well intended offer to spread margarine and warm snot alongside delicately thin cucumber slices, on bread that could double as pan scourers. It is important for me to pursue the subject of the Mermaids' crap pool table.

"Course I bleddy remember lad. 'Er was pissed at them bleddy seagulls weren't 'er! Was that when they ad 'er fish and chips away Maccy? I can't remember!"

"Nope! It was the time one of 'em crapped all over 'er new hairdo! I dunno why she was so bleddy annoyed. Some women pay a fortune to have streaks put in their hair! Where is she?"

"'Er's still at 'er sister's sobbing her heart out because I didn't get the bleddy lottery tickets. She does know her numbers have come up!"

"How much did she win Bligh?"

"Don't you never listen, lad? I done told ya I forgot to do 'er numbers. That's why 'ers in a bleddy lather! She didn't win a damn thing! She slammed the bleddy telephone down on me."

In a lather! "Do you want this back?" After hooking the plate out of my glass with my little finger I offer the yellowing set back to their owner. Again, I think about the lather. I think too about the tufts of 'gorse' that grow lushly from the landlady's moist armpits that are so terribly visible when she reaches for a cloudy glass from the shelf above the bar. Not that she's been doing much of that lately. I'm not really sure why I even noticed her armpits. It's a worry.

I am reminded suddenly of female Russian shot putters. Blencathra would put even some of these mountainous females into the shade, literally. Next comes the horrendous vision of virgin white shaving cream dripping along her forearms, that in circumference might compare with my collar size. Unfortunately, it also reminded me of the half inch head that has settled on the top of my second pint before the enamel intake. It is enough. I can take no more!

I empty my glass with a swiftness that would have pleased the local gulls. "Gotta go Bligh; I'll ask some of the lads about playing for the Mermaid next season, but only if you get a light over the table and promise not to do us any food. By the way, tell me, how much didn't 'er win?"

"Ten bleddy quid Maccy!"

"And, how much didn't you spend on tickets?"

"Ten bleddy pounds, she always has a tenner, every bleddy Saturday."

"Then she 'aven't lost anything, 'ave 'er?"

"I dunnaw, let me think."

"Take all the time you like matey. Good night Lil"! I am careful not to wink at the old tart. I don't want her getting the impression I would be looking for her after

131

kicking out time, gripping two brown sacks in my hands, one for her and one for me in case hers falls off during intimacy. I pull the heavy door shut tight behind me, hoping she can't open it by herself.

I am looking forward to getting back behind a pool cue. I did play now and again while I was away. It wasn't quite the same as playing in the North Cornwall and South Devon and district Super League. For one thing, unlike playing in Chelsea or Hammersmith, gambling is not allowed during league fixtures and I did lose more than a few quid up there. The funniest thing about our local league was the rumour begun just before my extended disappearance to the Metropolis, that the Marisco Arms, the tiny part-time pub that doubles as a post office on Lundy Island had obtained its own table and that it was contemplating joining our set-up. With a rough sea it would take nearly a week to get there and back. There's hardly any parking for boats at Lundy either. I can't see it happening.

It was some time before I discovered the date I was given the information. It was April 1st and the unusually impish Blencathra had taken it upon herself for one day only, to become a comedienne. It was a wind-up and a good one. I knew that such a fixture was an impossibility in any case; playing pool against four men, a mud-splattered sheepdog and two large hairy sheep was a non-starter. Well, we wouldn't want to lose to them!

There was the possibility the white ball might end up rolling around in the Severn Bore if it left the table. Lundy's hardly the Isle of White. The place is so small, every time someone takes a piss the water level rises.

I was also aware that apart from once being a haven for fifteenth century pirates, feared Viking Raiders had once occupied the tiny seaborn picnic spot. I just couldn't get rid of the mental photograph of our opposition wearing short skirts over great thick, hairy legs, horned helmets and carrying broadswords. Of course, there was the added fear of being personally violated by these huge hairy and rampant Danes. If we beat them at the table, they might wanna beat us over the table, maybe worse. Then there's the return match. The Vikings had invaded Padstow once before. The illegals had burnt the place to the ground a thousand years ago. Padstonians are known to have long memories when it comes to rape and pillage and they might not take kindly to half a dozen horned and chainmail clad foreigners carrying flaming torches and pool cues wandering around the quayside late at night with local girls slung over their shoulders. There's one or two that wouldn't be missed much; and some that wouldn't mind to be fair. One or two might be glad of an invasion, if you get my meaning!

I intended to ask Bligh about any reappearance of the yanks before I left. I was interested to know if they had returned to the Mermaid during the day. Somehow, I had become sidetracked, ambushed, by the old feller's woeful tale.

I turn myself in the direction of the Sailmakers and switch my thoughts to the impending game. Once again, I am the victim of an ambush. Only this time it's one of a physical nature. No, it isn't a Viking.

Striding cockily towards me is the town crank and he looks mean. I attempt to ignore the face to face meeting. The gangly bloke soon blocks my way. He doesn't appear to be carrying binoculars on this occasion.

"Maccy Tamryn, so you're back in town?"

At this rather squeaky statement I turn myself sideways. I look at my reflection in the grubby window of a pasty shop that doesn't have any pasties on show, just a few crispy wasps. I must agree with my would-be way layer, who in fact had been christened, perhaps a little unwisely by his parents, Soul. It has forever been my habit over the years I have known him, of prefixing Soul Beswetherick's given first name with the much favoured 'Arse'. The fact that I have been back a while now would mean little.

During wintertime, some Padstow folk are apt to disappear almost completely. In spring when the sun hopefully returns, so do most of the locals, eventually.

"Ah Soul, good to see you and fully clothed, there's a novelty." See what I did there?

I know Beswetherick will not take kindly to my reminding him that I have little respect for his peculiar mannerisms and much favoured outdoor activities. The fact is, Bessie is, at the very least, a peeping Tom, albeit an amateur, not that I know much about such things. My experience is severely limited to the Birdseye's yacht and I don't think that counts for much. I have no liking at all for Bessie as he is about to be reminded. I am a good two stone heavier than he I guess, I am ready to counter any physical assault he might be contemplating. I am prepared, rightfully so, as it turned out. I am fully able to put aside any thoughts of the late, Andy Stewart's sixties rendition of 'Donald where's your trousers'. With the instincts of a veteran quayside scrapper, recently reminded, I deftly take hold of my opponents' shoulder as he comes at me with a nasty look in his eye. Bessie is lacking in co-ordination. He is also a shit swimmer, it seems.

With a swift dip of my right leg and by twisting my shoulder around in a downward motion I have Bessie swinging upwards and outwards before he knows it. He comes up and over rather easily. I watch with satisfaction as he hits the water, a dozen or so bobbing seagulls flee skyward in startled terror. The action had been so simple; Bessie might just as well have thrown himself in.

I walk across to a life buoy that hangs a few yards away and unhook it. Seeing Beswetherick bob to the surface after a few seconds, I am careful to toss the red and white ring close enough for him to make use of it. I know for sure my opponent can just about get around in the water as we have exchanged similar pleasantries previously. It's a local custom in any case.

"Good lad. Keep your hands where they can be seen Bessie. Sorry I can't stay longer, got a pool match to play lad."

Bessie is spitting mud and saltwater. I'm certain he is attempting some less than polite reply to my gentle teasing. I should get on and don't catch every word. I am rather pleased with myself, especially now I am reasonably certain the opposing team is likely to be one player short. I don't ask Bessie to translate as I don't like to disturb folk that are preoccupied with trying to continue breathing as much as they need to, to stay alive.

Chapter Fourteen

A Fool in Paradise

At my totally unheralded entry into the Sailmaker's public bar I stare, perhaps rudely, at the new staff member. To say she is well proportioned might be an understatement. If I am to be honest; I can do honesty in times of need and propriety, I feel she doesn't seem to be my type. There's no harm in looking and look I do, with some growing consideration to quickly changing my type! She is beautiful. More than that. It would be wrong of me to comment; out loud anyway. I stare as she stares. It is unexpected. I'm not sure what she's staring at. I can't possibly state the objects of my own visual targets. There are a couple of clues obviously!

I think back to my sudden brush with Bessie and it didn't prick my conscience. To my annoyance it affects my concentration.

Lenny has noticed me enter the bar, he already has my pint waiting. The inevitable and direct question comes. I decide to be indifferent.

"So, what do you think Maccy?"

"What about mucker, I idn't sure what you mean?"

"The bleddy price of Conga bleddy Eel! What do you think I mean, the new barmaid for Christ sake, Maccy."

"Dunno, I 'aven't hardly had a chance to look boy." I am certain Lenny will continue his line of questioning as I would have, had the foot been inside the other boot and on somebody else's leg. So, I look the girl up and down; mostly up, as I can't see much of the down due to the height of the bar. I could reach over to make a more thorough observation but an action such as that might see me rewarded with something inedible from the bar menu; a knuckle sandwich. Her dad might be standing behind me? I turn, there is no sign of anyone who looks like a parent.

I believe she is acutely aware of my scrutiny and subjects me to a similar viewing. I should be flattered but something is bugging me. There is something familiar. I am unable to decide what it is, there is something.

"Yeah, very nice Lenny." My mind is what some would suggest partially absent at this point, but not for long.

"Hello Maccy. Lost your voice, 'ave e my bird?"

Here it is, the voice I recognise. The make-up I don't. When I say make-up, I don't mean that the girl might have a bricklayer's trowel in her handbag, or a rusting cement mixer parked outside her house, not unless she is a jobbing builder by day. No, it is a visual, audio thing. I know the sounds. The sights are unfamiliar. 'My bird' is a common enough greeting in this neck of the woods, but I must confess that when it is directed at me, I get a queasy feeling, said to resemble the sensation of a gut full of lively butterflies, in hobnailed boots. I wrack my brain, unable to bring forth the vital information I need. It is in there but reluctant to show.

The pool match is underway, I am called to participate, which completely chops off my various tangled lines of thought. I detest losing at anything and set all my available concentration to the tabletop. After five unsuccessful minutes at the table, I am completely thrashed, I return to the bar. Lenny is called up for the next frame. I am left alone with the lanky girl. She is definitely pretending to watch the tabletop competition, she continues to do so as I speak.

"You know me?" I half smile my question and have little time to wait before receiving a reply along with a knowing, girlish giggle that carries a hint of warmth and rustic charm. This is me getting all lovey. 'Rustic charm' I am not myself! I was earlier!

She turns her head but not her elbows towards me as she replies. "Not completely Maccy, I'll be patient, my lover." This is my second favourite localised endearment. I

137

must stop myself from reaching out, as to my dismay, she sidles away to attend to the damp Bessie who has shown up for the match and obviously intends to play his part.

The carpenter sneers un-longingly at me. Perhaps he still had a great gobbet of seaweed lodged inside his mouth and is frightened it will suddenly and explosively appear on his chin if he attempts to provide live commentary. I'm reminded of once being told: don't order spaghetti on a first date due to wayward strands of the pasta sticking to my chin area. It could be similar with seaweed! Me? I am satisfied with my swift and conclusive actions to his attack on me at the quayside. I have no thoughts of rekindling the earlier violence. Further physical contact with the dripping idiot is the farthest thought from the small part of my mind that I believe remains perfectly intact after the short opening exchanges with the girl.

She has somehow demanded my attention. Physical contact of the affectionate kind is in the planning stages. I believe right now we are thinking in tandem. 'Great minds work alike!'

I resist the temptation to remind the dripping Bessie that he once again has his cue in his hand and ignore the village idiot by setting my vision to lock onto her well carved stern as she turns away. I can see her fully now. With my mind still partially absent, I must have spent the remainder of the evening in a semi stupor. Nothing new there!

I can't be positive, I more than likely did walk up Padstow Hill with Lenny. I must have slid back into the first class sleeping compartment at some late hour that night having eventually downed a gallon. The homeward journey, as usual, would remain a mystery. Like my erratic driving of Ma's car! I intend to spend most of the day wandering around Truro City centre, that bustling capital of the Duchy. Thriving hub of the county they say. Yeah right! I find the capital half empty; I guess all the shoppers have buggered off to Falmouth for the day. I would have myself if I hadn't been searching for restaurant work.

Burger bars and chippies are nowhere near the top of my agenda. I have no intention of looking for work in Newquay, a dreadful place! And so Truro is my target.

It just so happens that Wednesday early closing had been done away with about twenty-five years or so previously; it seems word must have got out to the erstwhile Truronians eventually. Returning early after a fruitless job search, I jumped from the bus on the Padstow road and walked in roughly the right direction across the fields, climbing the tall Cornish hedges that would soon be covered in Primroses, Daffodils and dossers! I jumped the gates I knew would lead me home. My erratic memory of the previous night is still firmly in place. Once in my wooden pad I do my housework in no more than ten minutes. Five minutes longer than my usual efforts. I slept for an hour or so before once again taking to the fields in the direction of Padstow. I could have cycled but left my bike still leaning against the grass at the side of the carriage.

I crossed over Little Petrock Creek by way of the ford and again found myself on the familiar path that was once the busy branch line between Wadebridge and Padstow. Now it's a grown over track for cyclists and dog walkers. It makes me wonder, but for these, might we still have trains. I headed for the Sailmaker's. The woman, for girl she is not, had invaded my thoughts at regular intervals during the day. A day that had almost come to be my last when walking across Truro's Boscawen Street.

There may have been few shoppers about, but buses still operate, and don't the drivers like to see pedestrians run? One can get the impression they lie in wait. It's the same in West London. The difference there is that if you escape one, another would instantly appear. A man could easily be inserted into a large bright red sandwich. Just when you think there aren't any at all, three come along all at once and none are going in the direction you need, unless you've recently changed your mind about your destination. Or simply moved to a new house.

Truro is a little different from Battersea, where you might only see two buses idling, each one going in opposite directions. Until the driver decides he has a victim in his sights. A quick flash on the indicator and away they go, straight at the nearest poor bugger that might be confused by the unevenly cobbled streets that hardly discriminate from the pavements. Or worse, if a driver comes across some lovelorn visitor lacking in concentration, like myself. They can read your mind and speedily shake you out of your stupor.

I called into the Mermaid first, as you do.

"Maccy my lad, am I pleased to set eyes on you?" It is difficult to tell if the old guy is excited or confused. A bit of both I decide! So, everything is as it always is!

"What's the problem matey?"

"No bugger 'aven't come in 'ere at all today, except that Calhoun. You're the second. She isn't gonna like it. Now Frank 'ave gone, I dunnaw what us are gonna do."

"Where's Lil?" I ask and at the same time wondering how the ten quid a day Frank used to put over the Mermaid Bar' counter would make such a big difference.

"Dunnaw, she 'aven't showed!"

So, now we're up to twenty pounds a day. The Mermaid has never been a goldmine, now it seems it resembles a copper mine. For once, I feel sorry for Bligh. Not because I think Blencathra will do the old feller any serious or permanent harm; I admit I don't know her that well, but who does? I feel certain she'd not hurt a hair on his head. Apart from anything else, he doesn't possess many and those he has mainly sprout from the bulbous section of the leaking central protrusion that adorns most of his facial territory. She'd have a hell of a job to cause any serious injury there without a vicious pair of tweezers.

"Pull us a pint Cap'n. Let's think about this. See if we can't come up with something to help."

I take a good mouthful from the offered misty glass and begin to ponder Bligh's sad situation. The sudden opening of the wide door gives me hope; maybe a late coach load of lager louts has pulled into the harbourside carpark. It is only Lil, which I suppose is a bright spot. I pay for her drink and she takes up her usual seat just behind me.

"What do you think Lil? I ask, without turning my head. How are we gonna get some more business coming in to this place?" I don't expect a sensible answer from the old girl.

Bligh seems to have more faith in Lil. He cocks his head in anticipation of some gem of a solution. He is about to be sadly disappointed with her pointblank reply.

"Sell the bleddy place Bligh. You'm past your best ol' buddy. Time to sell up and 'ave us a younger man behind the bar. A big strapping lad like young Maccy here, he could do it."

Bligh's face drops at Lil's surprise suggestion. My own stays in place as far as I know. For a while I feel even sorrier for the miserable landlord, though Lil could be right.

"Bligh, maybe it is time for you and Big Blen' to take a rest." I am more careful than Lil not to be so blunt. I begin to see the wisdom of her words. Words that sprinkle a single drop of water on a seedling somewhere in the deep section of my brain, calling for drastic action.

"Can't sell Maccy. I told you, it isn't ours to sell. We have never paid them bleddy yanks back."

This admission from Bligh seems to be the signal for the heavy door to open once again. Right on cue, it is the grim reapers. Stan and Ollie are back. I nod in their direction and watch their approach to the bar. Bligh stiffens, not enough to alert the undertaker. I begin silently to wish that big Blencathra was around, though I wouldn't have the nerve to call her 'big' to her face. Blen' would be more than a match for these two. They wouldn't antagonise her. She would have them both by the goolies and back out on the quay by now, where they would have to rearrange their wedding tackle.

"Virgil!"

"Guess we should talk, Bligh. Where's my ugly sister?"

141

"She's away. Don't knaw when she'll be back. It's her you should talk to. I can't tell you anything, on account I dunnaw nothing."

Bligh is holding his end up, for now, but I feel these two are on the verge of intimidation of the old feller. I quietly rise from my stool to show my support.

"Can I get you gents a drink?" I ask, an attempt to keep a mood of friendliness.

Hardin nods his answer. Virgil speaks up. "Two, small, cold beers should do it, thank you sir."

Another mistake, 'Sir'? I don't think so. 'Ugly sister?' That may be true. I suppose a brother can say that about a sibling but neither remark goes down well with me. There's an unwritten law, not so much a by-law more a bar-law, that when one's landlord is under attack, either verbally or physically, the regulars must show their support; more so when it's the landlady. Obviously, there's no need in Blen's case. Blencathra may have the build and physique of an Easter Island statue. The pantomime begins!

I am beginning to seethe at Virgil's impertinence. I keep my thoughts to myself. I stay poised to pounce at any time.

"So, tell me Bligh, when do you expect my sister to return?"

"Drekly I reckon!"

"Directly, is that what you're saying?"

"Ais, drekly, soon or thereabouts."

"Can you narrow that down some?"

"I don't believe I can."

It is time for intervention on Bligh's behalf. With the initial intention of employing politeness, I make it known, albeit subtly, I think the line of questioning is intimidating my friend.

"Now listen here, you buggers have heard what Bligh has to say. I reckon you should think seriously about leaving now while we are all still on friendly terms. Nothing to say you blokes can't come back when Blen' is here. It's her that you need to see, you can't right now unless you are in Plymouth and you bleddy idn't, which is a great shame."

The taller reaper leans towards me. I half expect some form of physical contact. It is a ploy on his part. The taller yank reaches for the half pint of lager and reverses a little. If the forward movement had been meant as provocation, it hadn't worked. My knuckles stay unemployed for now. Virgil says nothing as he picks up his own glass with noticeably less threat. The Americans retreat towards Frank's replacement table and settle into the mismatched chairs. Lil makes a grunting sound. Nothing unusual there; I would say it was something which might have put her customers off, but maybe they liked it!

I lean closer to Bligh. "How much are they after Bligh?"

"More than Blen' and me have got Maccy. There isn't any hope for us lad, no bleddy hope!"

"We'll see about that Cap'n. Best we leave it for now. Let these two assholes empty their glasses and be on their way."

I decide to stick around while the two are still present. I am keen to return to the Sailmakers and find out more about the young lady who is continually on my mind. She would have to wait. I would have to wait. I am still irritated with my crap memory. Somewhere at some time we must have met. I can't for the life of me remember where or when. I look at the redundant dog and don't expect any help. He looks with interest at the two Americans and bares his teeth. The Alsatian is not smiling. I don't even remember when it got here!

The reapers take almost an hour to empty their glasses. Both send half-hearted glares in my direction as they prepare to leave. I'm pleased. They have taken heed that Bligh has friends that will support him in time of need. I give the nervous landlord a friendly wink, Lil a careful smile; I don't want there to be any confusion, as I depart. I am thoughtful as I meander towards the Sailmakers. The

Blighs are in trouble. What should I do? I don't ever remember meandering before.

I reach for the door and here it struck me, right between the eyes, like William Tell had missed the apple and had given the beholder, me, a third eye socket. It has opened wide. Suddenly I remember that tiny speck of my past where the girl and I had interacted. It was at the Well, Padstow Paradise, that tiny secluded local beach where we had spent a summer under the lean-to, mostly leaning, followed by a spate of falling.

I'd made a friend or two in London and had more often than not, draped myself over a sofa or floorboard in one place or another to get a half night's sleep. There was just one time I decided I needed to be back amongst my own. The summer had shown signs of becoming a roaster. I could not see the point of wasting my time in the 'Smoke' and sleeping in some new-found friend's greenhouse when I could be on the beach. I had dragged some of my new mates back down with me and along with Lenny and Michael, we had a memorable time. The carriages had quickly become health hazards; strewn with empties, dogends, discarded condom packets and sun-bleached Kentucky Fried Chicken bones, pizza boxes, certain items of women's clothing, some of which are still turning up to this day.

The Well had quickly become a nesting place, where we looked after the Chicks. I remember clearly now. She had been one. We had turned our tiny part of the foreshore into a naturist's haven. She, like everyone, had not been averse to disrobing.

We didn't indulge in all day orgies or anything like that, more's the pity. We just constructed our own little colony that existed without the constraints of any local by-laws. Luckily by-laws are non-existent hereabouts. Anything could and sometimes did go, but only as far as I'm aware with full consent. The Well is perfectly secluded and beneath the under hang of some ground erosion. We put together a lean-to that served as kitchen, dining room and dormitory. Just over the other side of the grassy embankment still stands a small stone built ruin, a Victorian Beach house that at one time belonged to the local squire and his family. Here we had dug a hole for our waste. I have many times tried to remember if we had filled it in at the end of the summer. We had made every attempt during our stay.

If the weather had been against our continuing occupation of the nest, we retreated to the wooden carriages. There were times when they resembled the Paddington to Penzance Express; standing room only. There were times when some never came out of the carriages, just as there were occasions when some never left the beach enclosure.

If we didn't fancy a dip in the ocean, we had our own private swimming pool. Not more than a hundred yards away from the nest was a real pool that many years ago, someone had thoughtfully fashioned with the help of concrete and the natural rocks. It would only fill itself at high tide and then the water level would gradually decrease until the next full tide when it was naturally replenished with fresh seawater, plastic bottles and rotting flipflops. As a tacker, I had learned to swim there, Dusty too, with Ma's firm guidance. If a Padstow kid can swim, here's where he or she learned to. If not, it won't be a Padstow kid.

Locals, on hearing of our residency had arrived at the haven uninvited. If they had been sensible enough to come loaded with beer, large bottles of wine of any hue and little food they were never turned away.

The girl, Jennifer, from the Sailmakers, had been one such. I begin to remember more details of her visits. I am certain we had never become particularly close in a physical sense. I was so certain that it pissed me off a little now to recall my lack of adventure. I have every intention, as I open one of the double glass doors, to eventually put things to rights. I have changed my type. I am disappointed. She is nowhere to be seen. In my annoyance,

145

I get completely legless and fall arse over tit in the doorway as I leave.

I awake with water trickling slowly down my forehead. I can hear a soft, gentle cooing in my ears. I suppose for a short time I must have begun to make my way back along the path to Little Petrock and home and must have stopped on the embankment for a doze. I had done plenty of times previously; this did not seem to be the case. It doesn't feel like rainwater. This is different; the cooing cannot be some lovelorn wood pigeon calling softly to a chosen mate on a branch of the next tree. I am not stretching into consciousness on a cold girder on the extensive Iron Bridge a mile from town. I am lying comfortably on something much softer than a railway embankment that is missing its rails. I am not alone.

Until now, I have never heard of a wood pigeon that could talk. "Hello my bird, sleep well?"

I keep my eyes intentionally shut at the familiar sound. The cooing is humankind. The water is from some tempered cloth on my forehead. I am in some personal heaven. There was me thinking 'Heaven' was somewhere else, Mevagissey perhaps!

I resent the intrusion of some local music Jock and his ridiculous attempts at humour. If I could lay my hands on the radio that must have been somewhere in my vicinity, I would crush it. Its interference in my temporary utopia is pissing me right off. I make a mental note that if I ever meet the immature DJ on a darkened ex-railway line, I will not mince my words. DJ's do tend to be immature. I refuse to awaken completely for fear of spoiling the desert island effect.

"Maccy, do you know what the time is?" The question, to me, although irrelevant, seemed not to matter much, etc!

"Nope, I have no interest whatsoever. I don't give a monkey's nuts what time it is. I know you, don't I?"

"Afraid so!"

"The beach."

"That's right my bird!"

146

This was the explanation for the vision-like appearances of Bessie whenever I looked at her.

"I remember you wandering about naked. I wish I could remember more."

"Me too. I mean I remember you wandering about, not that you were completely naked. I do believe you were shy Maccy Tamryn."

"Maybe. Put it down to a good upbringing."

"And me?"

"I didn't mean it like that. I'm sure you were well brought up."

"I accept your apology."

Still my eyes are closed. Somewhere close to me is heaven, having recently been moved from Meva'. Although I have forever been certain in my mind it is a place I would never visit, it had somehow come to me. I pray the girl is still of a mind to wander about naked. Another reason for me not to break the spell by looking. I was beginning to become hopelessly pathetic.

"I have to go Maccy."

Shit, bugger and bollocks! Her semi-whispered statement is a sign. The spell is broken. I open one eye at a time. It isn't easy!

"Go where?" I feel incapable of extended sentences right now and it doesn't bother me. I put my hands behind my head that must be nestled on the softest of pillows. I look around at her with my eyes half focused. I don't believe they are bulging; the pillows are elsewhere.

"Work, it's eleven O'clock, I must go."

I appreciate her honesty. My head is a church jumble sale. "Eleven O'clock when? Should you be going out this late at night?"

She got to her feet, then she was gone.

Chapter Fifteen

Guinevere!

She pulled the door tightly shut and disappeared. I am left to work out, all by myself, what part of the day I am in and my exact location. Not that I need to confirm I am in a prone position. I am unaware in which part of Padstow Paradise I am currently laid out. I remembered the radio ape and my silent promise from earlier. It is morning. DJ's seem to be much calmer during evening time. I can do without hearing these monophonic morons. Just do what you're paid to, play the bloody music and shut your gob.

The DJ is psychic, he did both. I listen to Shaking Stevens and This Ol' House. A lively ditty that makes me wonder why the vocalist is permanently nervous. It could be, he is waiting for it to fall down. It helps me come out of my stupor. The DJ returns after the regulation three and three-quarter minutes and manages to utter more words in one minute than Shaky did in his allotted time. I consider smothering the tosser with a pillow. I resist. I'm not ready to stand up on wobbly feet yet, let alone attempt to kill someone I can't see.

In allowing my eyes full rein I could see above me thick exposed, darkened wooden beams. I am in one very large room. A studio flat not unlike Alice's. No dead cats here either. At one end is a kitchen effort, just a smidgen better than my own. To one side, I can see a row of recently laundered female garments that perhaps should not be on display at all to a stranger or me. At the other side of the room is a small TV and stereo player, the radio is still on because I can't reach it. I have no intention of throwing other people's belongings out through a partially open window. It would be awesome to see a seagull with a radio dangling from its' beak..

If I could see through the thick stone walls surrounding my surroundings, I would realise that below my present position is the 'sail-makers' as was. I discover this is the very loft that George and Frank had visited all those years ago when part of Frank had remained in some form. I hope the separated limb isn't still here tucked away behind a wardrobe or in a cupboard under the kitchen sink.

I continue to lie quietly, attempting to conjure her back as a vision, dressed, or not, in a pair of what is hanging in the kitchen. I stay where I am until I feel I can discard the now drying flannel that still covers my forehead. The effect isn't the same as when she was holding it. I hadn't the heart to tell her I wasn't suffering from a hangover. My head had just been fizzing. I was suffering. It wasn't due to alcohol. On sitting up, I consider how I got here. I realise by being able to see only sky through the nearest window, I am in an elevated room. I know there will be a series of steep, well-trodden, granite steps leading to this one roomed penthouse.

How was I delivered? No way could she have put me over her shoulder! My conveyance will remain a mystery. It is of no matter; I am safe, sound and sober. I have been suitably succored. The fear that she might have suffered, at the very least, a double hernia or dislocated shoulders by delivering me here, soon evaporates. It is the fact that I feel clothes less, which made me look beneath the thick quilted cover. Nothing to worry about, everything is in its rightful place. What makes me a little nervous is the fact that everything would have been visible at any time. I don't recollect this is anything to do with me.

I do know my hair isn't long enough for anyone to drag me here. I must have been carried somehow. I would worry about that detail later. On second thoughts, I won't worry about it. Why should I? I'd only got drunk and incapable of anything. It isn't a crime. Maybe it is a crime and I am now permanently incarcerated here in her room. I'd thank god for that, if it turns out to be true.

In less than half an hour I was showered and dressed. I had gagged the DJ by disconnecting him and stepped outside to be confronted by the mutt. We shamble past the chippy and towards the nearest quayside café where I choose hot food that won't disrupt the workings of my insides any more than they already were. We wander along the quay in possession of hot food in the erratic shape of a fried egg nestling between two slices of bread and on a proper plate, rather than a flimsy paper effort.

I'd like to see a seagull with a plate hanging out of its beak next to the radio! I sit down on the polished wood bench inside the abhorrent slate-hung shelter and consider my position before considering the state of my mind. It is bit of a mess. I quickly change my subject. The dog waits for a share of my breakfast.

I query my lackadaisical memory as to where the sandwich had been obtained from. It is of little importance, I soon stop worrying about it. It had been paid for, think I remember that much. What to do with the plate, I have no idea! I keep a ready eye out for low-flying members of the Cathartidae family.

Padstow gulls are one thing you just can't forget but would like to. It's possible they are descended from some huge South American flyers. And then they came. One at a time my lively audience built up. They wandered around in front of me begging, sobbing incessantly for my breakfast. 'Bugger off' didn't seem to work, they don't get so much as a crumb though I am wishing I had something to offer from the Bako-foil and baking powder menu.

My thoughts turn away from girls and gulls and back towards Bligh. He owns a dilemma, which to be fair is more serious than my own. There must be some way in which I could help he and the still absent Blencathra out of their predicament.

The girl didn't escape my thoughts completely. Her smiling face manages to insert itself into my mind occasionally. I am certain she will reappear just as fully in my life sometime later in the day. Why shouldn't she? I had behaved myself as far as I know, it had been obvious that we had not come to any temporary joining of the parts or any permanent parting of the ways. She had left in a mood of affability.

The Beast of Padstow gratefully finishes off my breakfast by licking the plate. At least its' tongue is still in good working order.

I know right now I need to direct my energies, at least those that have surfaced so far, towards Bligh and Blencathra's transatlantic relations problem. Not much of a 'special relationship' there by all accounts.

The seedling grows. It had been planted by Lil. I may have the resources to counteract the American's possible takeover. I am unsure how to put my proposition to Bligh and Blen' without causing offence. I have never even run a badly presented flea market stall, selling out of date cans of coke and crushed packets of biscuits alongside rusty spanners that didn't fit anything anymore.

The one and only time I ever attempted a car boot sale I forgot to put the crap in the boot of my car. It all stayed in the yard, neatly stacked. It's still there to this day! I had busted a gut that morning. I'd cleared out the remaining junk from the carriages, before going to Ma's and starting on the garage followed by the lean-to barn, and my bedroom. Being followed by a lean-to barn and a bedroom is particularly weird. It lends a whole new meaning to 'don't try this at home'. Maybe it doesn't. Does to me!

When I say lean-to, re: the barn, I don't exactly mean it is affixed to something else like a regular lean-to. The barn leans on account it is a tad flimsy. When the wind gets up the barn will lean in the prevailing direction. We keep well away from it most days. The Cornish weather can be unpredictable.

I have digressed, I had spent half a day in Camelford trying to sell the car. I did get some interest but no firm bids, which was good as the car wasn't entirely mine. In truth, none of it was mine. It was Ma's. My main consideration was in getting myself home again. I teased a handful of Sunday morning browsers and read a borrowed newspaper until I got bored and just drove away.

It had been such a bloody waste going all that way with nothing to sell. So instead of presenting the empty boot to Sunday timewasters, I had pointed the pointed end at them with the bonnet up and a secondhand car salesman's lop-sided smile on my face. You know the kind. So, I suppose I had in fact run a badly presented car boot something or other. I was glad the car hadn't sold, it would have been a long walk back to Little Petrock.

As I was saying, the Mermaid is to me, a second home. It isn't even in any small way comfortable. In fact, it isn't anything like as comfortable as the train carriages, it isn't as inviting either, far from it, but one thing it is, it's my local. I intend it will continue to be so, a bit like Frank: Until death us do part or not in the case of the missing limb. That one piece took off rather early for the old feller. Frank was following himself in a manner of speaking. Perhaps Frank might materialise fully in the Mermaid Bar one day and can tell us all about the other side.

I wonder if he has been reunited with the missing bit now that he's passed over. He won't have any clothes that fit properly. Frank could be wandering about now with an arm that he has no place to put unless he has found a decent tailor where he is. Another thing, if the part isn't replaced, he won't be able to play the harp.

Again, I make my way unsteadily towards the double glass doors of the Sailmakers. I find Leonard is in place at the bar and as always, ready to receive me like an old-fashioned petrol pump attendant but without the oily rag. She is there of course, and I smile like a limp jellyfish. Do Jellyfish smile? Who knows and who cares!

I could no more ignore my Florence Nightingale than I could Lenny. They are both here, expectant of some lively rapport. I feel I have entered the bar with some great bubbling, boiling pox erupting from my face. 'Look everyone, here's Maccy and his famous exploding boat race'. I have to be careful in case a slobbering stream of lava began to trickle a path down my chin. I see a small chance to quell my imagined discomfort. "Oi, Leonard, you'll never guess what happened to me last night!" Just as the last excited word emits itself and before I catch the fully loaded, perfectly aimed glare from behind the bar, I realise that I have no idea what had happened to me, if anything, I don't have a clue. How the hell could I tell Lenny or anyone else that might be interested!

"Go on mate, tell us."

I slide a nervous glance over the well-polished bar. "Forget it. Let's go and sit down. I need to talk over something important with you."

"Idn't you drinking nothin' Maccy, you feeling rough?"

This is the sort of thing a woman can do to a bloke after just the one horizontal but as far as I know, innocent, liaison. My head is all over the place, what with.... "Excuse me. Don't mind my asking, but what do they call you maid?" I knew she was watching from behind her armrest and as I stand up and approach once more, she gives me a look that I believe to be one of, you're gonna be dead fluffing' meat if you're not very careful.

"Jennifer!" Just in time, I remembered!

The look changed to one of limited affection as quickly as it had appeared.

Of course, it is. I should have known, I was in the presence of Celtic royalty. Nope, as far as I know Jennifer isn't some secret love-child of Prince randy Andy, Steady Eddie or any of that wayward bunch of yuppy royals who occasionally frequent the pubs and yacht clubs across the estuary. Jennifer, the name as any good Cornishman will tell you, is derived from Guinevere. King Arthur's own queen. It suits her, it will do for me. Much as I hate to do so, I have to get back to my conversation with Lenny and talk to him about my idea and so having eventually ordered and received a pint and a semi-vicious smile from her majesty, I return to the table and Lenny.

"Lenny, from the way I see things, the Yanks are here to take over the Mermaid from the Cap'n and Blen'. Best

153

you keep this to yourself matey. It seems Bligh and Blencathra borrowed the money to get the Mermaid from her Yank family. Problem is they haven't ever paid none of it back. I don't have a clue what it cost, I'm sure they can't raise the dough to repay the loan."

"That's bad news Maccy. What's your plan? What can we bleddy do. Have a whip round from us locals?"

"Well I'd say there are two ways of lookin' at things. First, I'd say right now the place isn't worth much more than they haven't paid for it, on account, there isn't any more business now than when they started." A whip round from a dozen locals won't help. Fifteen quid was going nowhere. I can see a way out for the couple. "I have an idea."

"What idea?"

"We two, you and I, could make Bligh and Blen' an offer for the pub. Buy the place and get some newer faces to stand at the bar with the older ones. Or, we can have the whip round or do bugger all, which will amount to the same. What do you think?"

"We, me and you, run a business? You're having a laugh Maccy."

"Why not?"

"Cos I'm too bleddy young, you're too young, we both are."

"Lenny, think about it at least."

I had already been doing sums in my head. I have a fair idea how much the property is worth. I know there is no real business to buy, perhaps just a token payment; fixtures and fittings and stock, the goodwill as I believe it's called in business circles. They don't just teach bake and flake at college. Ten to fifteen grand might cover the ingoing. The property could be worth one hundred thousand, easily mortgageable, due to its potential as a thriving Bed and Breakfast. I must be honest and confess I have no idea what the upstairs rooms were like. There might not be any for all I know, apart from Blencathra's black-sheeted boudoir.

All I had to do is speak to a brewery. Any brewery will do; I've heard breweries are apt to fight tooth, nail and cheque-book to get in to established, freehold pubs. I can't see the Mermaid would be an exception. It is in a prime position. It has very little else going for it, it does have prime position. Just the one snag, I'm eighteen!

I ignore Lenny's whining. I am certain I could talk him into anything. I'd done so plenty of times over the years. Good and bad. What did years matter? At least I am at the age of consent?

If Lenny and I could get fifteen grand or so together for the business and talk the bank and brewery into providing the dosh for the property, we are up and running, trotting anyway. I believe between us we could float the Mermaid out of the eighteenth century and into the twentieth. It would be prudent to miss out the one which had occurred in between. It does seem there is a two-hundred-year gap, especially when Lil appears.

Another thing that bothers me is my non-existent accounting skills. Let me put it this way, Lil is better at applying her make-up than I am at doing sums. Bligh is better at wiping his nose than I am at arithmetic. As far as I know a logarithm is a piece of floating driftwood. I had no idea what Algebra was all about. I always thought letters were for posting! I would need to talk downright friendly to the Birdsalls. I know accounting had been their game before they had retired to their own posh quayside, knocking shop. It occurs to me they do in fact own, albeit a little on the small side, a very expensive looking house-boat.

So now I could have dodgy accountants or at least I might, as soon as I had talked them into coming aboard so to speak.

"Lenny, we need to find out if the Blighs do have the deeds to the place."

"I don't know Maccy. What would I need to do?"

"It's easy, you know how to pull a pint don't you, you've seen it done enough?"

"Ais, I reckon I can do that. What about the money, where am I gonna get my half of the dosh?"

"You could sell that bleddy car of yours. You never drive the bleddy thing anywhere and if we get the Mermaid you won't have time to go anywhere. Besides I bet you haven't taxed the bleddy thing since I went away. Is it even Mot'd?"

"Keep your bleddy voice down Maccy. For Christs' sake man."

Before leaving the Sailmakers and my still half-filled glass, I need to see how the land laid with Jennifer. Leaving Lenny to think about the idea, I sidle over to the bar and prop myself on my elbows.

"Might have a proposition for you my queen."

I am getting way ahead of myself but why not? She's a great looker and obviously she harbours some thoughts of a relationship of some kind with me, though I have no idea of its potential or longevity. You don't let someone sleep on your couch that way if you didn't feel a little something and even more especially if you only have a couch and no proper bed. Not forgetting the invisible pillows. There was the brow mopping too and another thing, how the hell did she get me up the bleddy steps to the loft? And she did leave me naked under the quilt. All questions that might have the right answers. I just had no idea what they were.

I explain my plan to Jen', she is surprisingly supportive and immediately full of ideas, which takes me completely by surprise. Lenny and I leave to get whatever information we could from Bligh. We have to act fast. Blencathra will be back soon enough. I want to get this idea off the ground and somehow fix it into Bligh's head as quickly as possible. I am certain the old feller is on his last legs. I mean in the pint pulling sense. The Cap'n looks as fit as a butcher's dog, the pair of them have just lost the interest they never had. The Cap'n is lean, mean and fit for his age. The only thing wrong with him is his nose needed a new washer, maybe a pair. It is increasingly obvious Blencathra is no longer interested in trade building. She could be our biggest stumbling block. I wouldn't consider calling her a mule, but she can be stubborn. She will have to be talked around. I am certain I know who would be doing the convincing. Bligh isn't up to it. It will be down to me. So long as long as I don't rile her, I'll be safe, probably.

Our first task is to submit our plan to the Mermaids' leaking landlord and get his opinion. I realise my heart might be running faster than my brain. I will dilute the plan a little when putting it to the landlord. He could dilute it himself with little effort.

I pass on my plan of action to Lenny as we walk around the quay at a leisurely stone kicking pace.

"Seriously Len, what do you think about the idea?"

"Seriously, I dunno Mac. Let's see what the old git has to say. I could get eight or nine thousand for the car easy. What about you, can you get your half of the dosh?"

"Good question." I would hope to find out the answer later that night. I am confident a quick chat with Ma would give me the nod. "Don't worry about me matey. Shit and Roses, know what I mean?" On thinking about it, Guns and Roses might be more useful where Blencathra is concerned!

I dare say the Yanks are carrying armoury, don't they all?

Chapter Sixteen

Lil Keeps Mum

"Ah now Maccy lad, I've been waiting ta see you. You'll never guess what 'ave gone an' 'appened now. I just 'eard they 'ave catched a bleddy great, 'uge man-eating whale up down at Stepper Point. Big as an 'ouse, big as my Blen', maybe bigger. They do say it can't be brought inside the quay as it's so bleddy big. I 'eard it does 'ave a trainer stuck in its gob too."

"Christ! I never heard anything about that, Cap'n. Poor sod. I hope it isn't anyone we know."

"Ow the 'ell should I know?"

"Bleddy hell Cap'n, what are they gonna do with it?" Lenny is hooked!

"Dunnaw lads must be a bleddy biggun though. I 'aven't never heard of such a thing. Why don't you boys go look and come back n tell me? I can't leave 'ere, Blen'll be home soon and she will want me to be here when she gets here."

"Come on Maccy; let's take us a look at this bleddy whale. I got my doubts 'ow big the bugger might be, might just 'ave been a young kiddy it swallowed."

"Can't Lenny, we gotta talk business with the Cap'n. It's why we're here remember."

"Me? What have I done? Whoever told ya was having you on. I ain't been anywhere to do anything I shouldn't have."

"What about this bleddy whale, Maccy?"

"Lenny my old mate, forget it, there idn't no bleddy whale. It's just Bligh pulling our plonkers, your plonker at least right, Cap'n?"

"Ais, sorry boys, I'm just pulling your togders. T'wern't really a whale, t'was my little joke about Blen' comin' home. Not very good was it, I must be getting' past it."

We shake our heads in mock solemnity at Bligh's admission.

"Listen Cap'n what time do you reckon 'er's gonna get back to home?"

"She'll be here in an hour, Maccy lad. She did just telephone me from Bodmin Road Station and she's gettin' herself a taxi. I suppose I'll have to pay for the bugger. Dunno why she couldn't have hitched a lift from a bleddy lorry driver, if she could get one to stop for her. Taxi driver will need a psychiatrist soon enough!"

"She's a bleddy woman mate. Anything could happen. Hitchhiking is bleddy dangerous."

"Might be for the bleddy lorry driver. I hope he's got a spare pair of trousers, he's bound to shit himself, best they be brown!" Bligh cackled mischievously.

"Right, now then Cap'n, we gotta have us a proper yak before she gets back here. We don't have a lot of time."

I look around the bar before pursuing the subject. Just for the present I don't want anyone else knowing what Lenny and I are planning, except of course Bligh and Blencathra. I spend time filling the old geezer in on the details and once I am done, Leonard and I wait. It is as if we hear Bligh's brain slowly engaging. There is hardly a sound but an imagined humming and whirring for what seemed like minutes and by watching the strange, almost unnatural looks that criss and cross the old geezer's face I even wonder if he might be in some excruciating pain. I begin to think I have come up with a plan to fill in the quay with concrete and turn it into a carpark. Somebody will, one day. For a moment or two I have the time to think about Jennifer. I wonder if Bligh will give us a reply before closing time.

Strangely enough his answer arrives at the same time as Lil. I buy her drink and make a mental note to not get into a habit of it for two reasons. Firstly, she might get the wrong idea. Secondly, if Lenny and I achieve our objective

159

and become the next owners of the Mermaid Bar, we couldn't be seen to be buying all our customers their drinks. It would defeat the object. In any case, she's had more than her share from me! I sense a less than sudden reply is imminent. Bligh seems to take on a different persona to deliver his answer. Lenny and I wait and listen with baited interest.

"See now boys; if it were me, I'd say give me the money and here's the bleddy keys. Only tidn't just me that should be considered. You do have me bleddy convinced. Who's gonna convince my Blen'? Another thing, where are us gonna live if us idn't here? I idn't going over to bleddy England, no bleddy way."

"Main thing is Cap'n, how much did ya borrow from the brother and how much will they want, to settle the loan?" Leonard has suddenly come alive in the discussion. To my surprise he is asking all the right questions. I let him get on with it.

"The way I see it is, best not to tell them you got someone who wants to buy the place from you. If they get to find that out, my bet is they'd want a lot more than you could get away with if they didn't know."

"Ais Lenny, I'm understanding ya lad."

"First thing, you get paid for the business you have already. Won't be a lot. There isn't a great deal for us to take over?"

"Knaw I suppose not, now that we have lost yon Frank things idn't looking so good."

"You would have to get a valuer. The brewery would do that for you. They would tell you a figure for the trade, that's the business and what they do call the goodwill. Maccy and I would have to pay you that. As for the building, we two would have to get us a mortgage, that means you'd get paid for the bricks and stuff too, see?"

"I do see Leonard. I'm gonna tell Blen' myself what you boys have told me, every bleddy word, proper. Do you know what I think? I do think she might just like the idea, especially if she can put her feet up and take it easier. They

160

bleddy bricks do worry me some. Us haven't got any bleddy bricks. We do have a rockery but it idn't much to look at. Bricks? I don't know what to do about these bleddy bricks, Maccy."

This is my opening. Lenny has done us proud, put our case perfectly. "That's right Bligh, you can both take it easy." I resist the urge to mention that in the time I had been back from Chiswick, Blen' had done bugger all or less and Bligh had done a tad more badly. Taking it easier would be as easy as falling off the quayside. I should know. I pretend the brick question and rockery answer didn't even arise.

What was important now was that I could get away for the last half hour and see my Jen now that the ball is well and truly rolling. There was just one other thing I need to get done. Even though the Birdseyes are even now walking in the door, this isn't the right time to go into detail with them. That should be for another day.

Lil! I had totally forgotten she is here. By the look on her face she has heard more than enough. I know how to keep her quiet for now, I need to have a word before I leave. I get Bligh to draw off a double Gin and scoop up a dusty bottle of Tonic. Winking at Lenny as I leave him, I take my life in my hands as I sit down next to the grinning old tart.

"Now Lil, I do believe you might 'ave overheard our little business discussions." I place the glass and the bottle in front of her and wait patiently for a reply.

"Never 'eard a word, Maccy. Don't you go worrying. I know to keep my gob shut. You ask anyone about here. You haven't put any bleddy ice in this, nor a slice of lemon, you bleddy shyster."

Lil has more secrets than a Swiss Navy Admiral. She wouldn't want to spill the beans. Another thing, she would eventually benefit from the situation.

She and Bligh might have more time to carry on their own secret shenanigans. Yes, I had sussed the buggers. The Cap'n is canoodling with Lil whenever Blencathra is away. "See ya Lil." It's my turn to wink and I did. Lil smiled back and I swear there was telepathy.

"Lenny, I'm off to the Sailmakers, got stuff to do. Cap'n, Mum's the word until you get done what needs to be done."

I believe I might have skipped a step or two on my way towards the Sailmakers. I am not disappointed at entering through the glass doors. It is a quiet evening. There is no comparison to the Mermaid Bar. I am content to spend a half hour idly staring across the bar, sipping a last pint, before being ushered out at closing time. The queen gives me instructions to wait for her at the quayside. You can bet I do as I am told. I hardly move and having bought myself a nice expensive cigar before leaving the inn, I am at peace with my world.

Five minutes later all but a couple of the Sailmaker's lights are extinguished. The queen and I are strolling hand in hand towards the Drang.

I wake early and find a cigar. I stand alone, leaning on the tiny iron railed balcony that overhangs the empty cobbled street. The mutt seems to be following my lead – excuse the pun - in surveying the harbourside. We are two of a kind in many ways. The dog doesn't smoke of course. The narrow, cobbled lane just allows a distant view of the Camel estuary and further views out over the Doom Bar into the Atlantic. It is different here in the winter. In a couple of months, the old alleyway will be swarming with whiney, complaining emmets and their obnoxious, swearing kids. There will soon be dropped ice cream cones, polystyrene chip trays and empty lager cans everywhere. I don't drink lager!

I would purposefully steer clear of the pub for a day. I want to allow some time for Bligh to do his work with Blencathra, now that she is most likely home and I want Lenny to have time to think about our partnership.

For the time of the year there is an unusually warm air current drifting inland. I notice a series of tiny flickering lightning twigs some miles out on the horizon off Stepper

Point. The twigs become branches as they travel closer to land. I watch mesmerised, perhaps it isn't the teasing light show. Maybe it is thoughts of the sleeping girl. I'd looked in on her three or four times since she had decided to sleep on.

Now it is a time for thinking. I want the Mermaid. I hope to have my mucker Leonard as a partner. I want Jennifer as a partner of a different kind. I have no idea what she wants. I don't want to give up the carriages. I would give up anything else to get all these other things. I would even give up the dog; it's not's my dog anyway!

I've done my playing. I've done my fighting. I'll do some more if called upon obviously; I've done my time at college. Now, I want to do my time in my beloved home town. I believe by having achieved my goals at the Chiswick Catering College, I did intend to find myself a top job at a big Truro City hotel; to be fair there is only two or three. Now I'm not interested, it's no longer what I want. My future is presently in the hands of the lovable but sometimes cantankerous couple, Bligh, a sixty or seventy year old story-teller and husband to Blencathra, a throwback of the legendary Cornish giants, a spouse few grown men would attempt to dispute a point with. I believe I should be patient. I need to be patient for all my hopes. I know I will need a medium sized portion of luck and a fair wind.

I stare out from my tiny railed vantage point that allows me look across the lower town and out to sea. Just below me in the Drang, I notice a heavy coated stranger sitting alone on a bench doing absolutely nothing. I have seen him before. It is the bloke who'd held the door open for me at the pub a few nights earlier, the man whose wallet I had found. Calhoun!

I spy the Admiral clambering about on the deck of the tidy yacht and promise myself as soon as I heard, hopefully some good news from Bligh, Lenny and I will sit down with them and make a business plan.

In my temporary idleness, I take myself away from the small balcony and the flickering, now distant lightshow and back to that summer at the beach and the reason behind my one-sided and short-lived exchange with Bessie and my first meeting with Jennifer.

Now although the 'queen' had on occasion been a member of the dossers at the enclave and for reasons that I can't begin to fathom, I had not recognised the ample physical attractions she is in possession of. I can only think she didn't have them at our first meeting. She has flourished!

She, along with a couple of other girls, had complained to us lads of a feeling that they were being watched from a rowing boat behind a grassy bank a few yards back from the beach. A bit like JFK but without the noisy painful bits.

Lenny and I, plus one or two other lads, had climbed the bank and had been just in time to see the back of a man rowing for all his life is worth. I had just enough time to recognise him as he flailed a path through the water with just one oar. We couldn't chase him further as we didn't have any kind of boat. I did catch up with the perv' a few days later and led him to believe he'd get a good smacking if he ever found the urge to return to the grassy knoll bank! As far as I know, he never did. He was most likely in a queue at the chemist for paracetamol.

I don't think he ever did make another appearance at St George's Well after that day. He had appeared out in the estuary in a mickey mouse rowing boat. We didn't make a positive identification, partly due to the huge binoculars that were held in front of his face. It hadn't been long before some of the others had discovered the lone 'sightseer' and with fifteen or twenty kids yelling 'pervy pirate' and other mild obscenities at a person, that person is likely to make a hasty exit or at least attempt to, which he did, eventually. Now it can only be assumed that Bessie had taken up some new, less dangerous pastime.

The fact that we had decided unilaterally to clear our sandy little haven of many small rocks and glass bottles, along with various other heavy unwanted items, only lent haste to his escape.

I can laugh to myself even now at Bessie's antics employed to get out of range while trying desperately hard not to be recognised. It can't have been easy to maneuver an eight-foot rowing boat while your head is below the gunwales and you've inadvertently dropped one of your oars in the water. Bessie was going around in circles for some minutes due to his untimely mishap and all the time trying, successfully unfortunately, to dodge missiles that were coming his way.

Oh, those were good days and weeks at the Well. They were memorable for many reasons and like all good things, best not repeated. These things are never the same second time around. A weird local once told me regrets are pointless. I asked her how she knew, she told me she had never experienced one. You work it out!

I have an important meeting and leave the almost silent flat as quietly as possible.

Chapter Seventeen

Kicking the Devil's Arse!

The early morning storm and light show had waltzed away in the direction of Hartland Point and Lundy Island after having first dropped a heavy load of H2O on the sailing club across the estuary, which was rather pleasing to see. The heavenly entertainment over, I had returned inside. Jen' was up and about, the pair of us shared breakfast before I left for an important meeting. I have one stop off point before my visit with the Birdsalls. I stroll to the rear of the grey Victorian chapel and pull open the seriously creaking back door, almost expecting Christopher Lee to appear. He was nowhere to be seen, not even in a mirror. As a movie Vampire it's hardly surprising. I pick up a fresh pint of milk from the step as I enter.

I know I'll find Michael here. The table is brushed smooth. It is obvious my religious mate had recently ironed it. The fifteen reds are set and the colours placed on their respective spots, waiting.

"Best of three, Maccy?"

"Just the job matey."

Michael pulls at the string that dangles from the overhanging light hood and accompanies his action with his usual request; 'let there be light!' Sometimes I think he takes his intended calling a little too seriously.

It has been a habit of mine to visit the chapel at least once a week. I'm not overly religious, partly because my mate has a vision of becoming a Methodist Minister. God help us! Snooker helps me think. Lenny, Michael and I have spent many an hour up here in the huge loft above the altar, where the table stands like it has arrived there in some mysterious 'beam me down Scotty' sort of way. I half expect to see a blue police telephone box in here one of these days.

Snooker hails back to our schooldays. If Michael, Lenny and I fancied an unofficial day off, it was here in the chapel's loft we would become most invisible.

Michael holds to the idea the loft isn't part of the general 'Household of God' and for one of us to 'Fight the Good Fight' means we might need to get out of a snooker behind the black which is exactly where I left the white after breaking up the pack and potting a fluky first red.

"Open thou eyes that I may behold wondrous things out of the law of the baize Maccy. Psalm one hundred and nineteen verse eighteen, part two. Part two is my own addition."

"Nice one Mike'!" Michael has saved the points by applying check side on the white ball. My mate must have silently called upon the boss man in the first frame as he easily wraps it up with a thirty break and follows his win with another obscure quote:

"For thou, Lord wilt bless the righteous; with favour wilt thou encompass him as with a shield. Psalm Five Chapter Five. Scotch, Maccy?"

"Let the words of my mouth, and the meditation of my heart, be acceptable in thy sight. Nineteen, verse nineteen, part one! That's almost all my own."

"I'll take that as a yes then."

"Oh, how great thou art, Michael! That's not mine. I think it is a line from an Elvis song. I'll ask him later if he comes in for a couple of frames." He usually brings the food. I think Elvis was a Methodist!

Michael pours us each a decent measure, a top up with water; I'm not sure if it's tap or the more holy variety, which is most likely the same thing. I win the second frame and we prepare for the decider. The white skids across the table and bounces skyward from the bottom cushion.

"Bleddy 'ell Maccy, don't know my own strength."

"Reset?"

Michael nods and retrieves the white from a box full of jumble sale remnants. The second time the white enters a corner pocket. I am four points up, plus a second scotch..

"Damn, blast, kick the devil's arse and spit right in his eye! The Lord rewards me according to my righteousness Maccy! Some of that's mine."

"Methinks your boss has gone over to St Petroc's church Michael. You best pray louder or give me the match."

"No frickin' chance Maccy. You 'aven't bleddy won yet boy."

Like I said, Michael tends to F and Blind. Trainee minister or not, he's still a mucker and play on we did. The great one must have returned as Michael took the hard-fought decider. Perhaps I should go to chapel more often. Amen.

I leave my mate to gloat alone and amble the hundred yards or so to the Mermaid. The manky old dog appears from nowhere and joins me in my walk through the cold deserted back streets. The dog stinks. It has a habit of rummaging through dustbins and roadside skips, as I do myself at times. Just the one obvious difference, I'm not looking for food!

Even now with its great long pink tongue lolling out of the damaged side of its face it is taking up floor space by my feet as Bligh fills me in with the latest news, which is sparse at best.

I buy the last packet of outdated Cracklers and drip feed the dog as I listen to the Cap'n. I watch with amusement as the bits of half chewed pig fat continually fall from the side of its mouth before it can swallow them. The mutt should know that by lying on its opposite side, it would be able to keep the food in place until it can be chuted down the gullet and go through the normal reproduction process and into a plastic carrier bag. I have no idea who the mutt belongs to or if anyone cleans up behind it. I doubt there is such a person. I think about tying a carrier bag around its arse, but it would never get emptied.

"Cap'n, what did 'appen to this bleddy dog? Do you know?" I was interested, just.

"Ais, it was bleddy unfortunate and that's a fact, Maccy lad."

Stating the obvious is a habit Bligh has perfected. 'Bleddy unfortunate' I'd agree with that. If I lost half of my face, I'd consider myself at the very least, 'bleddy unfortunate'. I wait silently bollocking myself for interrupting the unstarted flow of a more important conversation.

"Well you knaw how some dogs like to chase after the bleddy cars. This one was bleddy different."

Bligh doesn't have the capacity to come to the point quickly. I can see the old geezer is getting excited. Bubbling evidence appearing at a nostril's edge. Bligh is easily satisfied.

"The bleddy dog was swimming in the quay, bleddy good swimmer they say. The poor bugger got his hooter caught up in an outboard engine. That's what did happen, Maccy, to the poor bugger, I think. 'Ee was swimming too bleddy fast!"

Thank god for that. Not so much a shaggy dog story, more a shagged-out dog's story. And now with luck, we might get back to the important business, once my mental imagery of Bligh splashing around the harbour wearing a power boat on his face has retreated. I decide I can no longer be bothered to feed the dog. I throw the bag and its contents down on the uneven floor. I wonder if the dog will suffocate due to the plastic bag. I resist the impulse to help the mutt on its way. It isn't my dog, I am getting used to it.

The Yanks appear. Virgil and whatshisname arrive as if they own the place. I suppose they do.

Lil appears, looking like an extra for bait in Jaws. The kids appear, they'll be exercising their jaws. The Admiral and Alma arrive. They will just jaw! A bunch of anoraked walkers walk in. Today is disintegrating fast. It is crashing down around me like the contents of a family size packet of cornflakes. Suddenly there are customers everywhere.

Punters are materializing like puddles of puke on a Wadebridge pavement at the end of an average Saturday night.

We just need Frank and George to float in for a full house.

While Bligh is filling glasses for the hordes, I find myself a pound coin and head towards the antique jukebox. Satisfied with my choices, which are limited to around the year dot, I park myself at a table and wait for my chance to recover the still un-started discussion with the old geezer.

It doesn't happen. Blencathra remains invisible for some reason never to be revealed and I sit tapping my feet to Foot Tapper, which is a decent enough tune, but the old record is so badly scratched that it sounds more like Night Fever, which in some way cheers me up as I am quickly reminded of the warm, wet flannel wielding of my night nurse a morning or two ago.

Thoughts of Jen' are all I need to drag myself away to the Sailmaker's, especially as my last couple of choices are due. I had plumped for Jagger and his Nineteenth Nervous Breakdown. I pull the door shut hard deliberately on Ken Dodd's Happiness and go on my way to discover some of my own. The dog doesn't see me leave.

Jennifer is in place behind the bar. I am greeted with a heart-melting smile and the greeting: 'hello my bird' that affects my addled brain so easily. It is enough for me to settle in a round-backed chair with a glowing tipped cigar and a lively pint of V D. What else did I need? Nothing! She may be a few yards away, it is close enough for now. Sometimes things look even better from a distance. What am I saying?

I suddenly become instantly alert again. I can see the Yanks are at the other side of the bar and eating. I don't know how they could have got here from the Mermaid Bar without my seeing them. Somehow, they have managed it. My animosity towards the two puzzles me a tad. On thinking about it, they had helped old Bligh out with Frank and his removal. I watch the two from afar with a mild interest.

I wonder how Blencathra happens to have an American brother and another twin at that. I didn't really think about it when Bligh told the tale but now with time to kill, it is a puzzle. I come up with the explanation the word triplet wasn't around in Blencathra's mothers' day; all her kids were twins.

Absent mindedly, I flick a small pile of beer mats up from the rim of the round table with the backs of my fingers and attempt to catch them between thumb and forefinger before they touch down again. What with keeping one eye on the Yanks, another on the mats and one on Queen Jen, I soon lose my hand-eye coordination. The beer mats flap everywhere.

The Yanks somehow use my buttered fingers as a cover to disappear and from afar I hear Jen' laughing at my clumsiness.

I am beginning to feel like a stricken vessel nearing the Doom Bar on a stormy night until she lifts the bar flap and comes towards me.

"What's the matter my bird?"

"Nothing." I lie for some reason I'm not sure about.

I am thinking about Blencathra. She is a worry. She'd be a worry to anyone, if only because I know if Bligh can't get anywhere with her, I'd have to sit at her table and convince her of what is in her best interests. I am not looking forward to that probability. What language would I use? Would I have to take my shoes off in her presence, would she rip my feet off for being presumptuous about her future wellbeing? Perhaps the Cap'n isn't a member of a one witch coven. It is a two-witch coven, maybe three, Lil's a member and the old feller just serves their every whim, for money. I begin to wonder if Blen' hasn't at some time got hold of the poor Alsatian and begun to tear it apart out of boredom, one hellish, storm lashed evening, before it eventually fought back and escaped. What about Frank? Did she rip his arm from its socket in some secret macabre ritual? Has she still got it? Did the part-time arsonist suddenly snuff it because the high priestess and her disciples were busy sticking pins in a tiny wax doll? Why does George only turn up when Blen' isn't about? I'm forgetting it was Frank's old feller that partially dismembered his son. And then there is me. Even now, is she chanting some murmuring cantations and conjuring up some devil to make me sit here with my ridiculous thoughts, flicking beer mats?

What would Lenny and I find if we manage to get hold of the pub? Shrunken heads and dried scrotums adorning the mirror of her dressing table, the one where the Empress Blencathra can see no reflection of herself. She should have got pally with Vincent Price. And of course, there is the cellar......

I had forgotten Jen' was standing here.

"Ready?"

"No, no! What?" Stuttering is fast becoming a niggly habit of mine.

"I got finished early, thought we could get back to our game."

"What game?" My brain is still trying to cope with Blencathra's darkened secret lair that may be a cave somewhere up in the Plantation, the ancient but still flourishing hanging gardens that once formed a part of a now dismantled mansion that had long ago stood proudly on the tip of Padstow Hill. Even now the overgrown wilderness can give the impression of a great green scarf around the neck of the old town.

"Bedroom Rugby, scoring points between the bedposts."

Ah, now here is something to shake me from the dark side and not too soon. I confess her suggestion conjures up some evil thoughts of my own. I flip the remainder of the dog-eared mats onto the table and leave my unfinished beer. I keep my cigar, savouring it as we walk arm in arm back to the loft.

Later, I had lain awake for an hour or so and used this idle time attempting to arrange my plans. I saw fishing nets. Lobster pots around the door, rustic tables on the small forecourt with umbrellas and menus and wild roses climbing up the side from their ancient roots embedded in the banks of Lost Souls Creek that still runs past the back wall as it has done for hundreds of years. I see my name over the door. Macdonald Tamryn licensed to sell Beer, Spirits and Liquors. Staring at the ceiling is allowing me to put the Mermaids' future into shipshape order.

Leonard is a worry. Lenny is like a brother to me and I know him as well, maybe better, than anyone. I have a niggling doubt Lenny will not stay the course. My mate is apt to get excited at some new idea but quickly returns to safety and his seven day a week humdrum. Lastly, I see Ma holding court at a corner table, just the way she does at the Maltsters Arms at Little Petrock.

The ceiling canvas is blank now. I dress and leave her. The great heavenly orb has begun to achieve more warmth as I amble around the quayside towards the Birdseye's swanky floating palace, wondering all the way where on earth I had somehow gained the ability to think in such a way, the sun is now a heavenly orb, I am not myself!

I halt at the harbourside and lean over the edge slightly. I rap my cold knuckles against the seagull shit splattered roofing of the Birdseye's yacht. It would be my first and last mistake of the day! Alma's head suddenly pops up and a slim naked shoulder peers through the small hatchway that allows entry to the tiny accommodation. She allows one not unattractive and youthful looking breast to peek out and glimpse the late winter sunlight. It is a rough guess on my part, I get the impression the airing is intentional as when she realises who it is has come calling, she happily allows a full view of both by letting her dressing gown slip from her shoulders. I am not averse to enjoying the sight of Alma's attributes - they are rather pert, youthful. I feel

173

the awkwardness of another stuttering spell approaching. I clear my throat in the hope I can hold it off. I ask for the Admirals' whereabouts, assuming by Alma's peek show, he is absent.

"He's out Maccy; back later this afternoon my cock. He had to see the doctor at Wadebridge, bit of a twinge in his back. Poor old thing's been overdoing it."

No surprises there; only that it is just a bit of a twinge. It's a wonder to me after my eyeful a few nights ago, that he isn't in intensive care at Treliske County General or whatever it's called now. I suddenly feel a pang of guilt at this reminder of having somehow almost sunk to Bessie's level.

On reflection, the guilt soon dispels itself as I didn't indulge in anything other than taking the one sly peek, which if I was honest wasn't sly, as the pair had given me an open invitation by leaving the curtains slightly parted. Anyway, I didn't know what they were doing until I looked. Not so guilty then.

"That's alright Alma darlin'. I'll wander back over and see him drekly."

"Maccy, I am rather pleased to see you. I have a small problem that I really can't deal with myself and a big strong lad such as you could help me out with it, I'm sure." The dressing gown slips again. Yeah right, here we go, 'I've got something heavy I need lifting, you'! "What's the problem, Alma?" Well, fair's fair. I could be wrong, it doesn't hurt to be neighbourly. Not so long ago I would have been in there like a rat up a rusty drainpipe.

"Just a bottle to connect up Maccy if you wouldn't mind cock."

There's that word again, she just can't help herself.

To be fair to Alma, she shouldn't be expected to lug liquid gas bottles about. I find myself moving forward to jump down onto the deck and play the hero of the moment.

Alma has pulled her dressing gown closed again. I take it as a sign that she wants me in the lugging rather than humping department.

174

Nervously, I stretch over the rail and step on to the deck and into the cabin.

"Where is it darlin'?" I ask, while allowing my eyes to search for what I thought would be a heavy, Calor gas bottle.

"Here you are dear boy. Could you put this up there on the optic for me?"

It contains one litre and a half of Vodka. I look up over the little side dresser where four optics are lined up. One is empty; the other three are taken up by a brand of Malt Whiskey, a partial bottle of Dry Vermouth and the third is a half empty bottle of Navy Lark Rum. Beneath this row stands a bottle of Blackcurrant cordial, an opened bottle of Lime juice and a Soda syphon. Crystal glasses stand waiting. The Birdseyes have it all to hand, even a crystal dish of tiny bright red cherries and a container of multi coloured cocktail swords available. Suddenly I realise that so too was I. I am determined that Alma won't get her hands on my cocktail stick. She makes a try.

Alma snatches at my arse as I turn to do her bidding. She pulls me from my standing position onto the narrow divan that I had seen her and the Admiral cavorting on that late night. She is all over me like a second skin and intent on getting everything in the engine room up to full steam. I can see no simple way to escape her talons as they grip my suddenly clenched buttocks like limpets on a lifeboat. I think fast and let her have her way; if she thinks I'm up for it, she might relax her grip. I could make a quick and easy retreat. It works nicely, but not before we have a short spell of tongue wrestling. She and I have a glorious lingering snog, which I rather enjoyed before I manage to retrieve the minute amount of dignity I possess, and my freedom. I hope she hasn't pierced my skin. I don't mind telling the old girl is pretty well formed for her age. Everything seems to be in the right place. I don't spill a drop from the bottle.

I know that self-praise is no recommendation but for once, I am proud of my steely will and dogged determination, in

175

that I am able to halt her ladyship's advance. She is fine about it and doesn't cause a scene. I take a little time to explain to her that I have simply made a vow to become a one-woman man now that I have the queen in my life.

I accept some of the Admiral's Malt Whiskey and a splash of Soda, while she pours a large measure of Martini and the same from the newly fixed bottle of Vodka into the same glass, stirring it a little with a plastic sword and dropping in a slice of fresh orange. With the help of a tiny pair of tongs, she retrieves perfectly formed ice cubes from a silver container next to the mixers. Bloody hell, if I ever get the pub, I'll have to watch out for the Birdseyes. They could steal my early evening cocktail trade, once I've got one.

We sit opposite each other. Alma is sixtyish and in what you might call a higher prime of her life. She has calmed somewhat from our frantic early beginning but is determined she would still be on show. I don't mind at all that she had made her move. I took it as a compliment. In any case, not so long ago I had been planning something of this very nature, Lenny too. That didn't turn out well either!

I could have been in worse trouble. I could have been knocking at Lil's front door and might have been dragged inside by the contents of my wallet.

My thoughts turn to Big Blen' and her silk curtained boudoir and black satin sheets with sloping ceiling mirrors projecting dozens of different shaped reflections of our writhing, glistening bodies all over the cave.

I might have seen a vision of Blen' knocking at Elvis's bathroom door just as he was having a good, long snort of Peanut Butter and Coke and when he opened it, he took the whole damn lot, thinking that The Angel of Darkness had come for him anyway and he might just as well hit the road now and escape Neanderthal woman. They say his final words were: 'I'm gonna go read a book'! Bet it was about exorcism. I manage to switch off my wild imagination.

"Come on Maccy, just a little one before you go."

I thought Alma had given up on the rough stuff. "I can't Alma, it isn't anything personal. I must behave myself. If it makes you feel any better, I'm almost disappointed in myself."

"Poor Maccy, I meant do you want a top up cock. Your glass is empty dear."

It was an easy mistake to make; when you're in a light stupor and one that is alcohol induced. I have no idea why my brain keeps doing this stuff to me. Alma is still almost half naked and she is intent on letting me see what I was turning down.

"Just the one more Alma and if I ever go back to my bad old ways, I'll let you know first, how's that?"

She stands up and stretches her arm to the optic, an action that allows the shifting of her gown, just enough to convince me once more of the rumour about her hatred of wearing underwear.

"I've a good memory my lad, best you be warned!"

The whiskey is full bodied as is the Admiral's wife. The temptation to comply with her early demands is still bobbing about like a fisherman's float. Thankfully my anchor remains firmly in place.

I would pass on all that is important to Lenny, when I see him later.

"So Maccy, tell me, what do you need the Admiral and I for?"

I'd all but forgotten why I was here? "Lenny and I are gonna buy the pub, Alma. We'll need accountants, financial advice. I believe you and the Admiral were in that line of business?"

"That was our calling before our retirement. I don't know Maccy, as you already know yourself, people change and then find it rather difficult to return to former habits."

I distinctly smell a subtle hint of blackmail. She is having a pop at me because I had turned down the opportunity to enter her version of the bedroom Olympics. I glance across at her smiling face, she is teasing.

I explain to Alma I need advice, rather than regarding her and the Admiral as our official bookkeepers just yet.

As I step onto the deck the Alsatian jumps to attention: I didn't think he'd seen me leave the Mermaids? Had he been following me all along? Maybe my brain was fuzzier than I thought! We leave the little sex sloop with the promise of help and the added threat of future physical attacks on my person when the opportunity might arise.

Chapter Eighteen

Sleeping Giants!

Lenny is viciously stubbing out another cigarette into a leftover blob of ketchup on his now discarded 'All Day Breakfast' plate. As is well known, I have my own before daylight generally and before the café is open. Lenny is doing well, he has ignored the sign he can take all day, he has only taken a half day to play with his breakfast. A previous butt has been stuffed into what remains of a fried egg. It is mostly uncooked resembling something that should be floating around in a garden pond full of sexually active frogs. It's a snotty egg!

There is one other customer in the café. The heavy-coated bloke I'd seen sitting in the Drang that same early morning, Calhoun. He might be writing a postcard or making notes in a book, a diary perhaps. He nods in a friendly manner at my arrival. I nod back. He bothers me now.

The man is nobody I know. He might be from the Council Tax people, I doubted it, simply because I want to. It had been so far so good for a while at my gaff. I am getting junk mail and free newspapers full of more of the same stuffed under the door regularly. A Royal Mail employee has found me. I need to have a word with him or her, put the bugger straight.

Lenny is lining up a young waitress. Following his usual pattern of playing hard-to-get, Lenny is actively nonchalant if that is possible. It'll last fifteen minutes at best. I move into the seat beside him and look at his intended victim with nothing more than disinterest. She is a stick insect, an underfed stick insect that has been stung by a bee twice on the arse and twice more in the chest area. This might have involved more than one bee. Two for breasts, two for bottom and lastly the one that did all the stinging. Makes sense!

Although Lenny and I have on occasion fought over some girl or other, it is more a bad habit than anything of a 'I want what you got nature'. We don't really have the same tastes in women. I know there was that business with Alma not so long ago but that was a one off. Oh yeah, the Northern tart too. The one who didn't quite put her hot pants on before she left home!

Me, I like my women with brains as well as beauty and in no particular order. Lenny just likes his with all the right bits in the right places. This one is built for speed with just one small section missing, which should be located in the central head area. The pair of them will get on perfectly. The girl fumbles in her overall pocket for what turns out to be the little pad she writes her table orders on. A quick search for the pen proves fruitless as I knew it would. She is nervous. To be fair, Lenny makes me nervous too. He has the pen in his hand. Lenny doesn't own a pen. He is using hers in an attempt to idly alter certain parts of the anatomy of a half-dressed model in the newspaper. Lenny is very artistic. The waitress hangs on to his every unsaid word.

This is Lenny's way. He likes to play the 'I can't be bothered' scenario. He is performing perfectly. I wonder how he attained the pen. The girl seems to be unaware he has it. She could just be a bit slow.

Lenny looks up from the disfigured model and smiles. "Maccy, what's on my boy?"

"We got ourselves an accountant. I just spent a couple of hours with Alma and believe me it was bleddy hard going. Just coffee please and another for him." I point my thumb, just in case the dumbstruck girl is in any doubt as to who the other recipient might be. There is some uncertainty in her eyes!

"You wanna see the inside of the Birdseye's boat Lenny. Jesus it's like the Rover's Return in there, only bleddy posher." I don't normally watch soaps; it was on in the Chinese once while I was waiting for a portion of battered mushrooms.

"I bleddy knaw that Maccy, I should do, I've been aboard plenty times if you get my meaning."

"You have?"

"Yeah, why not, I was there first thing this morning. The Admiral was in Wadebridge at the doc's." I was in dock here in town!

Now I know why Alma was mostly undressed at the time of my own visit. "None of my business mate, but I'd have to say you're not doing too good a job. She was all over me like bleddy freckles a while ago. I fought her off, eventually."

"Mind your own bleddy business. It idn't nothin' to do with you what I do or don't."

Dear Lenny, he can get a bit touchy at times like this. I begin to feel that prickling sensation down my neck at his threatening response. I know what's coming. This is Lenny at his most predictable. I tense quickly and catch the edge of the round, Formica topped table before it smashes my kneecaps. The decorated meal remnants and condiments slip by me thankfully; I'm not particularly partial to congealed fried egg decorated with cigarette butts!

Lenny's blood is up. He is on his feet and that instantly recognisable swinging of the arms that makes him look like the guitarist in The Who, has already begun. Lenny's upper limbs are beginning to rotate. My mate enjoys shadow boxing as much as Pete Townsend enjoys pretending to be a windmill.

The bloke across from us stops writing, disturbed by the sound of the table's feet scraping on the tiled floor. I see Calhoun look up, he makes no attempt to intervene.

"Lenny, wait! No!" I put my shovel-like hands up in time to stop the incoming onslaught. Lenny's arms slow down. Listen mate, there ain't no need to get wound up. The old girl is just a bleddy nympho'. She wasn't complaining about you lad. We got more important stuff to get sorted in any case and another thing, we two can't get to fighting every time we don't agree about something. It wouldn't look proper behind the bar."

"Fair enough Maccy, I'm sorry, I knaw you're right."

That's what I love about my mucker, Leonard, he's so predictable in the furniture and feature rearranging department; face merchandising. We straighten the table and chairs, pick up what's left of the unbreakable crockery and wait for the waitress to return with our coffees, most of which is in the saucers due to the fear of Lenny and I fighting and bad nerves. Either that or she just didn't pour it too well in the beginning. Calhoun went back to his diary.

He might have written: 'In Padstow today, very cold, waitress bit odd, food crap. People strange. Friendly enough for a minute or two. Fight a lot. Nice place, other than that, very quiet! Wish you were here?'

Lenny and I finish our coffee and without recourse to any further physical contact, pay the underfed runner bean stick. We slip around the outside of the café and into the narrow side street that leads to the Mermaid.

Virgil and Hardin are in deep conversation with Bligh. Lil is positioned in her usual place but thankfully not in her usual position and although it is unlikely she can hear everything, she is straining to listen to the whispered goings on. Her ear is fully cocked, in a manner of speaking.

The two Yanks are giving the old geezer a hard time again, it seems Bligh isn't keen on the idea. There's a lot of arm waving from both sides of the bar, some finger pointing and spluttering, the latter mostly from the Cap'n. The old landlord is standing his soggy ground. Unlike most regular landlords, Bligh isn't comfortable with extended conversation with anyone other than those he regards as 'proper locals'.

He will yak with visitors occasionally whilst looking for a victim. There was one time he half convinced a coachload of pensioners and their parents, the great

Cornish giantess Magog was alive and well, drunk as a skunk and fast asleep in the beer cellar. His giantess was Blencathra of course. It is Bligh at his brilliant best. He would have his audience all agog doing what he does like no other, inventing and adjusting local history.

I had been subjected to many of these fairy tale recollections myself. Bligh considers any punter as a potential victim at any time, as fair prey, but it is the emmets that get the worst of it and why not? They should have something to talk about when they get home to Manchester, Liverpool or Wormwood Scrubs. I consider that I too - once Lenny and I have taken command of the Mermaid - would attempt to follow in the old geezer's fairytale footsteps. I can't see a problem having had the benefit of his teachings and having more than once been a victim.

I have a good deal of respect for the old bloke's sense of fun and adventure and no less for his wicked sense of humour. Well he did marry a Totem Pole.

It's possible one or two of Blen's predecessors would have proved ample to scare away the Spanish Armada. Francis Drake could have continued playing bowls on Plymouth Hoe if there had been a Blen' handy for the Armada shindig. Blen' could have been Batman's Robin, Churchill's right-hand man. She could have partnered Fred Truman in his prime.

"What about the waitress Lenny, you seeing to her?"

"Nah, just passing the time mate. She does have breath like a bleddy dragon. Her chest is flatter than Old Mother Ivy's field. Another thing, she ain't no bleddy cook."

"I noticed that, bad luck with the egg!"

Lenny's comment on the girl's culinary skills, or lack of them, is provoked by the fact that most wintertime cafés are run by just a skeleton staff; of one. The maid was ideal for the job! Chief cook, bottle washer, floor scrubber, supervisor and wages clerk all rolled into one. The café's owners are most likely laying prone somewhere in the

Seychelles or the Bermuda Triangle. This one is a tad meatier than a skeleton, not by much.

As for Old Mother Ivy, they say she was a local witch that did at one time go about Padstow cursing all and sundry and making good fields turn bad as well as doing the occasional abortion at the back of a pub, which was the ideal setting, if there could be one. Lenny and I receive our pints, when Virgil and the Lone Ranger eventually move aside.

I am unable to catch any of the conversation's contents but am just in time to hear Bligh's last words. "Look I 'ave done told 'e, 'er idn't 'ere, she 'ave 'ad to get back to Plymouth, as 'er sister, your sister, 'ave 'ad a bleddy fall!"

Virgil and Kimo Sabe are unhappy. They grumble indistinct replies and turn away. Virgil has one last retort before departing.

"Bligh, we ain't got a lot more time to be screwin' around with you, no sir. Hardin and me best be shootin' the breeze and getting our arses on a bird home. Just gonna give ya and my goddam sister one more chance ta get around the table and chew the fat. Ain't that right, Hardin?"

"Sure nuff!"

Poor Bligh doesn't have a clue what the two are saying. He shrugs in his own unique way.

Tonto and the Lone ranger pull the door shut behind them as they retreat, dissatisfied. It is a relief to see them go. I'm not particularly overcome with happiness myself to hear that Bligh is telling the truth regarding Blencathra. I am starting to think about another attempt at teasing the bus drivers of Truro.

"What the bleddy hell was they two buggers sayin' young Maccy?"

"Don't let it get to you Cap'n." I thought back to Kansas and Renee. "The yanks all talk bleddy strange. Now listen Cap'n, we do need to talk to Blen' and see how the land lies or have you already done it?"

"I did tell 'e Maccy lad, she isn't against the idea, no, it be me. I idn't sure I wanna go to bleddy England."

"What do you bleddy mean Cap'n, it's you that is dragging your bleddy feet?"

"I dunno iffen I wanna go live in Plymouth. I been up down that way before and it isn't right pretty. This is my bleddy home. Tis alright for her. She 'ave got dual personality."

I stare at my torturer and wait for Lenny's simple translation. It isn't long in coming.

"You do mean dual citizenship, that's what they do call it!"

"Now Lenny, I do know what I mean, she does have both the buggers. Trouble being, I'm never sure which one I be dealing with. It's all well and good for you two buggers to stand there saying what you do think, but I ain't so sure I wanna go live where she was born."

I hardly notice Lil is sitting at her usual table. For once I am grateful for her to butt in.

"Friggin' hell Bligh, you ain't even bleddy Cornish. You did come here from bleddy London when the bleddy war was goin' on. Yer bleddy lyin' shyster you!"

"Thank you Lil, you're a bleddy godsend. Cap'n, get Lil a drink, on me."

So, Bligh is a bloody Emmet! If I was honest, I'd rather be in Truro right now flipping burgers, or tossing Pizzas and Spaghetti. Even the chippy on the quay is beginning to look attractive.

"Shut up woman. Shut your bleddy gob. There idn't no call to bring that up here, we men are trying to talk bleddy business. Give your bleddy mouth a rest."

"Don't you go tellin' me what ta do Bligh; you idn't payin' me now my lad. I idn't takin' that sort of talk lying down. So, you just think on."

I don't know about Lenny. I am beginning to think I am at Wimbledon on the last day. In the middle of the mixed singles final. I have this horrible feeling it is going to go to five sets, between Lil Navratilova and Cap'n McEnroe.

185

"You cannot be serious, you pair. We don't wanna know about your bleddy horizontal pleasures, Lil." It was a slip of the tongue or as McEnroe would have it; 'get me the referee.' I resist the urge to see if Lil is flexing her muscles. Only Cliff and his umbrella, singing Summer Holiday is missing now. It's early yet.

So now it turns out Bligh isn't even from the Duchy. He's been English all along. Still is! The infamous Admiral Bligh might be turning in his grave. He was probably buried at sea. He might come in and go out with the tide! It occurs to me there's no way Lenny and I will be able to get any business done tonight. I decide to make a start at a gallon and bugger the lot of them until tomorrow. Another plan that looks like it might go up in flames. Jen' appears in the doorway. I'd forgotten about her not working tonight. It's an easy mistake to make. I haven't got used to courting properly yet. I'd done some before of course but not for much more than a couple of days at a time. I know it has only been a week at most. This time it's different.

If I am honest, I am pleasantly surprised at the intrusion as Jen' sets out to share the evening with me. She makes herself known to all after her surprise entrance. Even the kids get a smile before they take themselves into their usual corner for the umpteenth replay. It will be a while before we see the whites of their eyes again. Lady Alma and the Admiral are next. Alma nods and winks at me as they approach the bar in typical high rolling fashion. I'm not sure if these sly signals are to remind me to be silent about our morning encounter, as if I needed reminding, or if she has had time to talk to the Admiral about our plans and he has agreed to help in the book cooking department. I'll soon find out. For now, it's full steam ahead towards a good night.

Calhoun turns up. Calhoun is definitely Irish. The yanks arrive with the Alsatian. They are flashing the cash and in a better frame of mind it seems. They even buy a round! The special relationship is improving. Anyone that knows me knows I don't know when to say no and I spend the evening not saying it. George did not make an appearance though I suppose he might have done, who knows? Frank might have been hot on his heels.

And so, a few hours later I am again staring at the ceiling. I haven't been awake long and somehow the rhythmic breathing of Jen' gives me the impression I am out in the Padstow Sound and there is nothing but the ripplets caused by my own tiny craft to stir the perfect surface. The night before was just what Padstow is about between seasons; friends and strangers coming together, a bunch of people in the same place at the same time. Just the one enigma was missing, again.

I did get the chance to talk with the yanks once or twice. They proved to be good company. Apparently, they are cousins. There was no mention as to why they were here in town. They were obviously not ready to impart information until Blencathra herself was present. How can one bleddy woman decide the fate of so many? Did I say woman?

When I had the chance, I made every attempt to get Bligh to see the wisdom of moving to Plymouth and England. I was certain if he wanted to go, the Cap'n would be going and that would be that. Might as well make him feel better about it beforehand. Jen' involved herself in the hard sell, I was pleased at her input. Older guys will always listen to a pretty face and I confess that is something Lenny and I can never hope to compete with.

Jen' has never had to take to a rugby field and so she had never found herself in the centre of a kicking, gouging and bloodletting scrum. There's nothing quite like, thankfully, finding a thick finger stuck up one's backside and looking around to see who it belongs to. Most likely the same finger would at some later point be poked into another opponent's eye. Then there's the groper. There's always at least one that wants to find out if another is better endowed in the tackle department. You can't be sure if the action is just an attempt to put you off your game, which is more than likely, or if the groper is in fact physically attracted to you. You desperately hope this is unlikely. I do anyway! It's always a wonder to me that although the tackle tackling went on, no-one ever really got hurt through it. Watery eyes don't count!

One most memorable match Lenny and I played in was at Cargorrack. The pitch was up on a windswept headland above the village. There were Meadow Muffins everywhere. It was a windy day; every time there was a conversion kick the ball would sail away and down into the sea. Some snotty nosed little Russian kid is the proud owner of a great collection of rugby balls by now.

If you've ever played rugby up that way, you'll know what it's like to run around covered in cow shit and trying to dodge twenty odd manufacturers of the stuff. They just stand there looking stupid. I suppose if anyone could read a cow's mind, they might discover it to be wondering why we wantonly plaster ourselves in that which it has only recently discarded. It might be they think that's their reason for existing. On thinking about it, that wasn't the worst game we ever played in. I recall the day we were up to St Donie's Chapel. Lenny knocked out one of the opposition backs after he had made a comment about his sexuality.

I thought we were for it that day. The bugger went down like a lead balloon. The thing was that almost every member of the Chapel side was related, legally and occasionally illegally if you get my drift. The small crowd too was made up of fathers, brothers and cousins, to a man, not to mention the odd woman! Believe me, there are some odd women about that village! Luckily, the trainer was out quick with a bucket of icy water and brought the bloke around. What made us laugh was one stray sheep that had joined the circle of players waiting patiently for the bloke to wake up.

I kept my thoughts to myself; I did get the impression the two might have been more than passing strangers. I'm sure most of the locals are fine and upstanding but every place has its odd ones. Bessie is the living Padstow proof of my theory.

I am once again staring up at the ceiling and it is getting' me nowhere. My overhead canvas has stayed blank, apart from one recently extended cobweb and oddly enough, the intermittent and unexplainable appearance of the Irishman in the thick overcoat. I wonder why he should be appearing on Jen's ceiling.

I wake the queen and tell her it is time.

"Time, time for what?"

"You'll see."

Chapter Nineteen

Winter Draws On

"I need to talk to Ma about the money. I need to get to Padstow somehow my queen."

Jen' demanded she be allowed to come. "I don't have a car right now Jen'. I can't remember where I left it." I usually walk, cycle or ride the nag, depending on how much I've had to drink. There have been times that I have even awoken on the old rail tracks, forgot which way I was going and turned up back where I started, in Padstow Town, in time for breakfast."

"That's easy to remedy my bird."

I hadn't even thought about Jen' having her own car. I could hardly say how would you fancy going to bed with me? By the way have you got your own car? Not that I did the inviting in the first place, you can see my point? Within the hour she and I were parking in the overgrown lay-by beneath my place. She is already commenting on the cozy look of the two timber carriages I call home. She is impressed with my humble abode that is just one step up, or more likely down, from a treehouse. It's a good job it's not up a tree. Folks would find it far too easily.

The old Tamryn farmhouse, a few yards away, has stood for nearly three hundred years. It is big enough in it's ramshakleness for Ma, me and the kid. I'm an independent sort. Before my eighteenth birthday I had decided to renovate what were two pre-first world war railway carriages, more recently used as store sheds, full of old machinery, tools and bike frames, crap to give the bits their real name. I bought myself a rundown caravan for fifty quid from an Emmet in the Mermaid. He said he was on his last day's holiday and couldn't be bothered to take the ageing wreck home to Chingford, intent on replacing it with a motor-van, some sort of caravan with an engine, I'm told. A petrol run chalet. A plastic tent with an engine!

With the help of Lenny and Dusty, who would do almost anything for the price of a pint, we got the old van to Little Petrock and onto the farm. The remains of the van are rusting at the bottom of the quarry. Everyone in the village uses it. One villager might go down there looking for some useful item and more than likely climb out with something they'd put down there before.

The ancient quarry is a bit like a car boot sale without any money changing hands. Bit by bit, I had stripped away the useful stuff from the van's interior and re-sited them into the first carriage that we had emptied in preparation. I'd even managed to rescue the old-style electric-lights and fit them into my intended master bedroom; for the more romantic moments which might or might not occur. I built a double bed that was the full width of the carriage leaving enough room below it for storing all my unused crap. It is a large space.

We emptied the second with the aid of a neighbour's tractor. We pulled one to within four feet of the other and we had them both level. With some more of the better materials from the caravan, Lenny and I produced a workable lean-to kitchen. There's a two-ring cooker, a Budweiser fridge with its own flashing light; likely due to faulty wiring, a microwave oven without a flashing light, a lot of empty plates and some missing cutlery. In time, we turned the second carriage into another double sleeping area and started on the peculiarly shaped living section. Peculiar as in knocked together over a period and without a plan that had gone missing before it was made. It's never been completed. What you might call 'a work in progress'. The addition of a tiny stone built bathroom meant if I needed to take a dump, I could wash my feet at the same time, as they rested in the tiny bath which was once situated in the Birdseye's small yacht. They most likely have gold plated taps now.

Jen and I are greeted by a cat, without a care in the world, comfortably sprawled out across a faded, leaking beanbag, all beanbags leak! The Alsatian had unwittingly been left outside and the door shut. Chalkie moves position in order, in his mind only, the dog can't come in. I rectify the situation by nudging the cat's arse with my foot and with a little more pressure from the same limb, manage to entice the shivering dog back inside. One thing I hadn't realised about the mutt is that it is a complete coward where cats are concerned. Chalkie anyway! It's possible the dog was being chased by a cat when it collided with the speed boat in the quay.

The cat normally just comes and goes as and when it feels. I know it's not mine and the cat knows I'm not his. The arrangement works perfectly well. I thought we'd left the dog in town. It's not even my dog. I guess the dog has adopted me. Serve it right!

Ma, now in her almost, but not quite made it, and probably never will, sensible forties, was a flower child. She was one of the many who made up the advance party to the invasion of St Ives around nineteen sixty something. If your teenage kid was a hippy and you didn't know where he or she was between nineteen sixty-eight and nineteen seventy-five, they were in St Ives, smoking something.

A Dad? who cares? I never met the hippy again once I'd reached the grand age of two, who had cajoled Ma into his flower dappled Volkswagon Caravanette. I wouldn't want to. I dare say he's a music teacher up to Bristol, or some such. He has a four-bedroomed, three bathroomed, two-garaged, one-dogged detached, with two and one third grown up sprogs that have never seen the inside of a Ford Escort or a rundown state school, let alone their half brother and his full brother. He probably has a golf handicap below ten and membership of his local tennis club as well as an obliging secretary. His wife does aerobics and flower arranging. Someone else does her ironing for five pounds an hour and she doesn't know her husband has two more kids than she does. I'm not bitter, I'm indifferent.

The sad tosser with a ponytail would never know that he missed out on Ma's entrepreneurial talents that had supplied her with a half fortune in return for her skills at making concrete mushrooms. What do you find when you lift a ponytail? An arsehole, every time!

Even now the Tamryn Farm is known locally as the Magic Mushroom Farm, on account they seem to spring up everywhere you look. I saw some of Ma's handywork in West London. I was in the Fulham Palace Road one Saturday afternoon, on my way to Craven Cottage to watch Argyle get slaughtered in the Cup. I'd caught sight of a grey slab as I ambled along the pavement. I knew it was one of Ma's. I managed to see the Tamryn logo imprint on the underneath of the cap-stone as I crawled around crab fashion on my hands and knees through the neat postage stamp, West London garden.

I was in the mood to make an impression that day and I did. I hit my forehead on a sign advertising 'Rottweiler at home' just seconds before I vacated.

Chalkie, who in fact is black and has no white at all, which was my reason for christening him that way, is huge. He tends to think of himself as some sort of guard dog. He has his own entrance and exit and when not chasing some poor sadly confused pooch, or on a hunting expedition in the nearest fields. Unless he's chasing a tail that isn't his own. I often wonder what his name is when he's not at home.

In many ways Chalkie is like me, minus the heavy beer consumption. He likes to sleep, scratch, fight and I assume, unless he's batting for the other side, bonk his brains out. He is partial to eating the back ends of frogs. I can only guess that the front ends aren't so tasty which is a shame for the frog as having their back ends missing doesn't seem to stop their breathing or staring mournfully. When I walk up the little path to my front door, I look the other way. Chalkie scares the hell out of the dog. The dog scares the hell out of me. I most likely scare the hell out of both of them at times; two birds, one stone, etcetera!

Chalkie and Jen' take to each other immediately. Somehow, she achieves a line of communication between them. She strokes, he meow's, she coos, he purrs. The cat has it all worked out. All he must do now is get her to find him frogs with no fronts. It would be much better all round. I'm a tad jealous, not because Chalkie is nestling heavily on her pillows but because he has never shown any interest in me unless I am carrying a newspaper wrapped portion of cod and chips. As soon as the meal is complete, Chalkie with an upward swish of his tail would give me a quick glimpse of his pencil sharpener, or rusty sheriff's badge if preferred and be off to wind up the poodle at the posh little cottage down the lane.

It's owned by some long retired professional footballer that thinks 'Roasting' has nothing to do with cooking a Sunday dinner.

Jen and I make our way to the Maltsters where Ma is sure to be. Ma is holding court, mesmerising at least three travelling salesmen and the weird vicar from the Hell's Angel persuasion from across the road. I don't think he even owns a motorbike!

Ma deftly sends her would be admirers into a semi-permanent exile at our appearance. Family always comes first, second and last with Ma. With a speedy 'Ma, this is Jen, Jen', this is Ma', I leave the two to learn more of each other while I rightfully attend the bar area.

On my return, Ma is in her natural element, already running through my unhealthy and sometimes dodgy past. It is all a ploy by me; I could have spent some time doing exactly what she is. I would have omitted plenty. The telling would not have had the same effect and would have taken me a month longer. I'm rather shy and retiring when it comes to blowing my own trumpet. I'm not what I'd call musical. Ma is into my mid-teens now, recalling the tale of the now long buried Ford.

I suppose the old car could have been brought back to the surface by now. If not, it's still underneath the vegetable plot of the cottage now owned by the thick footballer. Ma sold off the cottage a few years ago to raise cash to keep me in college. That old wreck was my first car. It had been badly damaged during some illegal night racing at the old aerodrome. In the dead of night, we had managed, after losing various important sections of it along the roadside, to get the broken beast home. With the help of a digger attachment to next door's tractor, it had been quickly interred. Twotrees had been fooled by my driving with no lights. He had taken a wrong turning in the midnight chase. It was my switching off the headlights that made the well constructed Cornish hedge invisible and it was here that I left parts of the bodywork.

One of these days, the footballer might think he's found an Iron Age relic. It'll be full of beer cans, pornographic magazines and certain small pieces of clothing that had never been worn by me, nor any of my friends! I just wanna be there to see his face. Obviously, the soccer player would have no clue as to what the Iron Age is. He would most likely think it's something connected to a Chinese laundry. A final mention, though there may be more, regarding the footballer; he never did win anything other than a golden sock. If he had played at a decent standard he'd be living in a posh gaff, the other side of the Camel!

Attending college was a bit of a rush job brought on by Mrs. Twotrees. She had a vegetable plot with a shed. A nasty malicious rumour swept the quayside that a local lad had been zealously helping her with her seedlings. That lad had been me. The rumour was true. I left town a day or two early and not too soon. There's nothing worse than being caught by the fuzz.

So, I sit smoking a good cigar and listen to my two favourite women yak to their hearts content. Occasional strange knowing glances and nods from one or the other are directed at me.

I am starting to feel like Chalkie. Not that I was intending any violence towards the weird Poodle. I'm sure I resemble a Cheshire cat. It is an hour before I get the chance to interrupt. Jen' needed the ladies room. I didn't have the heart to tell her that it was still on the outside of the building, wall less and roof less.

"Ma, I need ten grand!" I don't do subtle well.

"You're after that bleddy pub down on the quay."

"I know the Blighs have done nothing with it, that's to the good. The pub can only go in one direction. I hope it won't move at all while I have it. I need a guarantor for the mortgage too. What we reckon is to get the cash for the business, get a donation from the brewery towards a deposit for the freehold and take a mortgage on the rest."

"I dunno Mac', you know I never liked the bleddy place. I suppose with your qualifications you should be able to do something with it. Just you and Lenny?"

"There'll be three of us Mrs. Tamryn."

"You can call me Ma, or you can call me Joy."

Ma is on form. I don't need to tell anyone she is great company at any time of the day. Jen' is already taken by her and in turn, Ma has my queen in the palm of her hand.

"Does Lenny have his own ten grand Mac'? You need to do all this just right. Iffen you idn't equal, things can go awry."

"Lenny has to sell his motor. He won't quite get ten thousand for it. I'm sure he'll find the rest. I don't believe he'll last the course anyway, you know what Lenny's like."

"I should do after all the years I've known him. Let me know when you need the money. Why on earth do you want to borrow money from the bank? Your share in the farm would cover what you need for that place."

"I thought about that but if we don't make a go of the pub, I'll lose a lot of money. You could lose a lot of money. It's too risky. If we are paying a mortgage, we're more likely to work harder at it. There's just one bleddy problem."

"What's that?"

"There're two yanks sniffing around the place and we think they want it. Bligh tells it that one of the buggars is Blencathra's twin brother and before you ask, I don't have a bleddy clue. Bligh and Blencathra borrowed the money from the Yanks when they took the Mermaid on."

"Iffen I was asked boy, I'd say you need to put the buggers off."

"Yeah right and how would we be best doing that?"

"Easy boy, get 'em to see how bad the place really is."

"That's easily done." Ma is right, as she usually is. Somehow Lenny, me and the Blighs need to put the yanks off, make it look like a waste of their money; make it look as though the place would never amount to anything. Very little effort needed on our part. Things could be best left as they are. At the completion of Ma's expert advice, I move away. I had noticed something odd in an inglenook at the other side of the bar. I walked a couple of steps forward and my instinct and my eyesight proved to be correct. It is the Admiral. He is not alone. He has female company. She is just young or old enough to be a daughter. I can't resist an approach.

"Afternoon Admiral, business meeting?"

"That's right young Maccy. You know how it is old boy."

"I do Admiral, I reckon I do." I know alright; while Alma is playing away at home, the Admiral is playing away, away. I leave them to it.

It is a while before I can drag Jen away from ma. It's obvious the two are going to hit it off. I couldn't be happier and never really had any doubt that it would be the case. These days Ma is a good judge of people. I'm not criticizing her for her past choices. Teenagers traditionally don't make good judges and ma was just that when she fell for me and my father in no particular order, apart from the obvious.

While listening to the incessant chatter I notice the sky has, what poetic folk might call, become leaden in hue. I feel sure heavy snow is threatening. It isn't long before I am proved right. It begins to fall, lightly. It is time to go. Even as we pull up in the lane that passes just below the carriages, it begins to flutter with that eerie enveloping silence that always seems to accompany snowfall. The heavier the fall, the more silent the whole world seems to become. Why is that? Within minutes the sky has closed right in. It is a perfect white curtain. Everything is disappearing beneath a cold winter layer.

This part of the West Country doesn't often get heavy snow. Just the odd dusting that looks as though it's been sprayed on.

We called at the well-stocked village shop on the short return trip and bought supplies to supplement the almost bare shelves in the outside cupboard that serves as a larder. The cupboard is collecting a layer of the fluffy stuff that will help serve the purpose it was built for. A perfect place for chilling wine. I light the tiny gas fire that is just man enough for the job of warming the sitting area. The bedrooms need no heating. Warm air tends to float up the steps. The coaches are built of solid oak, not much can seep through their aged thickness. Jen' has happily rummaged through my sparse winter wardrobe and is even now wearing a thick Guernsey pullover that has either shrunk or I have put on weight since last I pulled it over my head. She looks much better in it than I ever did.

The cat is white. Chalkie has meandered in, now his name fits perfectly, it won't last. He shakes himself and nestles on the bag. The mutt had squeezed in at the same time and is already in the space under the steps that lead to the kitchen.

The meeting between Ma and Jen' could not have gone better. It must have been instantly obvious to Ma that Jen' had her head screwed on. Ma would have seen straight through her in an instant. She would already be history. I know their conversation would have simply died had she taken a dislike to her. Ma might be a leftover from the wild age of Woodstock, it might have been Calstock! She is nobody's fool.

I'm at peace with my world. Jen' is staring into the gathering whiteness. The small gas fire is taking effect. Chalkie is purring like a favourite old car that's been finely tuned but so far unburied. The dog is doing something I could never do, nor want to. I think about the pub and my intended responsibilities. Despite myself, I'm reasonably popular about Padstow, always have been.

Some might see me as a bit of a Jack the Lad at times and they would be right to a point; I'm what's known as affable. That's what ma said to me one day a while ago. She had been nearing the bottom of a bottle of Claret and had suddenly assumed a mother hen role.

We all change and maybe it's my turn. It is early days but my showing at the Birdseye's a day or two ago was a good sign. Then again, the Admiral is evidence that nothing is ever set in stone. Maybe there's something of my father in me. It's possible he was just a love 'em and leave 'em type of bloke. Loving and leaving has suited my own purpose a time or two.

Dusty, the kid, is a lot like me. Maybe he's worse. He's not got the gift of the gab like I have but he has the looks of our mother. Dusty is love 'em and leave 'em, plus all the other bits obviously. I wonder what my brother will think of my plans when he returns. Would he still look up to me now I'm on the verge of becoming semi-respectable? Dusty is built like a brick toilet at just an inch shorter than me.

According to ma, my brother is presently in Spain, working as a holiday rep', catching everything but rays. Sleeping days, working nights and somewhere in between, he tells Ma he's god's own gift to everything in a bikini. Ma mentioned she had a call from the kid a day or two ago. He should be making an appearance sometime soon. I sidle up to Jen'. She is staring as if hypnotized through the window, it is dark now. The snow is falling thicker. I think we are likely to be here for a while, there is already a soft layer.

Blencathra would be stranded in Plymouth. We three are going nowhere. The Maltsters is around the corner, just a ten-minute crawl away. The Ring O Bells, a little closer but they wouldn't want riff raff like us cluttering up the bar. Besides we only go there when I don't owe Chris, the landlord, money.

To be fair, I do spend a large amount of time there during and after the annual, friendly cricket match between St Issey and Little Petherick. I use the term 'friendly' lightly and a tad unwisely. There is nothing else for it but to sit out the weather and entertain ourselves. I don't believe that'll be much of a problem.

Jen' has read my mind as she steps up into the kitchen and makes toast. A strange thought comes into my head without warning. I'd been looking at the cat and my toast and I wondered why it is that if you drop toast on the floor, it always lands butter side down. Drop a cat and it always lands on its feet. What would be the outcome if the cat had two slices of toast strapped on its back? Answers on a postcard! It is a measure of my ridiculous mood.

I think about the Mermaid and how cold it will be in there right now. If Bligh has any sense, he'll be following in One Armed Frank's footsteps and demolishing what's left of the furniture. I think about how the cold weather will affect the amount of fluid that will eject itself from his nose. He might be walking about the place in wellies. The two kids will be keeping each other warm, the Birdseyes will be snuggled up in their floating Gin palace. Bligh would be best off giving Lil a nod and a wink. Lenny will be holed up somewhere with a waitress. Calhoun will be in his hotel writing more postcards. I don't believe I missed anyone, apart from Frank and George; I suppose in their condition the cold will be the last thing to bother them. They should be more nervous of extreme heat.

Thinking of the pair leads me to wonder if I should ask Michael to send them on their way towards the light or whatever it is a trainee minister needs to do. To be honest, so long as they didn't cause any trouble or annoy anyone, I didn't see any reason to change anything. There's a chance they'll visit even more when Blencathra has relocated to Plymouth.

Jen', Ma and I attempt to play Scrabble. It is half-hearted and doesn't last long. We did reminisce over the colony at The Well and fill in some of the blanks. She told me she had worked at The Yacht, a fancy pub in the nameless village across the estuary. It's a lump of a place that does very little; even a permanent name evades it. When I've had a night on the beer over there it's been Rock and Roll!

I break out some long stored Dry Vermouth I'd made before leaving for London. I find half decent glasses in a cupboard. It is a surprise to me as I believed most of them had been broken or lost outside. Ma is already half asleep. Jen' and I become what you might call comfy, all entangled like on the long black and yellow plastic sofa that must be twenty years old. It had not been retrieved from the quarry. I had saved it from its owner before he had time to tip it.

The liquid is beginning to seep through me. I am just about to suggest we retire to the extra width and warmth of a double bed, when we are most rudely interrupted. It is the unmistakable sound of some prat outside knocking at my door.

The accompanying voice is instantly recognisable. It is most unfortunate. The prat is my brother!

Chapter Twenty

Up Shit Creek

"It's me Mac, Dusty, open the bleddy door."

Only my brother would turn up out of the blue or in this case, blue underneath white on the outside. As my visitor has Dusty's voice, it must be he. "What do you bleddy want, we're busy, bugger off?"

I love my kid brother to bits, I would do anything for him, but right now, I wish he could be somewhere else. I don't want any interruptions for a day or two.

"Iffen you were to open this bleddy door, I could tell 'e!"

"I don't wanna know. I'm not interested. Why should I open it? I'll open it tomorrow. Go and sleep at the Maltsters, let me know what the food's like!"

"Jesús, Maccy, its bleddy freezing out here. I'm gonna lose parts. I'm freezing my nuts off. I can't afford bed and breakfast, I can't afford a bag of chips. You will have to lend me the money! It would be better brother if I stayed here. You'll save a fortune!"

"Just have the bed then. Get a single. You don't need a double from what I heard. You can eat tomorrow."

"Maccy!"

"Wait, I'm thinking about the disadvantages."

"I'm not thinking of going anywhere else matey, I don't believe we could if we wanted."

"Go and let the poor sod in Maccy, you can't leave him outside." I knew Ma would speak up for the kid, it's no surprise.

"I bleddy can. He's not alone anyway. They can keep each other warm. I suppose I would save money letting them stay."

"You bleddy can't, let them in, now. He's your brother. Nothing counts more than family!"

It is a direct order. I do as I'm told. I would have anyway, eventually. Dusty is just what his name suggests, they both are. He is covered from head to toe. He isn't alone and why should it surprise me? It doesn't. To be truthful I'm just surprised there's only one. I do feel a tad embarrassed now regarding my lack of a decent invite. To be fair, if the roles were reversed, Dusty would have demanded money before letting me in.

The dog continues his work with sound effects. The cat leaps for safety, in search of somewhere to hide from the moving, shivering, mini avalanches that come in after I pull the door wide open for a split second only. Blizzards should be outside stuff. Dandruff is acceptable! I had lied through the door. I was full of questions but allow the newcomers time to get their snow clothes off before asking. I pour the kid a neat whiskey and Vermouth for his lady friend. I decline the offer of a brotherly hug. Not because I'm not glad to see my only sibling; I'm certain he intends to use me for the benefit of defrosting quicker.

The girl is different. I would not have been rude enough to turn her away. She is quite a looker, although right now she is trembling hard with the cold. Perhaps she is afraid of a reprimand from me for her strange choice in men.

Jen' searches for warm, dry clothes for the girl. Like me, she ignores Dusty's needs. He knows where to look.

Within minutes my brother and 'Selena' are settled. Blue faces fast changing to red and then glowing bright pink. I swear I can see steam rising from our late visitors who, it seems, have just completed the four-mile walk from Wadebridge railway station. Beeching has a lot to answer for.

It is a unexpected meeting for us all, with me expecting no one to come knocking due to the weather. We are all on a Tamryn wavelength with no sign of awkwardness. Dusty and I are brimming full of questions. The ladies seem content to listen and get to know their opposite numbers by quieter, more sedate conversation interspersed with the occasional dirty laugh. They hit it off right away. It makes it easier for Dusty and I to continue our delving into what each of us have been up to since our last meeting, though some of it would need no explanation, mostly on my brothers part.

I eventually get the chance to tell Dusty about my plans for the Mermaid. He isn't at all dismissive. He knows the pub well and is aware of how hard it will be in turning the place into a thriving business.

"Jesus, Maccy, you got your work cut out. Bleddy 'ell, what's Ma say about your foolishness?"

You see, my brother is hardly dismissive at all!

"Ma's behind me. She's offered to put the dough up. Told her no thanks, except for what I need for buying the goodwill, not that there's much of that, but we won't get in for nothing. We hope to get some cash backing from a brewery to buy the bricks and what-have-you. We need to get a business loan from the bank and Bob's your uncle, or he might be, we don't really know, do we, thanks to the old man. More likely Rob! Ma's behind you."

"You're right brother. We could have us one somewhere. The Mermaid is the arsehole of Padstow, Maccy. Isn't there anything better? Why would Ma be behind me?"

"I mean Ma is behind you! It's the Mermaid or nothing. Let's face it Dusty, the place can't get any worse."

"Fair enough, I'm after getting myself something, a passenger boat mebbe. Hi Ma!"

"You're not going back to the holiday job then?"

"Nah, had enough of that stuff, or should I say, they have had enough of me? I have thought about taking emmets up down to Newquay. Like running a bus service without the bus, just a boat. Just need to get a business mooring and a decent craft. Nothing too fast. Puke'll be everywhere otherwise."

"Sounds like a good idea Dusty. If it takes off, you'll make a fortune. Every bugger wants to go to Newquay sometime. I can't stand the bleddy place as you know; full of bleddy chippys and furriners. Puke is everywhere in Newquay anyway, isn't it!"

I notice Jen and Selena have sidled off into the kitchen. The sounds tell us they are preparing a supper effort. It is late, what does it matter? The chances of us all awaking at nine O'clock tomorrow morning in a heatwave are as remote as Blencathra donning a spangled mini skirt, dying her hair blonde and singing Waterloo to the accompaniment of the Salvation Army band on a nudist beach. Am I tempting fate? I could be.

"You remember old One-Armed Frank, Dusty?"

"I dunnaw let me think, was he the one with the missing arm?"

The scotch is taking effect. "No, he was the one that only had one arm. He bleddy went and died in the Mermaid last week."

"Bad pint?"

"Might have been, anyway, he died and they're buryin' him drekly."

"Best all round I do reckon. You can't just leave a body lying about, not being buried proper, it isn't right. It'll put people off coming in for food. It might entertain the kids though."

"True enough brother, drop more before you go on your way?"

"It's best I do. Me and me darlin' do have to go soon and find us a stable or some such. The scotch will warm me in my search. I wonder if the church is locked. You still got that bleddy caravan, Maccy?"

"Ais but it's down the quarry."

"We won't never find our way down there in this weather."

This is my brother at his best. He knows there is another double bed up the steps, he knows he and Selina will use it. Ma will be happy on the sofa. It isn't actually a sofa, I don't have one, more a pile of cushions on top of another pile of cushions. I like cushions!

Dusty and I aren't as thick as we sometimes look. It's just when we get together like this, we tend to get into highbrow conversations. It drives our Ma crazy, she will laugh along with us most times. It isn't so often that brothers can get along like we two. I can never quite understand why his voice has a slight Irish lilt to it, but it does and it it's always more noticeable when he is drinking.

Dusty raises his glass. "To One Armed Frank!"

"To Frank with the missing arm!"

"You know where the bedroom is Kid."

"Aw, Maccy if only you weren't my brother, I'd ask you to be, for sure I would."

"Listen to me Dusty, if Lenny and I can get our grubby little mitts on the Mermaid."

"Ais, go on, Mac'."

"You get your boat and you could use Lost Souls Creek that runs down the side of the Mermaid for mooring and taking on passengers. We'd need to do some repair work. Get rid of all the crap. Replace some of the stonework on the old steps. Get rid of the bodies and stuff, especially the more recent ones. Think about it; while your passengers are waiting for their cruise to Newquay they'll be in the Mermaid drinking themselves towards throwing up all over the side of your boat."

"I dunno Mac', it's a bleddy shit creek!"

"I know, but you and I have been up shit creek plenty of times. It comes natural."

"True enough, brother. It's a good idea. You boys do have to get the Mermaid first."

"That's right, but we can't do bugger all until this weather breaks. Reckon we might be here for another day or two, maybe longer. Tomorrow we can chat with Ma, tell her what our plans are, see what she has to say."

We ate Prawn curry and I sent up thanks to the big guy. For once Dusty had arrived with perfect timing. My idea for the creek and Dusty's boat could put the finishing touches to my plans. I am excited about my prospects.

206

There is just the one fly in the ointment; two flies, Virgil and Hardin Fly!

Two O'clock had long gone when we took to our beds. I couldn't be certain as my clock never gets altered twice a year like most folk's. I just leave it alone in March and October. I believe it catches up eventually. It's an old habit and will never change. We had decided Ma should know all we had agreed on regarding the sea-bus and the creek. It is only right and proper that she knows all the bits and pieces such as they are, especially considering my borrowing cash from her for the 'goodwill', which I shall remind myself, was her idea. Ma could easily afford the money, but everything would have to be done just right. Business is business as they say in business.

The snow has thinned, but it is still falling lightly when we leave the warmth of the white-crowned carriages after a late breakfast. There is a thick layer on the roof of Jen's car. There is little or no wind and the flakes flutter down evenly and the soft carpet slowly deepens. Our feet press the snow down into at least six-inch prints as we trudge onwards towards the Maltsters for lunch. We can't resist snowballing and the bunch of us lark about like schoolkids. Snowballs are thrown at anything and everything along the lane. We lob a few at the dozy cat, who had somehow thought this little outing should include him as he hops along behind us.

By the time we get to the end of the lane he has decided enough is enough and turns back to the beckoning warmth of the carriages. The dog is hardier and tags along a few steps behind.

Our ma is already in her regular place at our arrival in the Maltsters bar, she had left before us. She decides we are all in need of a good meal, which we are. After a couple of drinks we make our food orders known to the old feller behind the bar.

Ma pays the bill straightaway without any consultation with us. She isn't one to have anything she hasn't paid for;

pay first, eat second! I suspect the kid's pockets are near to empty anyway.

While we are waiting for our meals, Dusty and I explain to Ma our recent changes. I'm not surprised at her extra support, she is impressed but still issues the warning not to 'count no bleddy chickens', exactly the right attitude. I am grateful for the foul weather. The meal gives us the chance to relax and throw around ideas that might become useful. It is just a shame Lenny isn't here with us. I still doubted his ability to stay the course. Not that it will put me off. Jen' has already promised her support.

Dusty might even become involved in his own way. It won't matter what Lenny decides. Dusty reminds me Lenny is a keen engine doctor. He might help him in keeping a cruiser mechanically sound. Dusty is right, Lenny is a dab hand with a socket set. The mechanical upkeep of any motor-powered boat can be expensive in the wrong hands. I know the sea-bus business is Dusty's alone but there will be times when I'd need to call on him as he would me. The meal is excellent. The five of us kick back, relaxed and content. Until something seriously unusual occurs. I am drawing on a nice cigar when a large helping of shit hits the invisible fan in lively fashion.

Our Ma isn't in any way what you could call a troublemaker. For the most part she's quite docile, which is another trait from her hippy days. Ma doesn't flit around with daisies in her hair and she likes a bit of waccy baccy, occasionally. I suppose you would call her a Flower Woman rather than a Flower Child. All the same, our table is suddenly flattened as if One Armed Frank has suddenly arrived and is feeling the cold.

Dishes and cutlery are scattered about the floor as if by the actions of a bull in a favourite retail outlet. Ma is moving forward like greased lightning before Dusty and I have any idea what is happening. I feel she is about to kill the chef because her Fillet steak was underdone or overdone. This could not be the case; her plate is empty.

The kitchen is in the opposite direction. Her intended target is just inside the open door.

He is white from head to toe. Just the face is clear. I feel certain for some obscure reason, Ma is about to drastically rearrange it.

The well-wrapped, new entrant stands rabbit-like in headlights as Ma storms across the room towards her quarry. Her intentions are obvious. I just have enough time to feel a tad sorry for the recipient of her attentions before he is flattened. Dusty and I only reach our rampant parent after she has already thrown the straight right and has connected perfectly with the newcomer's red tinted snot-box. The punch is a beauty. Luckily, before she can follow up with a knee to the goolies, the man slips down. Dusty and I quickly have Ma's wrists under control. If she attempts a follow-up, she will also be sitting on her arse.

None of us have a clue what has caused her to go at the poor bloke the way she did. Ma didn't say a word during her attack. There was no time. Me and the kid had been quick once we realised what was happening. We'd pulled her away. The girls re-erect the upturned, unbroken furniture.

After the heavy punch, the stranger quickly regained his snowcapped feet and without a word stumbled backwards through the snow littered doorway. I believe it to be the Irishman that had been in the café and had sat in the Drang that early morning. The man whose wallet I'd found. It was Calhoun. Calhoun left the Maltsters like shit off a Cornish shovel.

Ma has already approached the stunned and aged landlord, who is to show just what an easygoing bloke he is, by not asking her to leave. If Dusty or I had caused such sudden and violent chaos, we'd have been shown the door automatically. Ma is a local, a good customer. Her promise to pay for repairs or damages is accepted but dismissed. Ma resumes her normal level of placid calmness. The rest of us resort to a shoulder shrugging competition. Anyone who knows Ma well would never ask her why she does something. I ask.

"What the hell was that all about Ma?"

"The arsehole owes me Maccy, that's all you need to bleddy know."

Her answer is to the point and doesn't allow for a reply. I don't venture further. I know one thing. She is talking bollocks.

The others look confused as do I. There would be some odd thoughts going through their heads right now as they had only known Ma for an hour or two. I couldn't blame either if they had followed in the geezer's deepening footprints.

Calhoun must have owed an extraordinary amount to get that kind of personal final reminder. Red bills usually come through a letterbox! There must be something else? I could have done with having Ma's help around the quayside on occasion. We return to the subject of the Mermaid and Dusty's cruiser.

At mid-afternoon, we leave the Maltsters. Dusty and I leave our signatures in the Almighty's visitor book by way of 'Peescript'! The bog has no roof! It begins to snow heavily again. It's easily above ankle deep on the footpath. We are thickly coated by the time we reach the warmth of the carriages.

Ma decides she will stay over again and sleep on the cushions, with the cat for company. He isn't going out for the night, and who can blame him? Freezing ones nuts off is likely to be just as unpopular with felines as it is with humans. Chalkie's are a bit closer to the ground.

Dusty can't help himself and broaches the subject that had been so quickly discontinued at the Maltsters. "What's the story Ma? Did the guy get a shipment from you and he still owes for it? Did he give you a rubber cheque?"

"I told you to leave it Dusty, you too Maccy. Believe me you don't need to know, you don't ever want to know."

"Did he sell you some duff weed?"

"Maccy, tell your brother, enough."

Just when you believe there is no better place to be than in the nearest pub with your loved ones, some virtual stranger walks in, your mother takes one look at him and she's up doing a Lennox Lewis impression. The bloke goes down like a crap Argyle striker in the penalty area; you ask why, and the parent says, 'he owes me!'

"Who is he Ma?"

"Maccy, I told you, leave it there boy."

"Nope, there's more to all this than just a few quid and a score of bleddy concrete mushrooms or some crap baccy."

"I can't tell you boys. It's all far too late now anyway. It's done and dusted."

My mind is working overtime. Dusty's must be in a similar predicament. As far as I know, he hasn't seen the guy before. I had, at least three or four times. Jen and Selena try their best to dissuade us from continuing with our questioning. Talk of how long the bad weather was gonna last and repeated rehashed compliments of our lunchtime meal will not be enough. It's obvious what they are trying to do and fair play to them. With a woman's instinct, they could see Ma was caught in a corner. Don't the women stick together at such times!

"Did you get a good look at the geezer Maccy?"

"Only while Ma had her fist stuck to his face Dusty, which means, not really. It was all so bleddy quick, you?"

"No more than you did, I'd say. He is early, mid forties mebbe."

"Yeah, reckon that was about it. So Ma, old boyfriend, was it?"

I can't remember Ma having any what you might call proper boyfriends around the place when we were growing up. She always put her time in to me and the kid and the business. She never seemed to bother much. That isn't to say there were no would-be suitors.

We wait, watching as the emotions in Ma's face alter. It wouldn't be long I was sure. Her head drops, her hands snatch at a recently rolled spliff. She puts it between her

211

lips. She lights the end successfully at the fourth attempt and draws deep. I have no qualms about her smoking the stuff, I'd tried it myself. It just made me throw up. Lots of things make me throw up.

"It was your father! It was the bastard who left me when I was caught with your brother. You were too young to remember him Maccy. He was hardly about much. He didn't hang around once he knew Dusty was on the way. I heard he'd been seen. Milky told me he'd seen him in the Ship at Wadebridge once or twice. Milky was one of our party at St Ives. He knew it was Padraig."

P. Calhoun, Padraig. Dusty's Irish accent. The wallet and the photograph, I believe I had been looking at myself!

Chapter Twenty-One

Butch and Sundance

I had decided not to tell Ma and Dusty I was aware Padraig had been around Padstow for weeks; I didn't know who he was in the beginning. I couldn't have been sure of anything, I did have a feeling something was awry. Ma and he had met in a similar way as Jen' and myself, just by chance.

They had first met at a party in one of the tiny two up, two down cottages in Hick's Court, a row of diminutive cottages that can only be reached by passing through an ancient granite archway entrance, a much coveted and magnetic, St Ives landmark.

One or two locals had joined the commune in a part-time way, as she tells it. Many had come down from London for long weekends, leaving their suits and office wear behind for a couple of days; that many times, would turn into longer stays. Many just didn't go back to their previous lives and settled into communes around the county. There were regular get togethers of the pot-smoking kind, not forgetting 'free love'.

'Free love'? No such thing, someone has to pay sometime. Marijuana, or whatever else it's called? Who am I to judge? As I've said, I tried the stuff myself; it didn't do much for me that I remember but of course, it might have affected my memory. How would I know? Whatever Ma had got up to back then was her business. There are things she wouldn't want to hear about me, there are plenty of things I'd rather she didn't know. It's the way of it.

Ma had explained the communes eventually began to disintegrate, probably due to the arrival of Alvin Stardust, Queen and co'. The least said about Gary Glitter, the better. Many of the members returned home and became average 'Joes'. Ma did in a way; she came here and although her dress sense has never changed much, nor did her cheerful outlook on life.

Ma looked for some way to earn herself a living on the family land. She had an idea. It turned out to be a good one, if I was honest, which is a matter of opinion, even to me. She has never looked back. She did what she set out to do with only the sweat from her own brow. I know, I know, ladies don't sweat, they gleam! That's what almost all members of the fairer sex will tell you anyway. To be honest, I have never seen Lil or Blencathra gleaming. Lil can be seen dreaming, Blen' steaming!

It seems Padraig had wandered around the Duchy in search of others that might not have returned to the big city. He found none of them. He did find Ma and she had let him stay. Their friendship would grow, take a natural course. I was born a bastard as they never did marry. I've been a 'bastard' on and off for a while now! My brother a slightly smaller one. Dusty arrived a while after I had got my small feet under the table, though they didn't reach the floor. They didn't reach far at all straightaway; high chairs will have that effect.

Padraig had already pissed off six months before, unable to assume a simple role as head of a young family. Poor Ma had three bastards in her little family back then. One of them at least was of the Irish and more importantly, useless variety. Ma said he went away looking for work. I don't think she ever believed that. It is possible he had told the truth.

She had never set eyes on him until yesterday and then she nearly blackened them both. She would have too, had Dusty and I not stopped her. Now I'm wondering if we should have let her carry on and do a proper job on the worthless tosser.

I don't know what to think to be honest; there's that word again. I can't tell what's in Dusty's mind. I do know one thing, if I'd known who it was that had walked into the

Maltsters, I might have smashed his face in too. But that's only a first thought. My second and third seemed to come to the same conclusions. The future doesn't look too good for Padraig Calhoun. I can't speak for Dusty, I think I know exactly how he would react!

Ma had recounted all this early family history with a somewhat poker face, something akin to sadness. She didn't show the fire fuelled animosity that had flared up at the pub. There was something else there, a smidgen of regret, maybe? Not unexpectedly there would have been anger too. Ma has been wanting to punch the son-of-a-bitch's lights out for years and now that she had got her wish, did she feel better about it? There was some look of satisfaction.

I wonder if this isn't all a final curtain drawing. A new beginning. I feel there is more to come but there is nothing for us boys to do but wait and see what might become of this skeleton which has finally relocated from a cupboard.

Slowly but surely, thoughts of Padraig drift out of the room. We continued our evening with just the occasional return of the ghost of an injured Irishman. Now and then, little references to St Ives came up like the time Ma got chased down Tea-Total Street by the local copper, for sitting on the steep curb and playing a homemade flute 'for a few pennies', amongst other reminiscences. It's to be expected. When families get together there is always talk of the long distant past and hopes of new plans for the future.

The bloke is now flesh, blood and slightly mangled bone. With my partly absent mind, I stare out through the foggy window. Still there is the fluttering, feathery fall of the snowy curtain. I guess seven or eight inches, maybe more, have accumulated now. We all just sleep where we are pretty much.

I might have dreamed of a childhood of happiness and contentment and acceptance of what I had, not what I didn't have. I now realised for the first time, it had been incomplete; it hadn't seemed that way for all this time. Up until now I thought, you can't miss what you haven't had. I might be wrong.

Ma had no need to stay at my place. She could have found her way back to the farm easily enough by treading the softer snow in and across the fields. There was no need. I guess although she didn't want to talk about Padraig anymore, she just needed company. It had been the opportunity to catch up on more of each other's most recent scrapes.

Each of the younger ladies had slipped in and out of the long exchanges as and when they had something they wanted to say; a question to ask about some childish interlude. It seemed we had been digging up our past, despite Padraig; it made sense, he wasn't in it for long. How things can change!

We had plenty to laugh about and occasionally there were one or two tears, some of sadness and those much more precious ones, tears of happiness, at some anecdote or escapade.

I recall all the latest stories from the Mermaid. Ma cracked up at my antics with Lady Alma when the two of us had been alone on the yacht. Ma is no prude and she knows the ways of the world well enough. Selina turns out to be broadminded. It must be something of a necessity when you're a part of Dusty's life. The continuing laughter allowed the flow to, well, continue really.

Surprisingly it turned out Dusty and Selina had not become a part of the holiday rep' culture at all. They had met quite early in their season long contracts and a mutual liking had done away with the need to become members of that doubtful group.

This was all a change for the kid as like me, he had almost been banished from Padstow; due to his own Don Juan style. We had both made quick exits and our reasons were of a similar nature. Maybe 'banished' is too strong a word. It was a good time to spread wings.

We did eventually learn why the kid had suddenly left the dubious concrete beauty of Lloret de Mar and why

Selina had decided to depart the place with him. She should get herself an optician!

It seems Selina is the daughter of a very important hotelier on the Costa Brava. The hotel in question is a big part of the holiday company's business. I work out the hotel owner is or was some sort of 'face' in the London underworld; not high-profile East End but scary enough by all accounts. I doubt he would get a job in Eastenders, too much of a scumbag. Anyway, the girl gets an ultimatum from the old man, get rid of the kid or get out. She got out and kept the kid, for now at least. It won't last.

Let's just hope the geezer doesn't change his mind and come looking for the girl with a bunch of his scar-faced entourage carrying violin cases and bags of quick drying Portland cement.

At seventeen, almost eighteen, Dusty appears to have all the makings of another me. He is less likely to get into brawls and such; not that he can't look after himself, just that he's a little slower tempered than I. He thinks he's cool! It seems he has finely honed his courting skills. Dusty has always been a talker rather than a doer and so he has always used his gift of the gab and the speed of his feet to get out of scrapes that might lead to pain. Not like me at all in that regard.

Not so bad then and at least he had, in a roundabout way, kept the girl out of one kind of trouble. Dusty's a good kid and it is easy to see he likes her, but knowing my brother and his easy come, easy go attitude, there is little chance of a long-term future for the pair. While she is here, it's my bet he won't let any harm come to her.

Like me, he is the protective sort and what some twentieth century folk called, laid back. It isn't possible for my kid brother to lay back further. I'm certain this shared protective streak is an extension of that which we both feel for our Ma. Not, I should add, that she needs protection from us, as the previous day's encounter had shown.

The early morning saw the end of the falling snow but an extreme drop in temperature brought a different problem. Ice! The laying snow has assumed a top crust above the ten inches below it. There is nothing else to do but sit the cold spell out at Little Petrock and at the Maltsters. We aren't going anywhere soon.

Although I am eager to get back to Padstow, Dusty too is chomping at his own bit, as he had been away longer. Far longer than intended, but the time had been well spent.

It is becoming a little like a Christmas in that that our small family is together. There is something different about a pub at Christmas. They feel different, they smell different; it's the atmosphere. It is this same atmosphere that is supplemented by the superb accordion playing of an Elvis lookalike who it seems, just appears out of nowhere on a regular basis to play and sing his heart out for very little cash or reason. Either he lives in Little Petrock, or he owns a sleigh.

With slightly tinted glasses and thick blue-black hair with long sideburns, accompanied by a permanent, almost nonchalant smile, the player could be mistaken in looks for the 'King' as he plays the glinting accordion and sings his way through innumerable old favourites that belong only to the folk of the Duchy. There is no need for Christmas carols here. We have our own favourites.

There are fairy lights all year round above the Maltster's bar but no tree of course. Still there is that feeling of seasonal togetherness, without the usual bitchy arguments that erupt when 'big' families get together every year to celebrate by beating the crap out of each other and stomping off home early to kick the neighbour's dog. A bit like yesterday.

We went back with Ma to check on her dogs and brought them back to stay at the carriages. Both Labradors steer well clear of Chalkie. The Alsatian stayed well clear of both. The ducks and chickens that share the Magic Mushroom farmyard, and occasionally even the farmhouse, stayed where they were in the wonky barn. They are well provided for.

The Maltster's landlady has a simmering pan of stew bubbling away permanently. I believe the ingredients had been prepared late at night and left on a low light to simmer throughout the night. It would be left for hours to bubble and thicken over the range, to be ready for the following lunchtime and anyone stupid enough to be out looking for a hot meal.

Bread has been made in the kitchen and it is already selling to the locals who can't get any of the regular plastic stuff that takes almost a fortnight to produce Penicillin. Even then, only a mild variety and makes one feel they're eating a grubby secondhand pan scourer from the village store. This is what a real Inn is about, ready for anything, as by their ancient nature they should be.

At night we didn't get out at all. Of course, the dogs have no choice but to brave the cold now and then, usually with aid of a sharp kick up the jacksy. It is far too dangerous for us with the ice. We have our own toilet, indoors now. We played cards, charades and scrabble until our eyes crossed and re-crossed. Thank god, I never owned a monopoly board. Sleep would come much easier and earlier if I had.

I've got an idiot box, it rarely goes on. The picture's crap because the coat hanger's crap. I have a telephone …. somewhere!

Now, what is it they say, speak of the devil and he will appear. I'm thinking about the Devil, I was thinking about the phone and it rings at the very moment. I find the noisy implement down the back of the sofa!

It is Lenny. "Yes mate."

"What about n?"

"Day after tomorrow? bleddy hell!"

"We'll be there. Make a start on organizing it Lenny."

"Yeah Strange's up the top of Padstow Hill."

"Tell 'em we'll settle up after the do."

"See you on Friday."

"Friday, we'll be there."

"Me and the Kid, Dusty's here, turned up last night and drank all my bleddy Vermouth. He's got a bleddy woman with him."

"No, I don't know either, short sighted or mentally disturbed, I guess." She was probably normal before they met. I knew enough already to know Selina wouldn't be upset by my lighthearted suggestions regarding her sanity. In any case, I can hear her giggling like a mad woman behind me.

"We'll be there."

"Yeah bye Lenny."

I look towards the others who had gone quiet during the call. "That was Lenny. It's Frank's funeral; it's the day after tomorrow, twelve O'clock. I need to get in to Padstow by Friday. Some of us should be there to see Frank off. We gotta give him a proper do."

I have some plans of my own for One Armed Frank's funeral. I can see Friday as a day to make my first mark on the Mermaid, I've made plenty of marks on the place in the past. This will be different. With luck, I'll be in time to organise the old boy's sending off. I must get back there as soon as possible, it's only right though I can't quite see how it can be done.

"If you were to ask me, Maccy, there's only two ways you'll be getting to Padstow on Friday."

"How's that Ma?"

"Next door's tractor, that'll get you there, or, you can get a sleigh and the horses can pull it."

"We don't have a sleigh. I'm not bleddy walking, Last time I made a sleigh, I got stuck and couldn't get out. I must have put on weight while I was still in it."

Perhaps the sun will be out drekly and we'll have a scorcher. So, it's the bleddy invisible sleigh or go next door and borrow a tractor from a farmer who once wanted to shoot me." Bloody hell I thought, what kind of choice is it? And then I have a brainwave: Dusty and I would ride to Padstow, we'll ride Ma's nags. Safer than driving a car I don't have. Ma and I do have one, we just can't remember where we put it.

Six or seven inches of snow - might be more in places - four and a half miles or so, Dusty and I riding horseback ala Butch and Sundance only without the Sun bit. The nags might dance a bit in the white stuff. Neither of us are what you might call 'butch', but we do have horses. We would have to start now to get there before dark. And we almost do, but Ma points out an early start in the morning might be better. She is right as usual.

Thursday morning sees us trudge through the snow to the Magic Mushroom Farm. We both know how to ride but it has been a while, a long while since I had been in the saddle. We never did try to saddle next door's cows.

Dusty and I would ride Ma's only two half decent nags. Ma and the women will be coming in on the borrowed tractor. They might just make the journey quicker than we will. They might be a tad warmer too.

As payment for the use of the tractor, we make a promise to bring back a couple of cases of beer for its owner. The village shop had taken a bit of a hammering. It had virtually run out of alcohol, which is rather poor planning in my opinion!

Chapter Twenty-Two

Mothers and Fathers

Ma had tacked up our rides. I had Jen's door keys jangling in my pocket. Dusty and I rode out of Little Petrock in the early hours with the hope of getting to our destination for breakfast. Our mounts would not get through an MOT due to the lack of any headlights or indicators, breaks etc. They would have to do.

Hopefully we two would be sleeping in the loft tonight and the womenfolk would meet up with us in the morning. They would be bringing extra feed-stuffs for our mounts as the last pet shop in Padstow is now an art gallery, stroke café! Doesn't make a lot of sense to be honest. All of the yuppy folk go to the other place now, across the river. I forget its name.

Dusty and I don't attempt any land speed records on leaving the farm, content to let our nags saunter playfully. A good horse should have a sense of humour. A decent rider should also have something along the same lines, especially in this weather! We had called back at my place and grabbed clothes needed to attend a funeral. Dusty had bagged up some of his stuff that had been left at the farm while he had been aboard.

According to Ma, neither of the beasts had been ridden recently and they behaved a little like we did when we walked through the still falling snow to the Maltsters. They teased us two something shocking initially.

We would be in the saddle for at least two hours, thankfully the nags had settled into an easy gait. It is well below freezing, perfect for riding I believe but what do I know? We'll most likely end up on our arses! We drop down into the narrow valley where the hard frost hasn't completely penetrated. The snow is mostly hock deep but much softer here as we follow the Little Petrock Creek before a steep climb up to the main road again towards the town. It was hard going to get up the steep winding hill that would take us on to the main Padstow road.

We don't meet a soul. The road is empty and quiet. No abandoned cars, which points to a good early warning of the poor weather. Perhaps if I turned on my TV more often, I would have known what was coming too. I could have made more of an effort at the off-license.

Once on the reasonably level, Winnards Perch road it is easier for Dusty and I to ride side by side and talk. Hearing is a little more difficult as we are wrapped up in the manner of Egyptian Mummies. The sky is clear and blue now. The air is still.

Dusty explained all that had happened in Spain and like me, doubted Selina would stay around Padstow permanently. Dusty saw no long-term relationship for them, a fact that doesn't seem to bother him unduly. I'm not surprised. Basically, they are two of a kind.

He knew she had used him to get away from a dominant father and had been more than happy to help her along and of course, I'd say she's making the repayments in the non pyjama wearing department if you know what I mean; I could be wrong, I won't be. Selina's father would not be coming here to drag her back home immediately and the chances are, if he did, she most likely would have already moved on.

Dusty convinces me he is serious about putting his sea-bus plan into operation. The kid has never been one for proper planning in the past. I believe it can work. I have faith in his idea. I'd say on a bad day it could be a two-hour trip at most to Newquay. On a good day, an hour or so. The Fly Cellars quay at the north end of Newquay is a favourite fishing spot for locals and holidaymakers alike and is equipped for passenger landing craft. Dusty will need a license. He'd also need to apply for permanent landing permission from the local Harbour Commission.

Most importantly the kid will need a decent craft. They don't come cheap. There is always the chance of finding one at a marine auction. Boats become available cheaply sometimes when a business has just gone broke. Creditors never expect to get their full return and auctions are the quickest way to get some of what's owed and for the cash buyer every chance of a bargain. Other than auctions, there are boat magazines and boatyards.

I tell Dusty what I think he should do. He agreed. "We can't do much this week Dusty. We gotta see Frank off proper. First thing Monday we'll get started on finding you a boat. You any idea what it'll cost?"

"About ten, fifteen grand for a decent secondhand boat. A new one could be anything up to seventy-five K."

"Ma?"

"Yep, she knows it's a good project. She tells me she's donating the same to you for the Mermaid's innards!"

"You'll have your work cut out brother."

"Why's that?"

"You'll be taking a lot of drinking trade out of town. It's the kids your age that have all the cash to chuck over the bar. The locals won't be happy."

"So what, business is business. If they can't take it, tough! With any luck, you'll get plenty in the Mermaid. It'll be the only Padstow sea bus-stop, so long as we can clear out the bodies from Lost Soul's Creek enough to get a shallow draught boat in there."

"I'm starting to think you've got yourself the safer bet Dusty. Could be me and Lenny will have a tougher time of things."

"If you two get the pub you'll do proper. Stop worrying. I'll be bringing folks back here from Newquay. I wouldn't wanna be running back to Lost Souls Creek with empty seats if I can help it, it wouldn't make sense. Another thing, there aren't any berthing charges at Newquay, far as I know. I can tie up at the town quay next to the Fly Cellars for free, same as the fishing trip boys."

224

My brother is right. He could well bring other folk into town and into the pub; I must admit the return journey might be as lucrative as the outward trip. I hadn't given that a thought. The sea-bus could turn out to be a success. The kid has his head on proper these days. Maybe he's not so much like me after all.

I look at my borrowed watch, we are making good time. We're on the last leg. We plough on past the football ground and reach the New Road which will take us downhill past the 'big house' and the deer park. The small herd turn as one and wonder as we pass. We let our mounts choose their way down a steep slope and once again we are in water. This is Lost Soul's Creek. Less than a mile will see us arrive at the rear of the Mermaid. It has been almost two hours since we left Little Petrock. We turn into the yard at the back of the building, relieved to get out of the saddle and hoping all our manly bits would quickly drop back into their rightful places. Right now, it feels as if mine are somewhere behind my ears.

There is no need to inform Bligh of our arrival, the couple will still be snoring in any case. We tie up the steaming nags under a lean-to and take off the saddles, laying them carefully over a wide bench that suits perfectly. The ride, or perhaps trudge would better describe it, had been without incident. Relatively crash free in fact. The horses had behaved well after their early playfulness. I had packed hay and carrots.

The still silent, old town has a thin covering of snow, not as deep as further out. We leave the horses with the hay we'd carried and make our way to Jennifer's loft to drop off our bags. We make our way to the quayside café which employs the dopey waitress, who probably still clings to the misguided belief that the sun shines out of Lenny's backside. We don't see a soul on the quayside. The pair of us need a hot drink, followed by a visit to the undertakers. Not that either of us are feeling under the weather. I have some last minute details I want to talk to Strange's about.

I'm certain Frank has no living relatives. I am taking it upon myself to do right by the old geezer. I feel rather good about being responsible, even though it will cost a bob or two..

The girl is busy with the only other customer in the café. We watch patiently as she writes the order on her pad. She turns and walks towards the kitchen.

"It's him Maccy!"

"Who's him, who's who, where?"

"The geezer over there, it's the bloke Ma decked at the Maltsters. It's the old man!"

Dusty is right. I hadn't noticed when we entered, but it is the same bloke. The same bloke I'd seen on the Drang the morning of the storm. The owner of the wallet. The pair of us stare as he studies a newspaper not even knowing we are here or who we are. The girl returns with his plate and puts the foodstuff in front of him before coming to our table. This is weird. If Ma is right and of course she is, we are sitting in the same room as our father and we don't know what to do or say. At least I don't. Dusty has other ideas.

"Oi, you, got the time mate?' Dusty shouts his unfriendly question, across the café.

The bloke's eyes look up from the paper. His head stays quite still.

"Almost ten O'clock, lad."

"Didn't mean that, arsehole."

Dusty stands and walks heavily to the table, he flattens his palms on the nearest part of the surface and stares into Padraig's face. He tips the table forward and all that was on it slides into the lap of the middle-aged Irishman. He falls backwards, covered in hot tea and unfinished, unstarted really, scrambled egg. I don't remember the kid ever showing real violence to anyone before.

"Have you got the time to tell us why you buggered off, leaving our Ma and us?"

"Leave him Dusty. What's the point? The man doesn't have a clue."

"Why should I leave him?"

Padraig gets to his feet, he takes some money from the same wallet I'd found. He leaves a note on the table and walks towards the door. He turns once, before making his exit.

"I'm sorry boys. What else can I say?"

So, he knows. The bloke with scrambled egg and tea sliding down his expensive coat has put the two twos together.

"Dusty, you go down to Strange's and tell' 'em what I want done. Tell 'em I'll be footing the bill for Frank's funeral."

"Why should I?"

"Do it!" I raise my voice to my brother and it really doesn't come naturally.

"What are you gonna do?"

"Me, I'm gonna go after him and see why he's come back here. Then I'm gonna get him to leave. Do as I ask, and you better help the maid pick up the mess. Tis only right."

I understand how the kid is feeling. I could guess what he is thinking but right now I'm thinking it's best I keep the two apart.

"I'm sorry about the mess love. Dusty'll help you clear up." I give the girl a tenner. I tell Dusty to check on the horses after running my errand to Strange's and leave the café, in search of our father.

I catch sight of the bloke striding up notorious Lover's Lane. Lover's Lane is what its name suggests and leads to the Courting Field. The Courting Field is on a steep hillside, it overlooks the Camel estuary and the long beach that fronts the posh place on the other side of the estuary. It isn't that posh; the posh inhabitants make it up!

There's a fair few Padstonians that have been begun up in Courting Field, they say. Maybe where even Dusty had got started. It's none of our business. I guess the posh lot opposite did it in proper beds.

227

The bloke keeps walking at a steady pace. I increase my own to eventually catch up with him by the time he steps over the old stone style. I pass the memorial. I can see the old lifeboat station over a mile away. I call out to stop him.

"Padraig!"

It is the strangest feeling, calling out his name aloud. He stops with his back to me and waits. So, he knows I am here, I'm not about to give him an easy time. I sit my arse on an empty bench and wait for him to backtrack.

"Macdonald?"

"That's my name, don't bleddy wear it out." I am being disrespectful. I can't help myself.

"And the kid, what's he called?"

"Dusty" For a second, I'm not sure myself if it is just plain Dustin, if Dustin can be called plain. I never could remember. "Why didn't you ask him yourself?"

"Sorry won't count much, will it?"

"No, won't even scratch the bleddy surface."

"What do you want to do, thump me as your mother did? Go ahead, I don't blame her nor would I you"

"It's Mac, or Maccy." I want to know plenty but I'm not asking. Why should I? I want Padraig to tell me his story. I'm not about to tell him mine. The onus is on him. If I did thump him it would be the end of it. It wouldn't do me or anyone else much good. It would change nothing!

"Look, I wasn't much older than you are now when you were born. I thought I could handle that, and I tried, but when Joy told me she was carrying your brother, Dusty, I knew I was out of my depth. Put yourself in my place."

"No, I can't bleddy do that."

"She's done a grand job in any case, I did the right thing."

"And how the fuck can you know that?" I am riled more than I ever have been. It's not a word I use unless I hit my thumb with a hammer!

"I'm not an idiot!"

"I dispute that. You lost two sons and the best woman you ever knew."

"Yes, what you say is true. I can see that."

I am holding my temper, I feel I should be giving Padraig a good slapping. I am never far from it. "You could've seen us more iffen you'd wanted. You married now?"

"No, I never did. Been home in the old country this last sixteen years. Made myself a good deal of money, got my own construction firm. I'm a builder, at least I was. She sure knows how to punch, your mother. Something she's learned since I last saw her."

"You expecting to build something around here?"

"Maybe."

"Why do ya say that?"

"I'm not leaving for a while. I'm staying in the Ship Inn at Wadebridge."

"There's nothing here for you, never will be, you might as well 'ship out'!"

I did start to think maybe Padraig could find a way to stay; we don't have to live in each other's pockets. Might not hardly see him in any case. Chances are he won't be around long going by his past record and he does make it sound like he has nothing better to do.

"There's nothing anywhere else for me either Maccy. My company runs itself now."

"It's your choice, but Ma idn't gonna be best pleased. You keep away from her." How do I know what the hell Ma would think? She might not even give a shit what this Irishman did or didn't do.

"I'll not ask her for anything."

I stand up and look Padraig straight in the eye. "Keep your distance or you'll answer to me. There's nothing Ma needs from you and the same goes for me and the kid. I've gotta go. Got a funeral to organise."

"Funeral?"

"One Armed Frank died in the Mermaid, it's the pub Lenny and I are gonna be owning soon."

229

"Can we talk some more, tomorrow perhaps? You're young to be owning a pub!"

"Who knows, maybe Saturday?" The funeral is tomorrow. Yeah, right, in your dreams.

"Will you bring the kid?"

"I dunno about that. Best not, lessen you like wearing your food regular." We parted in silence.

I had gone back to the flat with Dusty, I couldn't settle. I needed fresh air, I needed to clear my head. So much is going on right now. I am alone as I pace the ghostly silent quayside. Padraig is constant and annoying. Even the gulls aren't interested in me as I wander aimlessly. I must look a poor sight to them right now. I forget most of the birds are probably fatherless too. I sneak into the still closed, quayside café and make myself tea, I don't drink it until it's almost cold. Ma is on my mind. She will be in town soon, she might again have to come face to face with Padraig. I hoped she wouldn't.

Dusty and I had talked for hours when I got back to the loft. I still have no idea what is in his mind. We had hit the red wine heavy in the late afternoon, the kid is sound asleep. I should have been myself. The early start had caught up with him. I'd struggled. I intended to walk it off.

Dusty had seen Strange. The undertaker had agreed to my suggestion that Frank should make his final journeys to and from the Mermaid. I still had not told Bligh. I am certain he'd not mind Frank coming back to the Mermaid one last time; after all he doesn't seem to mind George dropping in occasionally. To be fair he doesn't have a lot of say in the matter; if George wants to visit, he visits it seems, unless Blen' is home. I'd think twice myself!

I am switching the worrying section of my brain from Frank to Ma. Being out here on the deserted quayside is about my family not Frank's funeral. I see the dim light glowing through a thin, cold sea mist that is slowly creeping in. I make for the Birdseye's yacht. I need to talk to someone like the Admiral. I am certain he'll be still be up and about. I see a light showing. I just hope the two aren't busy. I rap my knuckles on the roof in case there is some private function going on. There isn't. The Admiral's head appears almost immediately.

"Maccy old chap, what can I do for you? You're about late. Come aboard lad."

"Need a place to dock for a while Admiral. I saw your light on."

"Get you aboard my boy. What would you like, a snort of whiskey, rum, something else?"

"Got a drop of French Red, Admiral?" I don't like to mix my drinks. I have a big day tomorrow, we all do. I try not to wonder too much what 'something else' might be.

As the Admiral searches in a cupboard under the little cocktail bar for my request, I tell him my plans for Frank's send off and inform him that I hoped he and Alma would be at the wake, as part of the crew. Alma appears from the snug bedroom. The dressing gown is done up tightly. She speaks for them both.

"Of course, we'll be there Maccy. Frank was part of the ship's company, wasn't he! It would be a bad day if we couldn't spare a couple of hours to give an old crew member a proper send-off, wouldn't it cock."

"Thank you, Alma darlin' I knew you two wouldn't let Frank down. Frank was one of us!" Frank was one of 'us', more than I was. I am on a par with the mangled mutt. The dog had turned its nose up at accompanying us to town. I haven't been back long from the Smoke, Frank has hardly ever been away as far as I know. I doubt he even knew there is a bridge at Saltash.

"To be honest Alma, that's not my real reason for being here. I'm worried about Ma. Have you two met her?"

"Of course, we have. She was at the Chase on your birthday. You really put a lot of effort into the evening's fun and frolics, a night not to forget, wasn't it Admiral?"

"As you say, dear."

"I might have joined you young fellers Maccy but, I'm afraid my running days are well and truly behind me; oh well."

I believe the Admiral meant it too. The old boy can't run. He can't hide either, as our accidental meeting in The Maltsters a few days earlier had proved.

"Those days are well behind me now Admiral. I'm gonna be a reformed character. I'm going straight. Going into business, with a little bit of help from my friends."

"Alma told me you might need a helping hand with your books. We'll sort you out when the time comes lad. There'll be no talk of payment, other than the occasional gratis evening dinner, once you get yourself started in that particular direction."

I bring up the subject of Padraig's appearance and my worries about Ma and Dusty.

"So, Calhoun is your father lad. Well now Maccy, I can give you just one piece of simple advice, it might be good, it might be bad, it is well meant, and you'll have to decide for yourself. Let things happen; don't interfere, Joy won't thank you for it. She's a grown woman and she'll deal with the situation in her own way. She might just surprise you my lad."

"Don't let your father get you on board. Listen to what he has to say, it's only fair. Everyone deserves to be heard but if it isn't what you want, if it isn't enough, take no notice, it will only alienate you with your mother and perhaps young Dusty too if you try to force things. You all three have to make up your own minds as to what you will accept and what you won't."

The Admiral continued. "Joy will deal with it as she sees fit, Dusty too, you can't interfere. You just must deal with things from your own point of view. Listen Maccy, when you were at the pub and she belted the bugger on the hooter, did she consult you first?"

"No!"

"There you have it. Trust her Maccy, she'll do the right thing. If she doesn't, then she can only look to herself and not blame you or anyone else. You must have trust, isn't that right Alma?"

"Of course, dear. The Admiral's right Maccy."

I had made the right decision. The Birdseyes have put everything into perspective in a few short minutes. I can't live Ma's life, nor Dusty's; the kid will do what he feels is the right thing for him and I must make sure in my own mind I do the same, even if the two are different. It is my signal to leave. I thank my friends and resist suggestions I should stay and finish the bottle, as I pull the door shut and head for the loft.

"Everything alright Maccy?"

"I do believe it is Dusty. I was just having me a nightcap with the Birdseyes."

"What about the old man, Padraig, what else did he have to say when you caught up with him?"

"You can ask him yourself on Saturday, mebbe. He asked if we'd meet up with him. Could be we won't. What do you think?"

Dusty grunted some inaudible reply.

At eight we are both up, dressed and eating everything we can find in the tiny kitchen. I need to see Bligh early and explain why he would soon have a three-quarters full coffin resting in the Mermaid. There is also a small matter of two large horses in the Mermaids' yard. I'm not looking forward to this morning in all honesty.

Chapter Twenty-Three

Blencathra

I get the biggest shock of my life as I walk confidently past the empties and push the doorbell that hangs loosely away from its fixings. I have already checked on our horses, leaving them with a healthy breakfast. Healthy as far as I know, it wouldn't do for me. I don't do vegetarian.

Oh shit, bugger and bollocks! My impending explanation will need to be a world beater. I believed I was well prepared to explain to Bligh why there were two large, smelly horses standing and crapping around in his yard, only this is not Bligh. I hadn't prepared for this eventuality. This is a kettle of fish of a very different kind. The doorframe is invisible. This is Blencathra and I'm wishing I was invisible! My number is up. All this time I have been waiting to see her and now I can, I want to be somewhere else.

"Maccy, my 'ansome!" The booming voice is devoid of any melody. She looks the same as she did the night of the fight though there is a little more growth around her chin and on her top lip. No further scars of battle! I'm not even saying anything under my breath, I am speechless. Blen has a face like a pig's butt. I'm saying nothing and I'm trying bloody hard not to contemplate any other follicle growth. Blencathra can hardly be mistaken for someone else, even at the best of times. Like anything, there is always the exception such as the Yeti in Tibet or the camera shy Saskwatch the yanks claim to have. What about the Padstow Monster? I am facing her! Falmouth has the Morgawr, a giant squirrel lookalike, Bodmin has a cat that cannot drink milk out of saucers. It's a beastly habit anyway! Apparently, the large pussy gets its sustenance by eating the cow. It can also change color at any time!

Thank the lord Bligh had been lying about the breast implants. I can't help but throw them a cursory glance. They are dormant, wherever they are. I believe if they needed to be seen by a doctor, she would have to lift her skirt up! What seriously worries me is the old girl seems to be expecting some sort of physical contact. I haven't got anything against hugging and that sort of activity, this is different, much different, dangerous, life threatening?

For those that don't know, it's something known by us locals as the 'Stone Frog' effect! The stone frog effect begins when a princess turns a frog into a prince, only different. Lip contact with Blen' might be able to turn me to stone, it might be better if she just kicks the shit out of me and have done with it. I can visualise myself standing in Ma's yard alongside the mushrooms, with a flapping price ticket hanging around my cold, grey neck. I could join the legendary Hurlers at Minions. Those erstwhile folks turned to stone for playing rounders or cricket on a Sunday! Personally, I don't believe they were doing either. There is no evidence of bats, bails or balls.

I remember like it was yesterday, when I was a kid of around sixteen and Bligh had flicked cigar ash in my first proper pint. I threw up for the county that night and it was Blencathra who'd taken me outside where she had helped me complete my oral rainbow by trying to poke her arm inside me. It was all unnecessary. She could have just suggested we have a snog; it would have had the required effect. I had no idea where the diced carrots and tomato had come from! Not true, I know where they came from, I just don't know how they got there.

Lenny had had a lucky escape that night. Blen' had favoured me. Should I be grateful? I don't think so.

What could I do? I let her have her way. I clench my buttocks tightly as I bite my stiff upper lip which I believe is quivering a little, rather like the bottom one, so neither are stiff! I take a deep breath just in case there is no oxygen where I am going. I will hold on tight. I tremble convincingly as I give myself to her.

I have some things to tell Blen' she might not be pleased about. I might as well do what I can in the cordiality stakes first. It isn't so bad in any case. There are no bodily intrusions this time, thankfully. I wouldn't want Blen' getting the wrong impression and thinking we could become an item. I'm sure stranger things have happened, to someone else, somewhere else, Mars, Uranus? I still shiver uncontrollably as my own tightens!

It is like having a great weight lifted off me. Once the tree-hugging comes to a halt and the feeling has returned, it is down to business, Frank business.

"Blen' my lover, I've asked Strange's to bring Frank back here this morning. So he can leave the Mermaid for the chapel."

"That's alright Maccy, how thoughtful of you to see to that."

This isn't quite going to my hastily produced plan. In all honesty, 'hasty' doesn't work for me. It is more likely to be instant! First thing, Blen' is smiling. I believe she is. She isn't screaming or howling at me, nor clutching me beneath an overgrown armpit before dropping me in the quay with a bag of cement attached to my ankle. What had I been afraid of? She's a pussycat. She is putty in my hands.

Maybe that old bugger Bligh has fooled all this time Now, that is possible. I am in favour of getting out while I am ahead. I am about to leave Blen' with the promise I'd come and help set up a resting place for Frank's box later in the morning. I had forgotten one thing, two things. I am just about to receive a severe memory jolt.

"Maccy Tamryn, come back 'ere!"

Oh shit! It was all a bloody wind up. She is ready to beat the crap out of me now she's had her way. Nervously I turn back towards the still echoing yell.

"Yes Blen?"

"I do 'ave a question for 'e my 'ansome, if you don't mind my asking my lover. What the bleddy 'ell is two bleddy girt 'orses doin' crappin' all over my bleddy back yard? Are they yours?"

"Er… see, Dusty and I had to ride them in because of the weather. We two wouldn't have made it for Frank's do otherwise. Dusty reckoned it'd be alright to park the buggers out here for a night or two." Why not, wouldn't you? The kid would lie, exactly the same, maybe more successfully!

"Did 'e now? I'll see to the young bugger later."

I promise her faithfully one of us, Dusty, would clear up the deposits before we depart on the return journey. Again, Blencathra's lips widen and part in some sort of attempt at smiling. This takes me back to Easter Island and the great statues once more. I wonder if there are any retirement homes on the Easter Islands.

"Another thing you 'aven't mentioned my 'ansome. Bligh does tell me you and you and Lenny do wanna buy my bleddy pub? Best you buggers come here Saturday and we'll get down to it then."

So, I did get off lightly. And this time there was no clarion call to make me turn back. I feel like I've just come out of the headmistress's office without getting six of the best. I think about checking my pulse as I leave her standing in the yard. I take to the quayside and begin to relax again until I bump into the other Butch Cassidy and Sundance Kid, remakes of Laurel and Hardy.

"Mornin' Virgil, Hardin!"

"Morning Maccy." They reply.

"We're meeting up at the Mermaid Bar later to see the old guy off. You fellers are welcome to join us there for the doings."

"We sure will Maccy, and thanks feller."

"No problem." And there is no problem. I feel it only right to hold out the hand of friendship at this point; especially as the two yanks had played a big part in helping Bligh the night Frank died. The 'special relationship' lives on! I walk on. I'm stopped in my tracks once more. It is Lenny; a serious look on his face, I know he has bad news.

"I can't do it Maccy, you need to find another partner mucker, sorry."

"It's okay Len, I understand. See you in the pub later, yeah?"

"I'll be there. Will you still go after the old dump, matey?"

"Yeah, course I will. Probably won't get it anyway. The bleddy yanks'll snooker me. See ya later, it's fine, don't worry about it."

Lenny is off to the café for his breakfast, I guess. His news didn't come as a big surprise to me. Lenny is a good bloke, just not the most reliable when stuff gets serious. I had always expected it. Don't get me wrong; if I found myself in any physical danger, Lenny wouldn't hesitate to dive in and do his bit no questions asked. I knew he wouldn't be ready for something like this.

In any case he did promise he would help with clearing the creek if it comes to it, that will be useful. Right now, there is no certainty of my getting the Mermaid. Even if I don't, it won't stop Dusty with the sea-bus. The kid isn't relying on me. He can run the business from any one of the old town's quays or slipways. And I still reckon he's gonna make a fortune.

Dusty appears as Lenny wanders away and the two of us make our way to the Mermaid to prepare for Frank's arrival. Bligh let us in and between the three of us we smarten up the bar area as much as possible. We set out Frank's old spruced up table next to Lil's. The two tables should be enough to hold an unusually light coffin.

Bligh seems more relaxed now that Blen' is back. Lenny's news, although not entirely surprising, has thrown my plans into disarray a tad. I need to find at least fifteen thousand now, maybe more. We were putting the finishing touches to making the place presentable as Strange's turned up outside the door. Frank was brought in and we settled the box on the tabletops. Disaster comes quickly.

238

The Alsatian has also appeared and causes a moment of panic. One of the bearers has taken fright suddenly at the dog's ugliness. He falls backward against the first table while still holding on to his section of Frank. The table becomes firewood. Thankfully the coffin, unlike its tenant stay in one piece as the bearers floundered. 'Decorum'!

Old Frank might see all of this as some sort of tribute. Maybe he did see it all. Perhaps he and George are leaning at the bar, laughing their bollocks off right now at our pathetic attempts to produce a dignified send off.

I give the dog a halfhearted kick up the arse and it scampers outside. Oh, there's plenty that wouldn't kick an Alsatian up the arse but there's a real knack to doing it. The safest way is to make sure its arse is in front of your foot. The dog must be the right way around. Never put your toes to the wrong end of an Alsatian, deformed or not. They can be snappy about such things. The appearance of the dog suddenly reminds me; Ma, Jen and Selina must have reached Padstow by now.

An RAF dog handler pal of mine once told me; Alsatians do bite, but they will let go, Labradors bite and they tend not to. I'll stick with the Alsatian!

Another table is put in place and the still complete box is eventually settled across the two. I pick up the broken pieces of furniture and put them next to the empty fireplace. I didn't, I was tempted, for a second or two.

When I arrive back at the loft, Ma, Jen and Selina are already piling up sandwiches and pasties. They are all neatly placed on matching plates. It is a typical Cornish funeral buffet. There were so many, I think they must have made one for Frank.

"Lenny's pulled out Ma. I'm on my own with the pub."

"That's alright boy. You'll manage if you still want the bugger, do you?"

"Bleddy right I do!"

Between us we manage to carry the food around to the Mermaid and set it all up on the last surviving table that isn't already being used.

Lil is the last of the crew to arrive on the day. She walks to the polished coffin lid and picks up the folded plastic baccy wallet and Frank's old shiny Zippo lighter. She shoves both items deep into her overcoat pocket without a word. None of us have any cause to complain. Lil must think she has a claim and none of us feel the need to discuss the subject. She'd already had his small change the night he expired! To be fair, he may have owed it to her, I can't think what for at fifty pence! It makes me wonder if Frank received discount from Lil as he was never complete.

Nobody is missing. Bligh and Blencathra in her finest bell tent, which makes her look like a fully loaded rotary washing line, are present, the two kids whose names not so much escape me as I have no idea what either of them are called, are present. The Birdsalls are already on the Brandy. The whole crew is on parade, except Lenny. He'll be late. There is no sign of any members of the rodent family. It is agreed the food should be covered, in case they make a surprise attack while we are at the cemetery. The Yanks haven't shown up so far, I'm certain they will.

I couldn't remember the last time I saw Bligh and Blencathra both behind the bar at the same time. It is a strange sight to see them there together, smiling, after a fashion.

Virgil and Hardin arrive at the same time as the hearse; they inadvertently remind me of the 'reapers' once again. Not that they are unsmiling. They are like all of us, cheerful, considering the occasion. We can be forgiven by the fact that nary a one of us is related to Frank. I don't believe he left any kin. Lil had been the closest if you get my drift. Frank is the last of his line as far as I know.

As the bearers carry the underweight coffin out to the hearse we fall in behind. Thankfully there are no more mishaps. Once again, it is left to me to eject the ugly dog; he decides to become a part of the procession.

The funny thing is, I have a hard time pulling the huge door shut as we leave. Almost as if someone unseen is trying to leave the Mermaid Bar with us and wants to be last out. I wonder?

The old quay is silent. The last of the snow has all but disappeared from the streets. One or two locals and the odd flitting well-fed seagull are tearless as they witness Frank's final journey. If George had indeed come and gone while Frank was breathing his last, there didn't seem to me to be any reason for him to make any future visits. Is it a final chucking out time? Was Frank attempting to have his own personal 'lock in'?

The hearse did what hearses do. With the coffin aboard, the driver drives at four miles an hour to the entrance to Pauly's Lane and slows to a halt outside the imposing grey chapel. To be fair, driving at more than five miles an hour around the super-narrow backstreets of Padstow isn't advisable at any time of the day or night. Our party is easily able to keep up.

Michael's father is standing outside in all his flapping finery. He waits patiently with Michael for the bearers to carry the highly polished chipboard box inside. The service is short and simple, so a bit like Frank, I suppose! Very soon we are all walking towards the edge of town and the tiny Padstow cemetery known only to us locals as 'God's Half Acre'.

To get to the graveyard at the same time as the car and its now 'blessed' contents, we must go the long way around. We mourners walk up Duck Street past the gatehouse of the posh house and into the old New Road, or is it the new Old Road? Fifteen minutes would see us inside the crowded little spot that has so far kept its white covering and standing at the freshly dug gravesite. Frank can't break anything here I decide, as I wait for my mate to begin a reading.

Michael does well enough for his first official task. He reads the usual stuff. We stand around for a decent spell, like regular mourners before returning to the pub by the same route. My mate promises to join us later, for a scotch or two, a game of pool and a hot sausage roll.

Just the one wreath is set down above Frank. I have been careful to make sure the florist has the right words on the tiny card, it reads: 'From the Crew. Don't break anything up there, Frank.' It is perfect. It ought to be, it cost enough.

The food is uncovered and most of us pick at it. No one ever eats much at these gatherings. A few locals poke their noses inside the door, have a single drink and leave again. One or two stay longer, mostly keeping themselves to themselves.

Even the accordion player from the Maltsters has decided to attend Frank's 'afters' do. He perches himself in a darkened corner, which they all are to be fair and plays some of the quieter and more sombre pieces that are known only to us locals.

Michael, Dusty, Lenny and I play pool. I was certain the table would be needed today and Jen' had borrowed a spare set of balls from the Sailmakers, at my prompting. The originals are still in the quay as far as I know.

The games are friendly enough and we play with the audio accompaniment from the accordionist and the ugly dog. The Alsatian is in place; spread-eagled underneath the table licking its bits and pieces with annoying frequency. By now he must have the cleanest dog's bollocks this side of the Tamar. It's the slurping that gets me. Ma and the women sit yakking, as only two or more women can. Lil sits silently alone with her double gin and tonic. The baccy and lighter resting neatly in front of her.

Having waited a decent time since our return from the chapel and graveside, the kids now begin their normal routine. No one could criticise them, they had paid their respects today; in a way, they continue to do so. It's funny, there had been no invitations, no one had given orders to be here, but every one of us is on duty.

And then, as I had dreaded he might, but hoped he wouldn't, Padraig appears. He sidles a little awkwardly to the bar where Bligh and Blencathra are continuing from where they had left off before we went to the chapel. The newcomer discards the big coat. Padraig pays for and receives his pint of Guinness. He sits alone on the only bar stall that remains unbroken. Ma doesn't move a muscle. She doesn't stare, she doesn't glare, she does nothing.

Virgil and Hardin keep their own company for the most part, sipping half pints of lager and picking at the food while watching the rest of us quietly.

Conversations continue around the Mermaid's bar, but it is as if a total stranger is in our midst; which of course is perfectly true, except in Ma's case. Even the sounds of the accordion seem to form part of the hush that is gradually taking over the confines of the room. There is a feeling of impending doom in the Mermaid Bar right now. Rather apt!

Michael has noticed the kid and I have suddenly become edgy.

"Come on Maccy; you're not trying you bugger."

"Sorry matey, lost interest. Should you be playing in that frock?" I am staring at Padraig's back. Dusty leans heavily on a cue he'd been using in an earlier game.

"Get stuffed! Somebody you know Mac?" Michael questions.

"Nobody I know, Michael. I do have a gut feeling that will change sometime soon."

"Why, if you don't know him, how can it change?"

He's our father; he's mine and Dusty's old man."

"You're bleddy joking?"

"I wish I was Mike." I check on Ma again. I remember the Admiral's and Alma's words of the night before. Ma is still unmoved.

I wonder what Dusty is thinking. I can't help myself from checking on my brother. He seems okay and is talking quietly to Selina, commenting on Michael's ability to play pool. You can never tell what's going on in someone's head, even if he is your one and only little brother.

"Any chance of a game, fellers?"

The music stops completely now as the solitary musician rolls a scrawny cigarette and blows out silent, rising smoke rings that seem to hang in the air. It is as if the unknown local knows everything. The canine slurping falters and eventually comes to a halt at the quietly spoken words.

While I had been checking on Dusty and Ma, Padraig had come up beside me, taking me by surprise. I have no choice but to respond to his question. To tell him to get his builder's arse out of here and never return. I don't get the chance. Maybe it is a good thing, time will tell.

Michael jumps in head first. "You any good, mate?"

"Tell me after we play!"

"The Tamryn's are my friends." Michael points an unfriendly thumb in the direction of the glaring Dusty.

The last game has finished, the table is free.

Michael glances at me as if to say, 'you wanna play him?' And I am about to take up the challenge and my cue when Dusty decides differently.

"Me and you arsehole, best of three, five if you like; if I beat you, you piss off and don't show your bleddy face around here again, comprende?"

Bloody hell! Now I know what has been going on in the kid's head and he's picked up a spattering of Spanish to go with the French and Irish. My brother is becoming bilingual!

"Dusty, that idn't…. you can't…. Come on now, kid."

"Nothing to do with you Michael, stay out of this; you too Maccy, it's between him and me. I win, he goes. He wins, I'm outta here for good, and pronto." Dusty is showing off now!

My little brother has thought it all out in quick time. He is gambling big stakes. I'm not happy. I know how well Dusty can play. I have no idea how good Padraig is.

Dusty's sharp challenge becomes common knowledge. The Mermaid slips into a deeper silence.

Padraig nods his agreement to the terms laid down by my brother, his son. He could ignore the kid's threats and

244

walk away but I didn't think he would. I get the feeling Padraig's running days have finally come to an end here in the Mermaid Bar.

Chapter Twenty-Four

The Match

Neither man changes his mind. Neither man backs down. I toss a coin. The kid wins the call and breaks off the first frame with a dash of cocky confidence. A red drops, the white stands behind another; Dusty, with the gentlest of nudges, leaves Padraig snookered. One mistake will allow my brother to clear up and complete this first game. Those spectating seem to close in on the table, without actually leaving their seats. The room seems to shrink.

The kid has played a blinder. One slip could bring him down to earth. Padraig gets out of the snooker but leaves Dusty a free table. The white shaves the black after his second attempt; it slides hopelessly into a middle pocket. Dusty's early confidence wanes a little after this first mistake.

Padraig takes his chance well. He uses one of the kid's colours as a free ball, a legal move that allows the Irishman to pace around the table with a spare shot. He systematically works away at his own targets. Just the black is left, the Irishman pots it calmly, without a flicker of emotion.

Dusty drops a coin into the box and pushes the slide in to free the balls for the second frame. The balls drop loudly into the silence of the Mermaid Bar.

I can see Ma is stretching forward in her chair to be nearer the action. She stays perfectly silent; her face is a tumble-dryer of feelings.

Padraig takes early charge of this second game. He wins it easily. Two nil!

Dusty again rummages through his pockets. Finding no change, he comes to me for the required coin.

'Don't play the player kid.' I say. 'Play the bleddy balls, play the table. Stop thinking about your bleddy opponent. You should know better. Pretend you're playing Blen', you're less likely to look then. I know I would be."

Dusty only nods his agreement at my well intentioned advice and inserts the coin. No emotion shows on his face.

As loser of the second frame, the kid must break first again. One of each colour drop and he has a chance to clear, which he does at speed. It is two one, though the cocky smile is gone.

There are no other sounds in the Mermaid, except the rasping, uneven breathing of the landlady, who gives the impression she could loom over the table from behind the bar, not to forget the slurping of the Alsatian as it begins its work again. It doesn't seem to affect the two opponents' confidence.

Padraig plays this fourth game like it is a decider. Cagey, tight, slow and deliberate. He is experienced and the quality of his play shows. Dusty slows his game down. Just the black remains, Padraig is first at it. He misses leaving the ball safe on a bottom cushion. Dusty is up, the kid plays a safety shot with the aid of left hand side on the cue ball. He returns the favour of cushioning the black at the opposite end, the white at the top. The two balls couldn't be further apart.

Padraig leaves a smidgen of a chance for the kid; again, he is off course, and luckily it is tight on the cushion again and safe. Any attempt at potting from this position carries the threat of an in-off. Padraig will know but still takes the chance. I am right; the white flies in dead centre. Two two, with one to play. The sound of the balls dropping for the fifth and final time echo around the now silent Mermaid.

Even at this point, the two players ignore each other and look to me to see which would break off in this fifth and deciding frame. There is no handshake. Still the relentless slurping comes from beneath the table.

I drop the fifty pence piece and must reclaim it before I spin it up again. Unbelievably, the dog stops what it its doing. Dusty calls Heads; it is tails and Padraig surprises me once more by letting the kid break. This approach is a gamble. One colour down and a clearance, or a snooker could easily settle the frame and decide the outcome of the match. Dusty pots a red and plays an intelligent snooker in the jaws of a pocket, a good shot.

Padraig plays a get out using check-side on the white; he plays the ball with side across the table and into the jaws of a centre pocket, it comes away at an unnatural angle, as it should do. It catches a loose yellow.

The kid pots three reds on the bounce. He has just two remaining reds to drop and the black and it will be all over. The kid misses his red. His opponent is in the driving seat now.

Padraig throws away all the diligence of the fourth frame and clears every yellow from the table. End of story surely!

The black is on its spot; Dusty's remaining reds are out of the way and the white is clear to drop the black. Padraig slows down. He glances almost inquisitively across at Joy. She shows no emotion. He drops his hands to the table and catches the white centre and right of middle. The black drops in the corner. The white runs back across the table, missing the kid's yellows; it reaches the opposite corner pocket and slips down with an unmistakable plunk. Padraig had employed running side on the white when it clearly wasn't needed.

Any pool player would know he should have played the white left and below centre to stop it continuing forward after contact with the object ball.

Dusty has won. The match is over. Or had Padraig won? Only one person could know for certain, the loser. The Alsatian starts up again. The dog can count!

Dusty takes me by surprise and crosses over to confront Padraig with an open palm, his opponent takes it. The pair shake briefly. Dusty speaks; to me.

"Maccy, remind me never to play him again."

"Why's that kid?"

"He's good, very good but the bastard cheats."

Dusty is right. Padraig had almost certainly arranged with himself to play the in-off. He took the match to the very edge and then threw it with a duff shot. I doubt we'll ever know the reasoning, that is what happened, I'll never believe differently. The unseen slurping shudders to a halt once again as the loser picks up his half full glass. He drains the contents, picks up the coat and walks out without a word.

Dusty leaves his cue at the side of the table and rejoins Ma and the girls. There is no look of satisfaction.

The mood that had drifted in with Padraig gradually lifts as strains of that most beautiful of Cornish anthems 'White Rose' fill the Mermaid Bar. The accordionist is present. Soon most of us are singing along. Michael and I play again, Lenny too before we leave the table free. Dusty does not join the mood of the room.

"I'm gonna get that bleddy table fixed one of these days, Maccy lad."

Bligh has left Blen' and come out from behind the bar to idle with us.

"I bleddy hope not pardner. That was the best pool I ever saw, best you leave it exactly as it is. All we need is a decent light. Anyway, you idn't gonna be here, are you? You'm gonna be up down to Plymouth!"

"Oh ais, I did bleddy forget that Maccy. Mind, I 'aven't decided I'm bleddy goin' yet ya bugger. I idn't certain sure I'm goin' at all."

"Oh yes you bleddy are Bligh. We are going to bleddy Plymouth and that's an end to it. We can live at my sister's 'til we can find a house of our own. If we can't, we'll 'ave to stay there with 'er. Tis time for us to move on my lad."

"Excuse me sis, but I sure don't reckon you'll be needing to worry yourself on that score."

Now this is very odd; the two siblings had been in the same room now for mebbe an hour and a half; this is the first time either have spoken directly to the other. Virgil had seized his opportunity to speak to his fractionally older sister.

"And what the bleddy 'ell makes you say that Virgil bleddy smart arse, Mr New bleddy York O bleddy Colligan?"

Virgil and Hardin raise themselves up and stride stiffly over to the bar where Virgil leans menacingly forward. Hushed words are exchanged and eventually widening smiles and agreeable nods pass back and forwards between the parties. This is turning out to be one weird day. I strain my own ears to hear what is going on; it is no use, it is impossible. I must wait and see what the outcome will be. Although it is none of my business, yet anyway.

Bligh scratches; he grins and scratches again at the fuzzy part of his head. It seems like he is juggling his teeth. He clings on to them thankfully.

It's like watching an operation in a hospital when you can't wait to find out if the patient lives or dies. Virgil, the surgeon keeps cutting away with his incisive mouth and Hardin seems to be using one of those horrible sucking things that keep the wound clear of bubbling, oozing claret.

And then it happens. Blen' throws her caber-like arms around Virgil's neck and I wonder if we might need to get Strange's back. Bligh looks like he wants to throw a hat in the air only he doesn't have one to hand.

"Maccy, my lover, bleddy well come 'ere. I got somethin' you bleddy want, I do believe." Blen' squeals a tad quieter than she had when suffering from the 'trots'.

"Oh shit, I dispute that, you bleddy haven't."

I cross the room and wait for my news from the ebullient Blencathra. I hope there is no more lip connecting required.

"When do ya want n, Maccy, my 'ansome?"

I'm fearful of answering her hideousness. "I dunno Blen. What do you want me to say?" I wonder if having full sex with Blencathra is the final haggling point. I quickly conclude she is unknowingly employing a double entendre; I could be wrong, she might have been doing it on purpose, which is the same thing.

"When will you wanna 'ave my pub, you naughty boy." A great bombardment of laughter accompanies her re-phrased question.

I'm getting the impression Blen' is psychic. It's how she must keep old George at bay. She sends him a message through the ether. 'I'm in tonight, bleddy well stay outta my pub.' No need for an exorcist when she's about the place. I look towards Ma and get the silent reply that I need.

"As soon as you like darlin'!" There is no physical threat, Blen' is behind a two-foot six wide lump of wood. Mind you, Doctor Lector was behind unbreakable glass and at least his was a fake mask. You don't get anywhere in life without taking a few unnecessary risks.

"Right you bugger, now before you start celebrating, what the bleddy 'ell are you gonna do with them bleddy animals out back?"

"Shoot 'em? So Blen, what's the news. How much did you get?"

"More than we'll ever need, Maccy."

It seems another family member – hopefully not another twin – has passed away and shared her fortune with the remainder. It's all I need to know; the finer details are none of my business.

The memory of Frank is not forgotten, he is never far from our thoughts. The wake morphs into celebration. I'm sure our departed crew member wouldn't have minded our merrymaking. If he'd still been here, he would have sat silently smiling and puffing away on a freshly made roll-up, before dozing off for a day or two. The man with the missing limb only acknowledging Lil occasionally with a silent pointed request for her to make another rolly and remembering her mother and George and the night the narrow, steep-sided, cobbled alleyway that is the Drang, echoed with the unmistakable sound of gunfire.

The afternoon is long and seeps into the dark of early evening. If I was asked, I would have to say Blencathra is already packing, at least in her mind. I can just see her stuffing cases and boxes and poor Bligh unstuffing them again and complaining, 'I don't bleddy wanna go to bleddy England! Tidn't fair. I wanna bleddy stay 'ere. I idn't bleddy goin'!' Now Blencathra is stuffing the old man into a suitcase like a music hall ventriloquist. Bligh getting the last word as the case clicks shut.

I have one last important thing to do before my eighth pint takes me over the edge of soberness.

"Thanks for coming and playing matey, you made the day for us all."

The accordionist smiles as he replies. "No problem Maccy, just doing what I 'ave to bud. It's my job!"

"What you have to?" I ask in slight confusion.

The musician winks and lays the sparkling accordion down without another word. I have no idea of his name.

When the evening is over, we Tamryn's sleep where we can at Jen's. It is cramped. The following morning brings further good news.

I hear from one of the fishing boat skippers, milder weather is approaching. Dusty and I decide tomorrow we will get back in the saddle and return the well refreshed and overfed mounts to the farm. The creek lives up to its' name once more as Dusty shovels the unwanted into its fast-moving flow towards the Maltsters Arms.

It is a chance to get out of town and a chance to forget some things. Forgiveness is a long way off, maybe it will never arrive at its destination.

It is a much easier return journey; the snow is thick water mostly, apart from some slushy, grimy crusts along the grass verges and in the centre of the narrow winding road. Even as we ride it is fast disappearing.

Traffic is moving on the roads again and I suddenly realise I'd broken my promise to bring alcohol back to the farmer. I soon stop worrying about it as I am sure the village shop will be able to restock quickly now.

We are climbing the hill just outside of Little Petrock when I first bring up the subject I know is foremost in the kid's mind.

"You don't have to like the bleddy man Dusty. You don't even have to see or talk to the bugger. Don't let him get to you. We two have enough on our plates. You and I have got plenty to be thinking about now."

"That's for sure. He's just bugging me. I'll get over it drekly, but he threw the bleddy match, didn't he! Why the hell did he do that? I don't understand why he cheated."

"I believe he did Kid. Face it, you beat a better man on the day. The better man lost but you gave him no choice; if he's got any thoughts of staying around, he had to lose, didn't you realise that when you challenged him? If he'd won; he'd have lost. He would have had to leave anyway. I don't believe he's going anywhere!"

Something has changed here. I feel Dusty has mellowed a little. It is the pool player that is bugging him, not the man who'd fathered and deserted him. Maybe there is a chance of a relationship, just a chance. For myself, I will just go with the flow and wait and see. There's Ma to consider.

"Yes, I expect you're right. He can play, I wouldn't argue with that. So you don't think he has gone for good Mac?"

"Nope, I don't Dusty. I don't think we have seen the last of him." I have the feeling Padraig will not give up so easily. "You told him to leave. He hasn't so far."

Dusty stops his questions. The subject of Padraig isn't raised again during our return ride. I get the impression the kid is still thinking about him and that someday he will forgive a little, as I might myself.

We'd had little time to discuss Padraig after his departure from the pub. It didn't seem right, we'd had enough of him for one day. The day was Frank's and The Blighs'. In a smaller but more poignant way it had belonged to the bespectacled accordionist. I wasn't sure why.

Dusty spoke first after another quiet period. "What about Ma', Maccy, how do ya think she's takin' all this?"

"Can't say brother, don't know. What are you gonna name this boat of yourn?"

Two screaming dive-bombing seagulls swoop down close to us and the horses spook just a little, they soon settle again.

"Dunno yet. Do you know that it's said a screaming seagull holds the soul of a tormented woman wanting to be released from her strife?"

"I never heard that before. Where did it come from?"

"I read it somewhere; a book, I think. Can't remember who wrote it."

"It must have been a woman!"

"I don't think so Maccy. T'was a man I believe that wrote it, can't remember which."

That's Dusty alright; he's read two or three books since he finished school and can't remember what they were called or who wrote them; we're so alike in most ways.

"Screaming Seagull!"

"Fair enough."

The horses take us home. We settle them into the wobbly barn with plenty of feed, before walking through the remaining streaks of slush to the carriages and collecting Jen's car which is now looking a lot less like a giant Christmas cake. The thaw had come quickly.

In less than fifteen minutes drive we would be back at the loft in Padstow. We pass Ma on the tractor.

The appearance of Padraig and the result of the pool match hadn't really spoiled the day. It might have altered some attitudes, mine and the kid's, at least. Ma's? I can't be certain, who knows? One thing I do know, Padraig had played two games, he lost one and I think he won one.

Chapter Twenty-Five

Lost Souls Creek

We will meet up for lunch at the Maltsters on Sunday. With Blencathra's stunning news, it is obvious the Mermaid is now well and truly up for grabs. It is time for some short term planning, swiftly followed by the long term variety.

Monday morning brings the time for prompt action. I give the phone bill a hammering. I get Dusty moving. He, Selina and Jen' oversee 'Boat-search'.

Nervously, I call all the local breweries. My voice is all fingers and thumbs. I've only been a businessman for an hour or two. I get myself an appointment for the next day at Plymouth Associated Breweries. I had managed to get a marketing manager at the other end of the line and outline my plans, as requested from the voice at the opposite end. The marketing director knows something of the Mermaid. He gives me the impression he is mildly interested and suggests a meeting at the first opportunity, which suggests to me he is more than mildly interested. Two can play at that game. It is an opening though, an opportunity to test the water. It isn't of the deep variety nor of the hot! I would have known, I've been in both kinds many times, it's early yet!

It is a difficult beginning; the bloke gives me the feeling he isn't in favour of chucking money at someone of my young age, which is not particularly bothering me as I know he is feining. I tell him I am an agent for Joy which seems to open a door a tad further. 'Bluett' can only be two or three years older than me. I at least give him the respect he deserves. Slowly, surely, he begins to listen more intently to what I say. Bluett is aware of the potential turnover of such a place and its location. He is aware of the past reputation of the Mermaid. It seems he might know, I am partially responsible for a lot of the shenanigans that may or may not have occurred there. At least I was absent during the New Year orgy.

I had played my part in the ups and downs, I can't take all the credit. Others have gone before me. The meeting reaches the hour mark. I feel I am slowly getting somewhere with this marketing man. I know my credentials don't amount to a great deal; though you could say in some topsy turvy way I am a respected local and I use this fact to my advantage. I believe it was my stint at Chiswick that might have swung favour. Bluett is getting us closer to the nitty gritty.

"There is hardly a pub in the Duchy that doesn't do food these days, Mister Tamryn. The Mermaid would have to become one of many."

Of course, a marketing director for a brewery can't count on any return from any potential food trade but he's aware quality food will bring more drinkers and we both know it.

There is a lot of nose scratching, ear pulling, pen tapping and eyebrow raising going on. I take this as a good time to bring up the subject of Dusty's plan to bring me extra trade. I enlist Ma again. 'Always save the best to last.'

"Well Mr. Bluett, thank you for your time and interest. I already have offers to consider. I have other appointments to keep. I need to get my arse in gear to keep to them." I get the feeling he doesn't mind chucking money about, just he wants me to catch it at his discretion. I am ready to go begging somewhere else but not averse to throwing a lie or two at him as a last resort.

"Others?"

"Ais, but to be honest I'd 'ave preferred it iffen you'd come up with some sort of deal for us. The thing is, I believed you would be our best bet. I do have to see one or two other interested parties but to be truthful, I don't need the financial backing of any brewery. You see we already have an offer." I'm an independent sort.

I well remember a friend of mine telling me he had just been to America. Just before he entered the airport, he trod in some dog crap without realizing it. He took his seat on the craft and made the journey. After leaving the airport he noticed some of the muck was still on his shoe. When he was ready to return home, he noticed his shoe was clear of any leftovers. My friend left his mark on The States. Bullshit can travel well too!

I push the chair back hard and make to leave, half turning away. I'm certain Bluett is hovering, swiftly re-calculating figures. I hope my statement might tip him over. I hope too I hadn't been too mouthy. I had no need to worry. Suddenly, this careless attitude on my part seems to do the trick.

"Just a moment Mister Tamryn, I haven't made a decision and can't right away. There are others here I need to confer with; I can't just say yes or no right here and now, you understand."

"Fair comment Mr Bluett and in the same way, nor can I. I believe us could breathe life into the old place and take 'er up to between fifty and a hundred barrels a week. My belief is that right now it doesn't reach twenty barrels and even that might be stretching it." My figures are a tad exaggerated. My luck needs pushing. Dear Blencathra had quickly schooled me in the art of conversing with men such as Bluett.

'They buggers like to talk in barrelage Maccy,' she'd said. 'Just you remember that, and you won't go far wrong my lad.'

I remember well, Bluett's eyes brighten some at my false claims. I silently thank Blencathra as Bluett eventually changes tack.

"I might have an answer for you by the end of the week Mr Tamryn. You'll need a survey. You'll need a business plan and you'll need a small miracle in my opinion. You will need a licensee. You aren't old enough.

"A survey? Hmm, not in Ma's case; if I take her up on her offer, that won't be important. She does 'ave the readies and she can be very persuasive when she wants. A business plan? I just now gave you that. We intend to turn the Mermaid into the busiest pub in Padstow drekly. As for miracles? Nah, I don't believe we'll rely on those. If we need one, I'll find one. Ma will hold the license!"

"I'll be in touch by Friday Mr Tamryn. Thank you for coming to us at Plymouth Associated first."

So, Bluett knew I hadn't seen anyone else. I didn't have other offers to consider. I leave his office with a tad more confidence than when I had arrived. I just might have swung my first business deal; with a little bullshit and nerve, I'd held my end up, even though he had seen through me. Now I would have to wait until the end of the week. I had little else to do. There are no other appointments for me. The Plymouth Associated Breweries Ltd, Organisation to give it it's full title, being the only ones half interested after my long miserable round of phone calls. Ma will be surprised!

I take a quick glance around this small piece of Plymouth as I go in search of Jen's car that is parked at the back of the brewery. I can see why the reluctant Bligh isn't overawed at the thought of moving here. I'm sure some parts of Plymouth might be half decent. The Devonport area where the brewery is situated isn't one of them. The poor old boy is gonna miss Padstow for sure.

As Saltash and its hideous bridge, Tideford, Landrake, Liskeard and Bodmin are disappearing in my rear view mirror, I wonder how the kid is faring in his search for a half decent boat. There isn't any hurry for that. He has plenty to do with clearing the creek and getting a landing stage built. The more I think of it, the more I realise the size of the job. We will need some heavy machinery in there. The whole thing is gonna be a hell of a dirty job.

I take a break at The Ship Inn at Wadebridge and wander into the hotel. It seems a good idea for me to do some factfinding and snooping. Look around at what others in the trade are doing. Maybe I have other reasons, maybe I don't.

I'd already checked out the Malsters in the same way. The difference is, the old couple running the place are what you might call on their last legs. As landlord and landlady, although they do a first-rate job, retirement must be beckoning them in the same way it is now awaiting Blen' and Bligh.

I sit myself at the Ship's small bar, it could be the Bridge and begin to study my surroundings carefully, trying to take in anything that might be useful. My spying mission comes to a sudden but not entirely unexpected halt. I have company, unsurprisingly.

The voice comes from behind me. There is no need for me to look around. I know who owns it. It is Padraig!

"Can I sit here?" He points at the empty stool next to me.

"Can I stop you?"

"Would you rather I didn't?"

"Please yourself. Why should I care it's a free country, they do say?" I'm happy enough whatever he does. If he wants to talk his head off, that's fine. If he decides to leave, that's fine too. He obviously didn't expect me to be here, I might as well listen to what he might have to say.

"I had no idea you came in here. I'm staying here right now until I decide what I might do."

"It's a decent boozer by all accounts. How's the food?"

"Not bad. I hear that's your game; food."

"You could say so."

"I got the nod from a brewery earlier. Not in so many words but I expect them to come through and if they don't, it won't matter much. Just on my way back from Plymouth and a meeting with a marketing director. I believe they'll come up with some money. They want my business."

"What about the kid, is he going in with you?"

"Not exactly." I go into detail and explain Dusty's involvement and the difficulties he faces with the creek.

"He's gonna have his work cut out. I've seen the state of that creek. He'll need heavy stuff in there to trawl out all the crap. Is it deep enough?"

"Should be if he can get the right sort of boat. Needs a shallow draught job, flat bottom. Most times he'll have a high tide but that won't always be the case. If so, he'll have to use the quay out front."

"The kid's a bloody good pool player."

"He is, but you had him beat. Why did you throw it? He's pissed off with you."

"Not a lot of choice Maccy. He gave me an ultimatum. What else could I do?"

"You could have refused to play."

"What would that achieve and why should it bother you?"

"It doesn't!" I lie. "Why didn't you stick around?"

"In the pub? I kept my part of the bargain. It was what the kid wanted."

"If you say so."

"When will you know about the money?"

"End of the week, hopefully."

"I could let you have all you need."

"No thanks. I'm off, stuff to do."

"Thanks, Maccy!"

"What for?"

"Talking to me like this."

"I had nothing else to do, I was here, you were here, is all."

"How about when you have nothing else to do again, we talk some more?"

"I don't think so." I have little time for picking over the past and none for shallow, meaningless apologies. I need to put all my effort into my future, not my past and anyway, it's not my past, it's Padraig's. Mine is fine, mostly dodgy but fine. I don't have a guilty conscience. I'm not doing any soul-searching.

"One last thing Padraig."

"Go on."

"That day in the pub when Ma belted you. Why did you come into the Malsters then?"

"Just bad luck. I didn't know you were all in there. I had walked from Padstow and was on my way back here. Was seriously thinking about moving on in fact until Joy changed my mind."

"Ma changed your mind?"

"Of course, she did. I would have been disappointed if she had ignored me. I got what I deserved. It had been a long time coming."

I could think of nothing to say following Padraig's admission. I left him sitting with his own thoughts and drove myself back to Jen's place.

It is refreshing to get out of the car. I hate the bloody things near on as much as I hate the telephone and the idiot box. I wonder how the kid has fared in his search. I find them all on the floor in various poses, thumbing through the for sale columns of the local newspapers and various dog-eared boating magazines which have next to naked women posing on the front covers for no apparent reason. I stare at one or two. I don't consider myself to be perfect!

"Bleddy crap!" Dusty is not best pleased.

The three of them have called every boatyard and auction house they can think of. Nothing has come to. Still, there is no hurry, the creek must be cleared out and without heavy-duty machinery, it will be time consuming and backbreaking work.

There is only one thing for it; I needed a beer. There's always tomorrow. It is unanimous. We trundle down over the uneven cobbles of the Drang and out onto the now darkening quayside. The old town is almost silent. It's nearly the end of January and still very cold. The last of the snow is slowly disappearing but tonight will see another hard frost.

Lenny is at the bar when we arrive. He puts his hand in his pocket and pays for the round. This evening will be the last one I spend with Jen' for a while; she is on duty at the Sailmakers for the next few nights.

"How's it going Maccy?"

"Yeah, I'm getting' there mucker. What's new with you?"

"Same as usual, seeing the waitress from the café and that gawky bird in the gift shop at the end of the quay. Oh yeah, and 'er that does 'ave the Maypole Inn. She sends 'er regards to e by the way."

Same old Lenny, never can do things in one's or twos. "Look out for 'er old man matey."

"Why should I, she idn't bothered."

"No, but the old man might be if he catches you and his missus having a lock-in. You'll be locked up most likely."

"When you're ready to make a start on the creek, let me know, I'll be there to help out. I'll keep the engines shipshape on Dusty's boat too when there's a need."

"Thanks Lenny. Appreciate the offer. Still not cut and dried yet. There's a bit to do."

I'd thought about the creek. More than once I had looked around out there. There is stonework needing repairs; it isn't a job Dusty or I can do, we would be needing a proper stonemason down there. The overgrown nettles and weeds will be easy enough. Ma will deal with the wild roses. We will be needing a timber walkway for passengers to get on and off.

Dusty has heard a whisper down on the quay there is a shallow draught boat available in Calstock. The boat might be exactly what he needs. It has been almost a week now of searching and phoning and although that might not sound much, it is when your kid brother isn't the most patient young feller you know. The kid has been like a cat on a hot tin roof since the day of Frank's funeral. Jen' would be needing a new telephone when this was all over.

Lenny had kept his word as I knew he would. He, Dusty and I had been down in the creek bed clearing away the centuries of debris that is easiest to move by hand and allowing us to see just what else would be needed to get the channel serviceable; plastic beer crates, even older wooden beer crates that have two and sixpence deposit on them, whatever that means? Broken glass is everywhere in

262

the brown silt that lays thick at the bottom. There is stuff down there that is best left undisturbed. There are certain things that should never have been put down there at all. No bones about it, even if there are.

There has always been a whispered local rumour that in centuries long past the creek was the favourite disposal point for unwanted births. The story goes that a well at the back of the Maltsters at Little Petrock, now hidden under the floor of the old lean-to, was the dropping off point. Many a poor child who had never seen the light of day had departed this life via the well and the creek. Lost Souls Creek flows a few yards past the Maltsters. It's horseshoe shape allows it to empty out into the Camel at Sea Mills.

Padstow would have been just like any other ancient coastal port. A bustling place and when full of tall ships, would be full of strapping sailors in need of certain comforts. The men that manned those ships would have been like a magnet to the working girls from Redruth, Camborne, Illogan and St. Austell, not forgetting Lil! For a moment, I wonder which century she is left over from. The ladies of the night could do good business in such a place, with the occasional, natural error or mistake; a pregnancy, the result. For the girls, a child was out of the question. They could hardly continue their chosen line of work with a hungry kid hanging off a breast or clinging on to an ankle.

Old Mother Ivey would get a call. Her gory work complete, the creek would receive another offering. There is little chance now of our disturbing any of those long forgotten, young souls. I shiver a tad as we climb out at the end of the day. I've no idea why, I just shiver.

I had heard the rumours and when I was a kid, Ma always warned me to cup my hands over my ears if I had to cross the 'The Bridge of Tears' late in the evening, so I wouldn't hear their cries. Sometimes I did.

We had pulled out everything we could. It was never going to be enough. As we'd initially thought, and Padraig had confirmed, we needed heavy machinery.

We could only do so much by hand and shovel. There is no doubt we will be requiring some professional he-men and mechanical forces to complete the task satisfactorily. It is going to take a big effort.

That's for another day. In the morning, Ma and I need to make a visit to the courthouse in Truro.

Chapter Twenty-Six

The White Rose

The big day has arrived! Big in our eyes anyway. To anyone else around here, it's the same size as yesterday. Our application for the license will be heard at the Magistrate's Court in Truro. We have our references. Michael's father, the Methodist Minister hadn't hesitated when we asked him to sign the forms as a professional referee.

How could I go wrong? Thanks to Mike' we now have the giddy feeling that even God is on our side. Maybe Michael had done some unpaid overtime, put a good word in for us. I can't think what else it could have been. He didn't have many to choose from. To be fair, the minister is known to like a pint of cider occasionally. It explains a lot about his eccentricity. Ma agreed to put her name to the license. It won't be there long, before it's replaced by my own.

Surprisingly the brewery had been true to their word. By Friday lunchtime they had confirmed by registered post. The finances for the bricks and mortar have changed hands. Ma has signed all the necessaries. The cheque for the transfer of the goodwill and all the other bits and pieces has been issued, excluding Bligh's rockery. The proceeds will immediately go to Bligh and Blencathra. It is all black and white. No more unnecessary talk of surveys and such.

I hope the solicitor that has done the legal work will become a customer at the Mermaid. I might get the chance to squeeze back some of the mountain of cash he and his firm have swallowed up on my behalf. Too late for me to realise I might be in the wrong job! No, I'm not having second thoughts. I'm still pondering over the first variety. My last minute nerves have arrived early.

My brother might at last have found what he needed to become operational. He must have got out early to have some kind of epiphany. 'Seeing the light' for Dusty means he gets out of bed before it gets dark. There's a first time for everything mind you.

The application hearing is to be held at ten O'clock. Ma, Dusty and I are preparing to get to Truro and from there Dusty will need to get the train up county to Calstock Boatyard, in time to look over the craft.

There is no time to lose as we are meeting the solicitor for last minute advice on how to behave to the magistrate and the clerk from the agents who would arrange the transfer of the license into Ma's name and the cancellation of the Blighs' There's no legal reason Ma should be refused the license. She doesn't make a habit of thumping people! Yes, there were plenty of witnesses in the Maltsters, none that couldn't easily be bribed. As far as anyone in the legal profession is concerned, I work for Ma.

In our Sunday best, we are on the road long before eight. Dusty and I are as excited as two schoolkids, which to be honest, we aren't much more than. We are heading South, following the spine of the Duchy, the old, dirty A30. Jen' had agreed to lend us her car. Automobiles are not Ma's forte. Joy and cars don't mix. Ma is the world's worst backseat driver, she fares no better in the front. She may well have initiated non-violent road rage!

Jen, Selina and Lenny have promised Blen' and the Cap'n they would spend the day at the Mermaid, helping in any way they could, to get the Bligh's belongings safely packed and stowed. Again, I can see Bligh being stuffed into a suitcase, his bony fingers clawing uselessly at thin air before they disappear inside.

Everything is falling into place except the creek. For Dusty's sake, it bothers me no end. It will be a tough task to renovate the area. We have done as much as we can ourselves. We need to get a contractor in. The condition of the creek would not stop me opening the doors of the Mermaid. It might just hold up the kid's Sea Bus business.

Truro is Truro at just before eight-thirty in the morning. Eventually we find and squeeze into a parking space in Old Bridge Street, that might normally only have been big enough for a discarded shopping trolley. There was one parked there, it's in the river with a load of others now! As luck would have it, we are on the wrong side of town for the courts. We must leg it through the rush-hour traffic to get from one side of the city to the other in less than half an hour. It is close. In something resembling mild panic, we race up the wide stone steps and scoot past the towering pillars of the municipal buildings. There is not a second to spare.

Inside, the place is swarming with the suited and booted. I don't see a wig anywhere. Wrong kind of court I suppose. Police uniforms are visible all over the place, which I had expected. One stands out amongst them all. The wearer is close enough to touch. I believe he is eyeing me with something akin to friendship; most unexpected! Twotrees is actually smiling and doesn't look surprised at my appearance; he has seen our name somewhere on some official rota, he knew we would be here. We had passed him on the road out of Padstow. He wouldn't dare stop us, we know too much possibly! I suppose it could be said we have him caught by the fuzz!

The trouble with Padstow, apart from yours truly, is that when someone farts down on the waterside, it becomes common knowledge at the top of the hill within minutes and vice versa. The annual farting contest in Padstow is a great favourite. It could be.

I'm not so worried now. Too much had gone almost according to plan in the last couple of weeks and especially the last day or two. Relief has set in a tad. The plod now has no leverage over us. Every dog has its day as the saying goes. The Alsatian is spending his in bed, my brothers, not mine. I edge closer to my brief. I'm still half expecting an incoming storm. It doesn't help! Dusty has also noticed Twotrees. Dusty knows the whole story. I've never been a chicken counter. Math's has never been my thing.

"Bleddy 'ell Maccy, you got no chance iffen he is here for our doings. He'll have you strung up by your bollocks, mebbe worse."

"Everything is good kid. What will be, will be. Anyway, he's stationed at Wadebridge now. He shouldn't have any say about Padstow business as far as I know. What's worse?"

"Dunnaw but the son of a bitch might think of something."

"Have faith brother."

A hiccup did arrive. We check the order of play pinned to a notice board; our application isn't first up. In fact, we don't see it on the list at all. We hop nervously from one foot to the other inside the courtroom. The solicitor told us all licensing applications are heard early in the day before the courts get down to the real serious business of fining folks more than they can afford to pay for not paying their Poll Tax or having no TV license. He hits us hard with news we weren't expecting.

"Mister Tamryn, why are you here so early?"

"Are we? Ten you said, I remember it clearly."

"That's right, I did but it's only nine."

The brief is correct, the clock on the wall shows me it is only nine O'clock.

Dusty states the obvious. "You tosser, Maccy. Why don't you keep your bleddy clocks up to date? I could still be in bed!"

My brother is right. I will have to change my habits re: Summer and Winter solstices. I'm not sure he would want to be in bed with the Alsatian. Even I would draw the line at that.

"Tamryn, I want a word with you."

The voice is easily recognisable, it is Twotrees. "Shit! Yes, sir." I have no idea why I used that expression towards him. It was a first. I wander across. He invites me to sit down. I do. I wait in nervous silence.

"Listen lad. I know you know what I know you know."

I give nothing away. I'm enjoying a feeling of power. It will only be temporary I suspect.

"In my patrol car. The person who was with me. If you promise to keep your gob shut, I won't speak against your license application. You with me."

I feel it is time not to turn the screw any tighter. I'm going for a status quo. I'll make the promise anyway. I listen without interruption until he's finished.

"Fair enough! Mum's the word, TT."

"Good lad. Thanks, Maccy. Good luck."

The solicitor approaches us. "It won't be long now." He states usefully in a solicitor-like whisper.

The brief is spot on. We are on our feet! I had fretted unnecessarily. Twotrees isn't on my case at all. I find it difficult to comprehend I now have a copper as an associate. I check, the smile is still in place as he looks across at me from the other side of the room with far less ferocity now that he owes me a favour. I'm not even certain I saw him with an unknown lady in his patrol car. I wasn't about to tell him that. I hope she's getting therapy.

Question to the police representative "Is there any objections to Joy Tamryn being licensed to sell beer, wine and liquor at the Mermaid and Bow Inn, Public House, situated in the parish of Padstow?"

I throw a nervous glance at the brief who shakes his head and silently puts my mind at rest. Twotrees might be asleep. He isn't it seems, as he glances around at me once again. I wonder if he was canoodling with the woman in a lay-by when I was helping Mrs. Twotrees with her seedlings. I must concentrate.

The magistrate studies the flapping application forms in his fingers. He peers over the rim of his glasses. He reminds Ma sternly of her duty to keep an orderly house. Not to sell booze to underage kids. 'Do not serve anyone who may be intoxicated.' Hmm! As if she needed to be told about these. Especially as she won't even be there. She will own the Mermaid in name only. I will be its manager in name only. No one will be any the wiser! Next subject is the legal opening and closing hours. Yeah right, I think, what about the Maypole? Did anyone come here and apply for a license for the Maypole? There's a place near St Merryn that never closes. Believe me, I've been there, morning, noon, night and morning etc.

The announcement comes from out of the blue. "License granted, Miss Joy Tamryn of Padstow Parish."

I dig Dusty in the ribs with a neatly directed elbow. He lets out a strangled gurgle that is heard by the bespectacled overseer and his two silent partners. Twotrees gets a blown kiss. I can't help myself. For my troubles, I get a short sharp lecture on my courtroom etiquette and rightly so, I admit.

"I must remind you Ms. Tamryn, people will look up to you. They will hold you in high regard. Make certain you are equal to the task ahead of you."

It is Dusty's turn now to dig me. I keep my face straight as the magistrate might be psychic. He looks at us sternly. I straighten my face with difficulty. We are getting a polite but firm bollocking from the bench. I accept it with a nod and a 'thank you sir.' I resist the temptation to touch my forelock, partly because I'm not certain where it is.

My solicitor had primed us with all the right responses. 'Courtroom Protocol', he had called it. Twotrees stays silent as promised. I'm tempted to give him a middle finger salute. I don't, he has kept his side of a bargain.

Dusty and I leave Twotrees a distant memory. The stuffy courtroom is behind us as we three bounce down the wide steps. Ma did more bouncing than me and the kid, if you know what I mean. We can't help but loudly celebrate the result of our hour and a half in her majesty's company. At least we weren't in the dock and she wasn't even there anyway. In bed with a bunch of Corgis I expect. I'm thinking about a strongly worded letter to the palace concerning her lack of interest!

"Come on kid, we gotta find the car and get you to the station."

Providing it's a goer, Dusty will hand over a cheque for twelve and a half thousand quid in exchange for a shallow bottomed diesel engined coastal cruiser that will carry up to around fifty wallet waving, beer swilling, vomiting in relays, teenagers. He will bring the boat around to Lost Souls Creek. Well he couldn't drive it down the A30!

Ma and I return to the loft and are greeted by Lenny and the girls. The looks on our faces tell of our success. It is a time for celebration. The welcoming committee can't wait to get us to the Mermaid to make the most of our successful application. I believe they have an ulterior motive to rush us. We have hardly drawn breath since seven O'clock, which should have been eight if not for my tardiness last October.

I don't need telling twice to celebrate anything. It has not been a hard day physically; standing, nodding and smiling to get a totally disinterested stranger with a pocket full of petrol receipts and restaurant bills to agree that we are responsible adults, Ma anyway. We had been mentally tough. Worrying about the whispered words of Twotrees had been bothersome. I did think he would come through and he did. Twotrees had thought I had done or seen something I probably hadn't. I'd say that is a result.

I know Dusty will be contemplating a similar reward if he gets what he wants, what he needs. He should be waiting a little longer for his birthday! As he's a family member and it's a private party, we could bend the rules a tad.

As for Padraig, we will manage without him as we have done for so long. I had listened to his story. I had given him a hearing. I felt sorry for him to be truthful. I can do sorrow when required. The Mermaid and hopefully the Sea Bus are our futures now. The special woman that is our Ma is our present and will always be.

We step to one side as a mud-spattered JCB with trailing clods of seaweed appears noisily from around the corner of the quayside. None of us would be giving it a second thought. The driver nodded his thanks as he and the machine rumble on their way past the old station. We continue towards the Mermaid as Jen' suddenly appears. She turns and walks with us without a word. She smirks silently. The penny drops as we turn the corner and approach the Creek.

Finally, she informs me Padraig had visited her at the Sailmakers, while she was working the night before. He'd told her of his plan to bring in the machinery to clear the creek. He must have told her too, that two highly professional stone workers, a labourer and a chippy would begin the task of rebuilding the steps and landing area. One last thing he had suggested, 'Keep it to yourself love.' She had done exactly as she'd been told. She had kept her word to Padraig.

I have no idea what we'll find when we got to the pub, my pub. I see an overalled chippy is working away at the newly erected wooden walkway that could be hauled onto the granite surface after it has served its purpose of enabling passengers to embark or disembark.

Bligh and to my surprise, even Blencathra, her great arms folded to support the voluminous breasts, still minus implants, stand watching with interest as the chippy adds the finishing touches to his day's handywork. The Alsatian, one foot stiffly in the air, continues its work at the feet of the She-devil who might have relatives in Borneo. I wouldn't want to be in his place. The chippy, a tightened toolbelt holding up his trousers, looks familiar. It's Bessie!

"What's on Bessie? What're you doing here?" I ask, when my voice returns.

"Geezer in the Sailmakers offered me a couple of days work Maccy, cash in hand. What's it got to do with you what I be doing? Bugger off and leave me do my work, I don't have time to be fighting with you today."

"Me? I bought the bleddy pub. The Mermaid is mine." For a second, animosity is rearing its ugly head. The

272

unmistakable smell of violence hangs in the air and then, something unusual comes over me. Why spoil a perfectly good day by exchanging unpleasentries and physical contact with Bessie?

The carpenter must be of the same mind as he issues his own redeeming statement.

"Well don't just stand here bleddy yakking, get the bleddy beer in boy! I'm nearly done for today and I'm parched. Finish the job off tomorrow if it doesn't bleddy rain."

"Put away your tools and anything else you might have hanging out Bessie." Bessie and I could never be mistaken for friends. Right now, I can find no reason not to take a beer with him and the rest of the crew that, I would discover, were all on deck inside the Mermaid.

There is a new member present. I nod a sincere salute to the man that has taken it upon himself to interfere in my dream. Padraig, my father, winks. Even Dusty, just returned by taxi, is smiling. That has to be a good thing. It's a start anyway and I'll drink to that!

I make up my mind to do away with the ancient jukebox as I hear the unmistakable sound of the accordion once again playing that most beautiful Padstow anthem. Elvis is in the building again. The strains of 'The White Rose' drift out to greet and envelop me as I open the door to the Mermaid for the final time as a paying customer. I don't believe I'll be spending any money. I'm not sure I have any left in any case.

If there is any one tune that can affect the quirky minds of born and bred Padstonians and convince them the world is full of friends, it is the White Rose. The accordionist is smiling, he winks and continues. The Alsatian? Well the dog is now still and silent, its work seemingly done.

As for Bligh, he has liquid on his face once again. I am certain it has seeped out and trickled down from the corner of his old but still sparkling, mischievous, eyes. I could be wrong but doubted it, as I squeezed the hand of my Cornish Queen at the dawn of a new era for The Mermaid.

"You drinking my best bleddy whiskey, Cap'n?"

"Yes sir, I believe I am!"

"Fair enough!" What could I say? I had drunk plenty of his orange juice at times. Amongst all the changes that have happened during the last year or two - one thing, two - the Blighs, will stay the same. I do wonder if Plymouth knows they are coming. No matter, Padstow knows I'm coming. Hell is coming with me. I bring little else to the party. I'm bringing the party!

One thought does cross my mind before it gets decapitated from the rest of me; who the hell is the guy standing at the bar and talking with Old Bert? I've never seen him before. I have to ask.

"Bert, haven't you got a drink mate, your friend?"

"Thank you Maccy. Not really friends as such lad, my boss, he does own the café!"

"I'll get you some food gents! I'll check the fridge, see we do 'ave us any bacon! Ketchup or brown?"

"Now Mister Tamryn, you're the one who has been breaking into my café."

"I guess you could say that, although I wouldn't have put it quite like that."

"How would you put it?"

"Um, yeah okay. I would put it like that, now you come to mention it."

"Take these."

So now I have the keys to the Mermaid and the keys to the café. I'll have to get a bigger keyring. The huge front door opens and closes again with a slam. It seems now everyone is on deck, even a new recruit!

"Can I have a pint of Doom Bar, Maccy?"

"Yep, on me pal, good choice." I hand the café owner a pint.

"What's this?"

"Pint of Doom, what you asked for. Anything wrong?"

"It's sand!"

"Correct, from the Doom Bar!"

274

Epilogue

It has been almost five years of roller coaster riding, so much has happened over this period of my life. One short conversation with Lil had given me the direction in which to continue my education. It was she who had made the suggestion; I should shoulder the responsibility of becoming landlord of the Mermaid and Bow Inn at Padstow. The Mermaid could best be described as 'past it', In my young mind, I believed it deserved one last chance Surely we all deserve a second chance. In the case of the Mermaid, it had to be the last throw of the dice.

From the start, the idea appealed to me. Who would have thought an ageing 'lady of the night' would have such an effect as to point me in the direction of the rest of the next phase of my young life? Most my age would have listened to an employment consultant sent to our secondary school to spend five minutes telling me I could do this, that, or the other and whatever I choose would see me through to my state pension. According to how much I had taken in from teachers who were disinterested in me. The Job Centre employee would know all about me. Of course they would. How can a total stranger decide my employment fate?

It was Lil, she did it for nothing. 'We need a younger man' she had said. I happened to be in the vicinity, I became the potential 'younger man'! Not one of the crew ever stated I was too young for the job. I never gave it a thought myself. The innocence – yeah right – I couldn't think of another word, of youth, drove me forward, allowed me to believe I could pull it off. All around me I had consultants, the' crew', who didn't question my credentials, they just gave me free advice. I owe the 'crew' so much. My faithful schoolmates, a tad short of vision and thinking power had faith in my plan. No man can have a better friend than Leonard, that isn't a dog. Lenny has always been off the lead, as have I. As for Michael, a born again sinner, he shares with me, God's word!

As the man at the helm, it is up to me to see the Mermaid into the next century and beyond. I must do it. I should do it, I will and more. Next to me will stand my Ma, my loving parent. My loyal brother, Dusty. A disfigured Alsatian, who like me belongs to no-one in particular, The Birdsalls will cook my books. Neighbouring pub landladies will help me keep my feet off the ground, if you get my meaning. Not sure about onwards and upwards, moving forward will suffice.

The Mermaid's landlord and landlady, Blencathra and Cap'n Bligh, had done their best, more or less, to keep the pub afloat, their tide had turned and to avoid the rocks they had given way to me. One last but not least personal adviser deserves a mention, Bert, café cleaner and breakfast provider, a leading seaman and irreplaceable confidante.

Alongside lying to a justice of the peace in court and manipulating the local copper into my way of thinking, I still had to do what normal teenagers do, have a life. I am succeeding here. Various members of the opposite sex will help the expansion of this part of my further education.

What happens after this first victory in the business world will be entirely dependant on my wits. I will lounge around in my self-built abode and plan my next move. The timbers of two ancient railway carriages that provide a roof over my head will secretly record the way forward, my way forward.

An 'epilogue'? No, not essentially, this is not 'the end', it is just the beginning!